Fix You

Fix You

Beck Anderson

G

Gallery Books

New York   London   Toronto   Sydney   New Delhi

G

Gallery Books
A Division of Simon & Schuster, Inc.
1230 Avenue of the Americas
New York, NY 10020

Originally published in 2013 by Omnific Publishing.

First Gallery Books trade paperback edition March 2015

GALLERY BOOKS and colophon are registered trademarks of Simon & Schuster, Inc.

For information about special discounts for bulk purchases, please contact Simon & Schuster Special Sales at 1-866-506-1949 or business@simonandschuster.com.

The Simon & Schuster Speakers Bureau can bring authors to your live event. For more information or to book an event contact the Simon & Schuster Speakers Bureau at 1-866-248-3049 or visit our website at www.simonspeakers.com.

Design by Davina Mock-Maniscalco

Manufactured in the United States of America

10 9 8 7 6 5 4 3 2 1

Library of Congress Cataloging-in-Publication Data is available

ISBN 978-1-5011-0625-5
ISBN 978-1-5011-0626-2 (ebook)

To the Anderson men:
Thank you for putting up with my writer-ly insanity.
I love you.

Acknowledgments

Many thanks to the following people:

First, to my husband, Marcus. You are the one who taught me about true love.

To my kids, for enduring the time Mama spends parked in front of the computer.

To the Chix. You complete me and help me complete my sentences. We rule.

To my awesome editor, Jessica, for equal parts common sense and cheerleading.

To all of my extended family and everyone in my "other life" at school for your enthusiasm on this new journey of mine.

And to the team at Omnific, for giving me my first break.

Fix You

Prologue
The Long Way Around

It's a bluebird day. Warm spring skiing, clear skies, soft snow. On Upper Nugget, the turns come to me easily, and I feel for a brief moment like an expert skier, someone terribly suave and possibly European.

I watch Peter. He makes long, lazy turns, and they seem to rise from the bottom of his skis, as if suggested not by him but by the corduroy powder beneath him. *Turn here*, the mountain whispers, and so he does.

I try not to be exasperated. The boys are between us. Hunter looks more and more like his dad. At nine now, he has begun to stand tall in his boots. His brown-blond hair riffles in the wind.

Beau races to catch up. He looks very small on skis, a compact bundle of energy. At six, he still is a little boy, though heaven help the person who dares say that to his face. He tucks determinedly, in a constant effort to keep up with his brother and, more distantly, his father.

The wide, sunny slope begins to narrow. Now is when skiers like me start to tense up. The run begins a steady banking that will end in a slender trough called Second Chance. What had been an ego-boosting run for me quickly turns surly.

As I brace myself for the transition, I notice that Peter has pulled up at the top of the shot. I stop, grateful for the chance to gather myself and assess the risk-to-benefit ratio before me.

"Why'd you stop?" I ask him. He usually never stops, not even to let the kids catch up. The boys have shot on down the run, making tighter and more frequent turns as it narrows like a funnel. I can see the chairlift at the bottom and can almost make out the liftie with the shovel, smoothing out the ramp.

Peter holds up a gloved hand, not answering for a second. When he does, he is uncharacteristically winded. "Give me a minute."

"Is there something wrong?"

He smiles, shakes his head no, still leaning on his poles. "I'm pretty sure it's your fault. You keep me up at night."

I elbow him. If it wasn't so cold, I might blush. I shuffle my skis, trying to stay warm and ready for the next burst of skiing.

"You doing this?" Peter nods down the tight stretch of snowy hill.

I take stock. The right side of the run, the side I like because the angle is more consistent, has been scraped off. I can see icy streaks of hard pack where the powder is gone.

The left side of the run is moguls. The powder has been bulldozed over to that part by the morning's skiers and boarders. The piles of snow are menacingly uneven. The cat track leading into the trees at the edge of the run—the gentle, safe way down—calls to me.

"I'm going around." I can see too many opportunities for disaster today.

"Okay, Miss Cat Track Fever. See you at the bottom." Peter readies his poles for a split second and shoots down the run before I've even fully settled into my decision to follow the easier path.

As usual, the boys have all left me by myself, contemplating, while they take action.

I sigh, adjust a mitten, and push off to cruise my way down.

"Don't mind me!" I say this to the pines and the crunch of snow as I leave the run for another day.

PETER SLEEPS, BUT MOSTLY the Fentanyl has taken effect, willing the pain to leave and the body to rest. I suppose he made the right choice a few days ago. After a long five months, he's insisted on having himself moved to the hospice center. I had no idea, standing on the slopes with him in April, that we'd be here now, making decisions like this.

His thought is that the boys do not need their home turned into a hospital wing.

I guess I could agree with him, but I can't help the strong urge to surround him with known people, items, rooms, anything. It feels like we need to batten down the hatches and ride out the storm, and here he is insisting on taking a trip in a rowboat.

He's warned me for weeks. About the trip part. And he's not talking metaphorically anymore. He is planning on departing.

Again, I can't blame him. The doctors have tried increasingly creative and desperate ways to manage his pain. They have been increasingly unsuccessful. And lately, there've been very few discussions about beating back the illness. It seems to have won in its effort to camp out with us. When words like *metastasized* and *terminal* began to be tossed around, we stopped fighting on that front.

Now we're in a different theater of war. I guess we could call it the Managing the End campaign.

We could call it that, but I can't give voice to it. I hang on by a very, very tenuous grasp to full consciousness. But I haven't let the waves of hysteria win, at least not yet. A few times I've found myself locked in a stall in the hospice women's restroom, but I manage to rally enough to make it back to the room and Peter's bed each time.

Right now I sit next to him. I'm kind of cheating about the sitting. I've pulled my lounger up to the side of his bed, and my head and upper torso rest forward on it. This pose looks suspiciously like the kids in their school desks when they play heads up seven up.

I listen to him breathe shallowly in and out for a while. My mind drifts, and I think about the message I need to craft to the boys' teachers, one that explains they will start the school year late, owing to the fact that they have a gravely ill father.

I don't know when it is exactly, but that train of thought gives way to the weight of exhaustion, and I am out. I don't think *sleep* is the word, because this is the absence of anything. Total deprivation leads to blank unconsciousness.

And just as suddenly, I am upright in the chair, and I know Peter has taken the opportunity of my sleep to leave. His body, though it's been still for weeks now, is a different kind of still. Before I'm even awake for a second, I know he is no longer breathing.

I stand and begin to call for someone in a loud wail of a voice. Thankfully the boys are away. I can pretend later for them that Peter's passing was peaceful. Actually, his part of it was, relatively, but my reaction is proving not to be.

His eyes are closed, and in the relaxed state of death, his mouth looks strangely smaller, drawn. His hands are at his sides.

Nurse Ann comes in, alerted by my wet cries for help. She

checks his vital signs or lack of them, makes a note of the time on his chart, and gives my hand a squeeze. She whispers a soft, "I'm so sorry, hon," before she exits the room. Then she leaves me with myself and my grief and my gone husband.

The thing I am most acutely aware of, before I lose myself to the sobbing, is how spacious the room feels with one less soul in it.

The Spaces in Between

I don't know how to describe the time that passes next. Yes, there are stages of grief. Yes, there are plenty of abysses that seem to suck into them any attempt at normalcy.

But routine often saves me. When I feel things getting bad, I notice that the house has gotten overly bad too. Toilets need to be scrubbed, and dishes have multiplied while soaking in the sink. If I throw myself a life preserver of chores and errands and rides for the boys, not only does the house start to look better, but I'm able to hang on through the riptides of depression that want to pull me out to sea.

This routine cannot, however, help me overlook the necessities prompted by Peter's death. It is not routine, nor is it a standard household chore, to meet with an attorney to discuss putting things in my name that were in his. There is nothing fathomable or predictable about the way it feels to summarily strip his name off of the title to the car, for instance, or the mortgage to the house. Or to discuss the life insurance policy—the one I tried to talk him out of because we were both so young. I don't like the way the lawyer says that policy will take care of me and the boys for a good long while. Suddenly we're comfortable, and it's because I've lost my husband. That's the worst kind of fortune. It isn't routine, all of this. What it is, is treason, as far as I'm concerned. It's an admission that yes, I believe he really is gone for good, and no, I'm not waiting for him to come back.

The least I could do for the person who waited for me while I fumbled around for my keys for the nine millionth time in the grocery store parking lot is wait for him. It's the loyal thing to do. Either that or follow him in a prompt manner.

Yet I have no choice but to stay. The other people in the world who rely on me for their basic survival force me to cope with what has happened. That's actually one comfort: I don't have any options. I can't think about doing anything but sticking around, because there are two people who need me to be here, now more than ever.

This doesn't make it any easier, though. Gray days stretch into one another.

Months slip through the house surreptitiously, like uninvited spirits.

EVENTUALLY, I WAKE UP one day to both my boys standing by my bedside. Their eyes are wide with concern.

"What's up, boys?" I sit up, rub the sleepers out of my eyes, and try to shake off the weight of the anvil sitting on my chest, my familiar companion since Peter died.

Beau elbows Hunter. He's been appointed spokesperson.

"Mom, we called Gran, and she said to get your butt up out of bed and go see Joe. We told her you slept most all of the weekend."

This is what they're wide-eyed about. They tattled on me to Gran, and they're afraid of the consequences. The thought makes me want to cry.

"Oh, guys, come here." I pull both of them to me for a long hug. "Listen. I'll hop in the shower, and I'll call Joe for an appointment right after, okay?"

Joe is our family doctor. He is also my best friend's husband. And he used to ski with Peter. He's patched up every one of the Reynolds clan at one point or another. I guess it's time he patched me up. This is not something I look forward to, but the way the boys look at me is reason enough to suck it up and call.

Sure enough, when I talk to the receptionist at Joe's office, my mom has called ahead. Great. She's staged an intervention long-distance. Since I went to college, we've never lived in the same town, but now that I'm alone in Boise with the boys, she keeps tabs on us more closely. Mom and Dad live in LA, and we visit them there and at their condo in Indio a lot. And if I asked them to move in with us in Boise, they just might do it. I'm pretty certain that would be a disaster, which is why the subject has never been discussed, but they do take good care of us.

The appointment is for ten. I drop the boys at the sitter and drive through town in the pouring rain. When I get there, the receptionist hustles me into a room. I check to see if I'm bleeding anywhere; I don't think I've ever gotten such prompt service at the doctor's.

I sit on a chair next to the exam table. After a few minutes, Joe sits across from me.

"What's going on, Kelly?" He's a fit, glossy-haired Asian man who looks trim and put together in his white lab coat. I showered, but that's about the only thing I have going for me currently.

"I feel rotten. I think you may have heard why."

He takes a deep breath, lets it out. "Are you taking care of your-self?"

"Yes."

"Exercising?"

"No."

"Sleeping?"

"No. Unless it's the random times when I can, and then all I do is sleep."

"Reading? Taking the dog on walks? Entertaining the thought of seeing your friends? Learning how to cook? Thinking about going back to teaching?"

"I get the point. What's your point?"

"I prescribe activity. You need to get out of the house. If you don't make an effort at this, to exercise, or call Tessa up to have cof-fee, or to get a part-time job, I'll prescribe something stronger. Anti-depressants stronger. You catch my drift?"

I surrender. "Yes. I promise I'll do something." I start to tear up.

"Oh, Kelly, listen, we all love you, and we're worried sick about you. But it's been seven months. It's time to ease back into it."

I nod.

He scribbles on a prescription pad. "Try running again. It's good for you. Gets the endorphins going." He hands me the slip of paper. "That's the address of the store I like for running shoes."

When I leave the office, the sun has come out. I squint and stop for a minute before I get in the car. The smell of the rain on the warming pavement is clean. I remember that I like that smell. I decide to give reentry into normalcy more of an effort.

I go get new running shoes on the way home. I call Tessa, Joe's wife, to have coffee. The pain is still there, hanging on under the surface, but I try to live through it, kind of like running through an injury. It feels awkward.

Finally, I'm able to put two days together where I function almost normally. Then I'm able to go three days with only brief crying episodes when I wake and when I fall asleep. And yes, after a long while, there's the day I make it through without a tear shed. The day after that is spent in bed, inconsolable, but still, the tear-free day is on record.

There's always an ache under my collarbone, but every day that I brush my teeth and put on pants instead of pajamas, I call a good day. I wait for there to be more of those than the not-so-good days.

Departure

A few months after my visit with Joe I'm able to stitch a few "together" days together. After six months, I make it a few weeks. And now, with the time that's passed, apart from the recurrent ache under my collarbone and the voids Peter has left all over my life, I'm pretty sure I at least appear to be a functioning human being.

Today, for instance, the boys and I are taking a very functional trip to visit my parents. This is something regular people do. No problem. Tessa takes us all to the airport. I love her dearly. She and Joe take good care of us. In a town without family, they are our family. With Mom and Dad two states away, I've leaned on Tessa and Joe a lot in the last two years.

She looks over at me. Her sleek dark bob bounces as she twists her hands on the steering wheel, the conspicuous diamond ring on her left hand glittering with all the movement.

"Are we going to park anytime soon?" I try hard to keep the exasperation out of my voice. Tessa gets worked up when we leave. It's sweet, but her worry about details and departure times and whatnot does nothing to relax me.

She finally pulls her oversize SUV into a spot at the curb. The boys hop out, shoving each other to get to the tailgate first to unload.

"Boys! Just get your stuff. Get it and go wait by the kiosk. This is not a race. We're all getting on the same plane."

"Mind your mother, boys." Tessa pulls a suitcase from the back of the car. Hunter and Beau finally have all of their stuff and drag their luggage into the terminal, leaving me at the curb with my best friend.

"I want to kill them already, and we aren't even on the plane yet."

She pulls one last bag from the back of her car. It's a shiny tote with the Eiffel Tower on it. "Here's the remedy. This is my flight bag. Delve into these goodies and ignore the wombats until you touch down in Cali."

She reveals the contents: a stack of gossip magazines. From the looks of it, most of them are "Sexiest Man" or "Hottest Hunks" editions.

"Quality journalism. I feel smarter already."

She shows me one in particular, reads from the cover. "Look at this gorgeous creature. And inside, 'Twenty-five Things You Didn't Know About Andy Pettigrew'!"

I look at the tall, lean, handsome man on the cover. "I know nothing about him."

Tessa strokes the cover guy's tuxedoed body with a manicured nail. "Except that he's smoking hot."

"Thank you, Tessa. I'll take good care of these. I better go herd the boys onto the plane before they get detained by the TSA." I give her a big hug, and I probably squeeze a little too tightly for the light conversation we just had.

She pulls back and looks in my eyes. "Take care of yourself. That's what this trip is for. Run lots, sleep lots, rest lots."

"I promise." I sling the bag over my shoulder and head into the terminal.

One Morning Run

I wake up to a dim room. Soft, blue light comes from a monitor. I sit in a chair in the corner.

I see Peter. He sleeps in a hospital bed. His skin is gray; his face is thin. I shiver at the sight of him and pull the blanket more closely around me.

I am still trying to center myself, orient myself, when the wind howls.

It grows to a roar, and the window blows open. I feel the ice-cold air bite at my skin. I try to shut the window, but snow flies in. It's everywhere, settling on the chair where I sat, filling the air of the hospital room.

I turn around. Peter is covered in snow.

I rush to him, brush the snow away from him. I uncover his face just as the monitor starts to beep loudly.

Peter's face is blue. It is the face of a frozen corpse.

I sit up in bed. The alarm continues to beep loudly. I smack it off and turn on the lamp.

Sitting on the bedside table is my wedding ring. I pick it up, feel it between my fingers. I don't know why, but I can't put it on. I set it back down and try to focus on finding my running shoes.

I like to run now. That's a big difference between me before and me now. I used to run on the treadmill when we all went to the gym. I did it because I should. Now I do it because I will go stark raving mad if I don't. It's become very cathartic for me. It helps me work through stuff that I might not even realize is a problem until I'm out there breathing hard and sweating.

I have a loop I like to run when we're here in California. From my parents' vacation condo in Indio I run south to this little coffee shop, about two miles, and sometimes I stop and get tea. It's a hold-over from living in the South, home of *sweettea*—all one word— which is iced tea with bucket loads of sugar in it. Only now I try to redeem myself and drink green tea since everyone is under the impression that it's good for you.

Running is good today. I feel strong. The Indio sun is warm in a very crisp, blue sky. The desert air is dry and cool. I feel so full and happy until suddenly I'm crying. Grief catches me by surprise then hits me hard. Tears stream down my face. After that dream this morning I should've known I was in for something seriously cathartic. It was there, lying dormant as I put on my shoes and told the boys and my parents I was heading out.

I'm just outside the little coffee shop when I have to stop. I bend over, elbows on knees, and there's definitely some heavy sobbing going on. But I'm also trying to catch my breath so I can get it together enough to stop crying.

There's a light touch on my shoulder. Oh shit.

"Are you all right?"

I look up from my bent-over position. I was kind of hoping it looked like I had a side stitch and was trying to work it out. Clearly it just looks like I'm losing it.

"I'm fine." The sun is behind the person's head from my position. I can only see that it's a guy, and he's wearing jeans, a coat, and a baseball hat.

"Are you hurt?" He's still standing there. He has a coffee carrier in his hand, with two cups and a white bag balanced on it. He's not leaving, so I guess I'm going to have to stand up.

I pull myself up and wipe my eyes and nose on the sleeve of my shirt. He's much taller than me, and he has on sunglasses. I feel my hair kind of flop back into place from being upside down.

"No, I'm okay." I step a little to the left, partly because the sun is still shining from behind him and partly because I have a head rush from standing up so fast.

He does not take this as a sign that I am okay. He steadies me by the elbow. "You should sit for a second. Here." He pulls out a chair at a little patio table of the coffee shop and helps me sit. He plunks the coffee tray down and sits next to me. "Do you want coffee?" He checks the two cups, evidently trying to identify which is which.

My head isn't spinning anymore, and I'm beginning to feel the full brunt of complete and total embarrassment. It's early enough that there aren't other customers to see this whole travesty, but still . . . I sound sheepish when I answer. "I'm fine. I drink tea anyway."

He plucks one of the cups from the holder and hands it to me. "You'll drink mine then. It's green tea. I'm trying to make up for eating crap food."

I sit very still, hoping I can disappear.

"Are you sure you're not hurt?"

"I'm really fine."

"Why were you crying?" His head is tilted a little. He seems to want to know. To me, it seems like a very young question to ask.

"A girl could have a million reasons to be crying while running. Unpaid bills, hormones, lost job, pulled hamstring—"

"Of course."

"My husband died two years ago today." Why, why did I just say that? I can feel tears crawling back up my throat again.

He covers his face with his hands. "Oh, Christ. I'm an idiot." He melts into his chair. Maybe I feel a little less embarrassed now.

"You couldn't have known. I didn't need to say that. I don't know why that just came out of my mouth." I put both my hands around the cup of tea. Either the weather's gone cold, or the turn in the discussion has chilled me. I shiver a little in the morning air. I start to look for an escape route.

He notices that I'm cold. No one ever notices that kind of stuff. He's up and out of his chair, and he's got his coat around my shoulders. It smells like Old Spice and cigarette smoke.

What do you say to a guy after you just brought up the death of your husband? I'm flummoxed.

He sits back down, pulls the top off the other cup. He takes a cautious sip and grimaces. "This coffee is awful."

"I like their tea." Apparently, inane blather is now all I can manage.

"No, this is some triple frappawhip vanilla nonsense. Tucker can tough it out. I'm drinking it anyway." He pulls open the white bag. "Want a muffin?"

I shake my head no and look at him over the rim of his tea that is now my tea. His brown hair is cut short at the nape and around his ears, but some bangs poke out from under the bill of the ball cap. It's old and frayed, obviously a favorite. I still can't see his eyes behind the sunglasses he wears. He has a stubbly beard, maybe a day or two. He looks young—younger than me. Maybe in his late twenties? The older I get, the harder time I have telling anyone's age.

I'm staring. I should say something. "Do you live here?"

"Just a couple days of work, then back to LA. What about you?"

I shake my head again. "No, my parents have a condo here. I live in Idaho."

He gives up on the sweet coffee and sits back, picking at the faux wicker on the arms of the chair. "I bet Idaho's nice."

He sits up abruptly and pulls a phone from his back jeans pocket. The phone vibrates furiously. He looks at the screen and jumps to his feet.

"I have to go. I'm sorry!" He leaves the coffee, the tray with the muffin bag, all of it.

He literally jogs across the street. He climbs into a black car and drives off before I even remember his jacket is draped across my shoulders. I stand up to see where he's gone, but the car has disappeared already, turned off onto a side street.

"Umm . . . okay."

Totally bizarre. I take off the coat and fold it. I check the pockets. There's a green plastic lighter in one, and the rest are empty.

I turn back toward Mom and Dad's condo with the jacket draped over my arm. I walk, too stunned by the chance meeting to muster a run.

The Next Morning Run

I tiptoe into the living room, feeling my way around the boys, still sleeping on the pull-out couch.

Of course I'm going out. The guy needs his jacket back, after all. I spent a lot of time last night thinking about how to graciously return it, how to say something witty, seem cool, or at least less crazy—all of that. Then I spent a lot of time worrying that I'll cry again.

I don't think I will. The boys and I had dinner last night and we talked about their dad, and I did cry then. But a lot of stories made me smile and laugh too. Mostly I just felt that familiar tight ache under my collarbone. That's how I feel when I miss him.

At the front door, I take the jacket and stuff it into a day pack I found in the closet.

Mom comes down the hall. "Are you going out again today?"

"I want to give that guy his jacket, Mom."

Her brow furrows. She's always been a worrier. "Just be sure he's not some stalker. Don't tell him anything."

"The way he left yesterday was more stalkee than stalker." I put the day pack on my back.

Mom pulls me into a hug before I can get the door open. "You hanging in there? I know yesterday was hard."

"I have to go, Mom." I don't want to have this conversation right now. I want to run.

"Sure, Bug. Have a good run." She kisses me on the cheek, just like she did when I was five.

Even though my mom drives me nuts sometimes, spending time with my parents here in Indio is always peaceful. I get a bit of a reprieve from the taxi-service-mom routine, and the boys enjoy hanging out with their grandparents. This morning I've got a bit of extra time: Mom and Dad are taking the boys with them to run errands.

As I stretch out and find my rhythm, I start to worry. I feel like a loser with the jacket in the day pack on my back. I am not a marathon runner, and in my opinion normal runners with day packs look like they're trying too hard. Also, the mystery guy's departure was odd. Is he a wanted criminal? Because the way he took off sure seemed a lot like that.

I'm almost to the coffee shop. What am I going to do if he's there? Do I jog on up, pull out the jacket? Then what?

I slow down, check the bistro tables out front. No one. The inside looks empty too. I stop for a moment, look around. The only person inside is the lonely barista behind the counter. I check my watch. It's roughly the same time as yesterday. Mystery guy is a no-show.

I'm a little relieved, actually. All the guy did was help someone bawling her eyes out. I'm silly to think I'll run into him again.

So I've been spared some humiliation. That's what I'm thinking about twenty minutes later when I finally come up the street to the condo and stop to stretch and cool down.

I peel off the day pack and toss it on the grass by the sidewalk.

The shade of the big palm tree out front is a good spot to stretch. I sit and start with my hips, turning across my body to lengthen the outside leg. Beauty queens. That's what Hunter's soccer team calls these stretches. Mid beauty queen, I hear someone walk up the sidewalk behind me.

"Um, hello."

I unwind out of the stretch to face the voice. It's him. Same baseball hat. Same sunglasses.

"Hi . . . How'd you find me?" It starts me worrying for a second. How *did* he find me?

"I pulled up to the coffee shop and saw you leaving, running home. I kind of followed you. That sounds bad." He tucks his hands into his jeans pockets, his shoulders shrugging up. He's uncomfortable.

"You needed your coat back." I jump up, brush off, and go for the day pack. I will be gracious, cool, and let him get out of here without embarrassing him. He wants to be on his way; I'm sure of it.

"Did you have a better run today?" He doesn't look rushed.

"I did. Yeah, I did. Thanks for asking." I try to hold still.

"I'm Andrew." He puts a hand out to shake.

I wipe mine off before I do. "Kelly. Nice to meet you."

"Are you busy?"

He's asking me?Really?

"No, I'm not." I have no idea what to say.

He shifts from foot to foot. He looks at me from behind the sunglasses briefly, and then stares at the sidewalk. "I have some time before I have to be anywhere. I could buy you a green tea."

I'm quiet. At some point I should probably talk. "Or I have tea. Do you want to come in for some?" For once in my life I say something normal.

He smiles. "Sure."

I pick up the day pack and try to fix my ponytail a little as I walk toward the front door. "My mom and dad got this place a few years ago. They live in LA."

I panic for a second as I open the door. First of all, did I just invite a serial killer into my house? And second of all, I can't remember—is said house clean? The boys have been sleeping on the pullout in the living room, but did they put it in before they left this morning? I cross my fingers that the kitchen doesn't look too terrible.

"It's been great to come visit them here. More mellow than LA." I swing the door open, and all looks well. Thank God Mom makes the boys pick up. The same probably couldn't be said if we were walking into my house.

"You said you live in Idaho?" He stands in the doorway. He takes off his sunglasses.

For a second, I can't answer. I am too stunned.

Andrew is Andrew Pettigrew. Andy Pettigrew. Movie star Andy Pettigrew. "Twenty-five Things You Didn't Know About Andy Pettigrew" Andy Pettigrew. Holy shit. Too bad I didn't read that article on the plane when I had the chance.

Recover. Recover. Speak! My brain finally comes back to me. He asked a question. What was it? "I'm sorry. Yeah. I live in Boise. Come on in. I'll get the kettle on." I check to make sure my mouth is closed.

How did I not notice this before? Young, tall, scruffy beard, nice smile, lives in LA. Probably the sunglasses. Without them, his famous blue eyes are unmistakable. Jesus, I am a dumbass.

What was the last thing I saw him in? He started out in a couple of movies as sons of really famous guys. I remember the one with that one girl, set during the Revolutionary War . . . What was the name of it? Oh, God. Nothing comes to me to say to this person. How do I say something if I can't even remember the name of his last movie? It was huge this summer, for God's sake. Come on!

He looks at me for a minute. His lips part, as if he's about to say something. It's a question, a look with a staggering vulnerability to it. I'm not sure what it means, but the way I take it, it feels like he's asking a favor. Maybe a favor about recognizing him, or not making a big deal out of who he is. I try to say yes by keeping my mouth shut. Keeping my mouth shut for once in my life is hard—trust me, I am a total reject at following social cues and shutting up. However, I'm all in favor of not discussing the movie thing at this point since I can't remember a single title of any of his multiple hits. Pathetic.

I put the kettle on and promptly am at loose ends. I don't know how to make small talk with a man, much less a famous one. I put two mugs on the kitchen table, get a tea bag in each. Thank God I have something to concentrate on.

He sits at the table. "What's Boise like?"

"There's a lot to do. Plus it's a good place to raise kids." Hmm. I just mentioned that I have children. I should know something personal about him. How old is he? Surely I can recall something from pop culture that could help me talk with this person. Why, why did I not read Tessa's magazines when I had the chance? I will bore him to death.

He seems interested. "You have kids?"

"Hunter and Beau. We moved to Idaho, and I realized their names are like the top two hunting-dog names out there. It embarrasses them. Hunter is eleven, and Beau is eight."

He looks at me for a moment, deciding something. "They must miss their dad."

Oh. He went there. I don't know why, but I let go. There's been nothing normal about meeting this person anyway. "My husband was sick for five months before he died. It was impossible for the kids. I was a mess. Some days are still worse than others."

He turns the mug by its handle. "That's why you run." He's perceptive. And curious. Interesting.

"If I don't, I yell. A lot. Things are tough enough without me being a total bitch." I try to take a deep breath. I'm not crying. That's a complete miracle.

"I have a hard time imagining you as any kind of bitch." He looks at me warmly and then leans forward. What's he going to do?

He takes the teaspoon out of my hand. The teaspoon I've been tapping on the table incessantly. I didn't realize that until now. "Oh, God, I'm sorry. You make me nervous."

"Why?" He smiles.

I doubt he needs to ask that question. I mean, really.

"Remember when you were first learning to drive?" I take another deep breath. I'm not sure if I've been breathing in any reliable way since we crossed the condo's threshold.

"Yeah, I do, actually. Everything was a giant ordeal. My dad took me out in our neighborhood. I sneezed and ran the car up on Mr. Hattingfield's yard. Took out his mailbox."

"I haven't been very social lately—except with people I know. Heck, since the boys were born, I haven't been super social at all. Okay, I wasn't ever amazingly social to begin with."

"But your point?" I think he's kind of grinning. At me. He could be close to laughing.

"I have one. Stop smiling. You're not helping. The point is, I'm back at the aware-of-every-little-part-of-a-social-interaction stage. Like beginner driving, when you check the mirrors, and you have to think, *Turn on the blinker*. That's the stage I'm in. I don't even know where to look. Do I look right at you the whole time we talk? Do I look you right in the eye?"

I stop to breathe for a second. He turns the mug all the way around by the handle before he responds, his eyes on the tea bag. "You're fine. You need to breathe, and you need to not tap the spoon on the table. Other than that, I find you pretty socially capable. I might even venture to say charming."

"Where do I look?" This has devolved into a social etiquette class offered by a movie star to a woman whose mind has completely left her in her moment of need.

"You can always look at me." He looks up from the mug, right into my eyes.

I agree. I think I could look at him for a nice long while. *Gaze* might be the word I'd choose for it. "Yeah." It's quiet for a moment. "Oh, let me get your jacket." I'm grateful for a reason to walk out of the kitchen and breathe. I look for where I tossed the day pack when we came in. I seem to be okay. I'm settling into the idea of the movie star in the kitchen.

When I come back, he's up, kettle in hand. "It was boiling."

"Thanks." I set his jacket on the back of his chair, sit at the table, and watch him pour water into both mugs. Do I feel different now that I know who he is? I can't tell.

He hands me my tea. "What if we went running tomorrow?"

"What?"

"You and me. I'd like to get out, stretch my legs. We could go for a run."

"I don't know. I usually run alone."

"You could humor me." He tilts his head in a little plea. I can't imagine anyone resists that look very often.

"I guess." I'm pretty sure this is a hallucination. What in the world?

"Good. I could meet you here. What time?"

"It's supposed to be really hot tomorrow. Six?"

"In the morning?"

"Yes." This running thing still seems unlikely. "Why would you want to run with me?"

"When you do take a minute and actually look straight at me, I like it. And I have to say, the way you were upset yesterday? I kind of feel like you could use a wingman."

"Except you ran off."

"Yeah, sorry about that."

"Sorry about the way I cried like a blithering idiot."

"No, really. I shouldn't have run off, but I needed to. Word sometimes spreads quickly."

We're talking about him. Him being famous. But we aren't talking about it. "I thought you were a spy. Or a felon."

"I act like a total lunatic ninety percent of the time, I swear to you. You've probably heard. I earned kind of a reputation when I was younger."

Again, I try to remember anything I've heard, but my mind is a total vacuum. "So you have to go back soon?"

He looks at me, takes a sip of his tea. "I think Monday. When do you go back?"

"Sunday. The boys start school again on Monday." I try to stay cool, but I think I'm sweating from nervousness. That's attractive. "I've kept you talking way too long. You probably have lots to do."

He makes no move to get up. "You'd be surprised. Unless I'm working, I'm completely bored most of the time. Sometimes friends come out to LA to visit, but other than that, I'm completely and utterly dull. I buy sneakers on eBay for fun."

"What kind of sneakers?"

"Old Air Jordans, other basketball shoes mostly. It's kind of addictive."

This strikes me as funny. "You buy sneakers worn by other people? Like, used shoes?"

"When you put it like that, it sounds gross. They're collectible. Limited editions. One guy spent eighty thousand dollars in a year."

"Really." I can't help it, and I can hear the sarcasm in my voice.

"I'm not *that* guy. It's something to do. I said I was boring."

"Do you even play basketball?"

"Not particularly."

I laugh. It feels good. As absolutely bizarre as this is, I like talking to him. He's funny.

Suddenly, I'm struck by a new thought: someone will be home soon. Someone as in one of my sons with my dad or my mom. I'm not prepared for any sort of introductions of this new person. I need to get him to leave.

Nothing smooth occurs to me. I stand up from the table. He looks at me. "I'm so sorry, but my boys should be home soon and . . ." I'm about to kick Andy Pettigrew out of my house. I am the biggest idiot on the planet.

"I'm leaving. Say no more." He's already on his way to the door, returned jacket in hand. He smiles at me. "So I'll see you in the morning, okay?"

"Okay. And thanks for stopping yesterday. Most people would walk a little faster if a person was freaking out on the sidewalk like I was."

He turns, hand on the doorknob, thoughtful for a moment. "It just seemed like the right thing to do. No big deal." He walks down the sidewalk to his car and gives a little wave before he gets in and drives away.

So I'm going on a run tomorrow at sunrise with Andy Pettigrew. No big deal.

Still Running

I don't even give the birds a chance to start their predawn tweeting before I am out of bed, dressed, and in front of the condo, ready for Andrew.

I held my breath for most of my morning routine, terrified that I would wake up my parents or the kids. The stealthy thing does not come to me naturally, so this is nerve-wracking. This is still my secret.

Yet my movie-star hallucination continues as the same black sedan pulls up and parks at the curb, just as the sun begins to filter through the palm trees to the east. Andrew Pettigrew climbs out of the car. He wears a hoodie, with baggy shorts to match, but no sunglasses this morning.

"Good morning." His voice sounds scratchy. He joins me on the sidewalk.

"You sound tired." I don't know if I should wave or what, so I put my hand out for a shake. "Good morning."

He shakes it. "Greetings, Kelly." He smirks. It's clear he thinks I'm a dork.

"Are you ready?" The longer I stand here, the worse the awkwardness will become, so I take off down the street, jogging slowly.

"Okay. Be gentle."

Of course I spent way too much time last night planning this. We're going to do a straight shot down the street to the cart paths of the municipal golf course, not far from Mom and Dad's condo. At night the course is lit, but it'll be deserted now—too early for golfers.

We run for a while in silence. He looks over at me and smiles. I smile back. He runs a little ahead, so I pour it on a bit and pass him easily. He catches up. We run in this easy, playful pattern for a while. He seems to be fairly fit.

He nudges me with an elbow. "How am I doing?"

"I don't know. Are you okay? Do you run much?" I like this. Talking to him while he's next to me is easier. I can run and look straight ahead and feel much more functional as a human. I don't know when I turned into such a crazy person.

"I run sometimes to get ready for work. Usually it's when I'm told to."

"You tell me when you want to stop and we will."

"You tell me how you are today. You feeling better?"

I'd much rather just run. "I'm okay. Each day is a new day. Some are easy; some seem long."

"Why don't we turn around at the end of that path up there? By that palm tree." He looks sly.

Probably because there are palm trees everywhere we look. I stop and turn around. "This is an easy-run day for me. We can head back."

He makes a big circle, twice around me, and then heads back

the way we came. "Thank God. I was worried I'd have to fake an Achilles tear."

I enjoy hearing the rhythm of two pairs of feet for a while, and I watch the sun climbing higher in the sky. We run together, side by side. I feel calm, so much more sane than I did yesterday, or the day before.

"I can see why you run. You're at peace."

We're back at the condo again.

"Here we are." I feel good—that wasn't a complete disaster.

He looks at me. "See? We're making direct eye contact without any kind of prompting or cue cards for you. Well done. And I have to say, you have lovely eyes. It'd be a shame if you avoided eye contact for the rest of your life."

"Thanks. For the run and for the compliment." I kind of want to reach over and touch him. I almost chicken out, but then I touch his elbow, just barely. It's my attempt to say "Hey, you're cool" in a low-key manner. Of course, I'm a complete dork, so . . .

He looks a little surprised. Maybe people aren't supposed to touch fancy-schmancy movie stars. Or maybe people just don't. He grins. "My pleasure."

We walk to his car. He swings the door open, stands with an arm draped over it.

He looks like he wants to say something else. For once I keep my mouth shut and wait to see what it is.

He fishes his cell phone and sunglasses out of the car. "Can I get your number?"

"You don't want my number."

"Yes, I do."

"No, you don't." Seriously, is he kidding?

"Do too." He shakes his head. "This is insane. Why not?"

"Look at you. Come on."

He stares at me with those very blue eyes. "Don't be ridiculous. Give me your number."

I tell him. He puts it into his phone. I bite the inside of my lip. I haven't done this in a lot of years, but I think the way I feel is the way a person feels at the beginning of something. It's kind of a dusty memory, but, yes, it's coming back to me.

I look at him for a minute. The world creeps back into my brain and speaks to me about real life again. "I don't suppose you get to Boise much." If this is a beginning, it's the beginning to a very short story. We are never going to see each other again.

His sunglasses are back in place, and he looks over them at me. "You never know." He gets in his car, but pauses for a second to comment. "Like I said, I'm bored a lot." And then he's gone.

The Next Time

The next day, my dad helps me load the car. The boys and I are headed back to real life, back to an empty house in Boise. But on this trip, we're also headed back to a reality that involves me keeping a surreal secret. Dad puts the boys' luggage in the back of the car for the ride to the airport, and I spend the whole time wanting to tell him who I went running with the day before.

Mom comes out on the driveway and begins to tear up instantly. I walk over and give her a big hug. I don't want to cry. I'm cried out for now.

"Oh, it was too short." She takes in a shaky breath, and I give her a stern *stop crying* look before I hug her again.

"We'll be in LA for Christmas, Mom." I snap the car's hatch shut.

"Did you get that guy's coat back to him?" She's changed the subject, making what she thinks is small talk. Little does she know.

"Yes, Mom, I did. When I ran back to the coffee shop."

Dad's interest is piqued. "What guy?"

Oh, oh, oh, I want to tell him. "Just a guy, Dad. He left his coat at the coffee shop."

"You gotta be careful these days, Bug. People kill each other from Greglist."

"It's Craigslist, Dad. And there was nothing creepy about it. He left his coat, and I returned it. End of story." There was a bit more to the story, actually, but still nothing worth divulging right now.

We say our good-byes, get the whole crew to the airport, and all I can hear repeating in my head is "end of story."

The boys and I fly back to Boise. I don't say a word to anyone about Andrew. I'm really tempted more than a few times, but then I remember that look, that silent favor I promised I would do for him. So I keep quiet.

I do get the names of his movies straight, though. I hopped on the computer when we got home and Googled him. And I may have done it a time or two since then. It feels wrong, kind of like I'm running a background check on him or looking through his underwear drawer.

It's amazing what you can remember when you're not standing in front of a famous movie star. I didn't have to go far to remember last year's big bank-robbing movie, *Thief at Midnight*. And that girl in that Revolutionary War movie, *Redcoats Rising*? Her name is Amanda Walters. There's a picture of him with her at some awards show right around then—about five years ago. They must have dated. It's at the top of the Google search.

There are more than a few old news stories out there from around the same time, with titles like, "Andy Pettigrew's Wild Night Out." My stomach flip-flops a little when I see those. He mentioned a reputation. For what? Partying? Lots of women? It's clear I could probably dig around for a while and find out more than I care to know.

But I don't.

I leave it at that.

There are a lot of reasons I don't want to know about his past. The big one right now is this: what's the point? He was nice. He was a good listener. I'll likely never see him again. No reason to drag out the old dirty laundry.

However, there are *many* Web sites devoted to his wonderfulness. I can't tell without looking more closely if any of them say he's dating anyone right now or not. I've decided to preserve our relatively pleasant exchange in my mind and not mess it up with any bizarre fan musings I might find if I look further. I'm keeping my little brush with fame unsullied by tawdry gossip, thank you very much. It's fun from time to time, as I sit and watch the millionth soccer game, or fold the millionth pair of boys' socks, to think about Andrew. I smile every time, and it makes my heart happy whether our paths ever cross again or not.

So the Reynolds clan falls back into our routine. School days are busy with the boys' swimming and soccer, homework, all that stuff. The school year has started without me in the classroom for a third year in a row, and I wonder a lot about what's next for me.

The days pass pretty quickly when the boys are in school. I get them up, get them to school. I check email, pay bills, all the boring stuff. Then I usually run, shower, and get ready. Sometimes I meet Tessa for coffee or go to the Y and lift. Or I do errands or clean the house (not that I enjoy that, or do it well, or often enough). Most of the time I turn around and it's time to go get the boys. It's weird. I do like to read, and I've been known to have other hobbies too. But since I got married, and then had kids, and then lost Peter, and then gave up my job, it's as if my life is a funnel. Things have narrowed and narrowed to a point where sometimes it seems I exist to take care of the house and the kids.

It's probably time for me to get a new job—a new kind of job. Teaching reminds me too much of my old life. It reminds me of Peter. I feel better thinking about a new direction. But I don't know what the new direction is yet.

As early November turns cold and crisp, I have to admit, I'm getting to be hard to live with. I try to run every day. I work on repainting the boys' room. I do just about everything to keep the ache under my collarbone from turning into a chest-crushing depression. But with the holidays around the corner, it's difficult. There's no way around it.

But I continue to try, so today I run before I pick the boys up at school. To add to the gloomy onset of the saddest time of my year, Boise is blanketed with a thick, gray layer of inversion, a cold, frosty smog. It hurts my lungs. It makes it ten degrees colder in the valley than it would be if we were on the top of the Boise Front, the foothills outside town. Yuck.

When my cell phone rings, I'm more than glad to stop to take the call. "This is Kelly Reynolds." I don't recognize the number, and it's not a local area code. It's probably the Shriners or the Kiwanis or the somebodies asking for a donation.

"Hi, Kelly. It's Andrew."

There's a pause. I'm drawing a total blank. "Hi there. Can I help you?"

"Andrew Pettigrew. We met in Indio?"

Oh my God, I'm an idiot. "Hi! I'm so sorry. I was just trying to figure out who I knew named Andrew. How are you?" I feel the blood rise to my cheeks despite the cold. I'm thrilled, I'll admit it. Andrew called! This is some sort of miracle or defect in the time-space continuum.

"I'm good. But I need a ride. Are you busy right now?"

Clearly I'm suffering from early onset Alzheimer's. What is he talking about? "I'm in Boise, on a run, but—I'm sorry, where are you?"

"At the Western Air terminal. Can you come get me?"

What? But I don't say that out loud, thank God. "Okay . . . I've got to get my car. I'll be there in fifteen minutes."

"See you then."

The line goes dead. I sprint home. What the hell? What the hell is Andy Pettigrew doing calling me for a ride in Boise, Idaho? When we haven't spoken in two months? When he is one of the most famous and sought-after men in the world, and I am a not-famous, not-sought-after regular person? Seriously, this is hard to believe. Running home, I think I probably set a personal record from sheer adrenaline.

And, oh, God, I can't even look at myself in the mirror when I get there. I'm in my running gear. I don't think I'm a feast for the eyes on my best days, but the hat I'm wearing right now is a hand-me-down from Hunter's last-season ski outfit, and my running tights are coated with Samoyed hair. Today I am not only *not* a feast for the eyes, it would be a stretch to say I'm even a junky, stale snack for the eyes.

I'll be damned if I'll leave Andrew waiting there, though. Yes, it's a private terminal, but I'm not going to give anyone a chance to call out the vultures that are the paparazzi. Of course, I'm not sure who that would be, given that this is Boise, Idaho, but the point is, I feel protective of him. I think we might be friends, and I'm not leaving him there for people to recognize and harass.

I drive way too fast to get there, and I also start to worry about the approaching end of the school day. I don't know where Andrew is headed, but this could be a close shave in terms of getting back to pick up the boys.

As I pull up to the terminal parking lot, I feel a little smile form. I'm going to see him again. I never thought that would happen. But I try to remain calm. There's absolutely no reason to believe he noticed me or thinks of me in any special way. This is a man, a famous man, who happens to be in my town, and there's no reason to believe it's anything more than that. Although a teeny, tiny part of me remembers that he *did* say I have lovely eyes.

I chew a stick of gum before I leave the car. I look a mess, but maybe the gum will distract from any terrible, sweaty odor I might be putting out.

Inside the door, I don't see him right away. There isn't a counter, just a woman sitting at a desk in a generic office reception area.

"I'm here to pick up a friend," I tell her. "He just flew in?"

"You can go on back." She absently waves me toward a door.

I go through it into a huge airplane hangar. The triple-story doors are open to the cold weather. A small jet taxis out, headed toward the runway. A man stands just outside the doors, silhouetted, a bag at his feet.

It's him. I can tell as I get closer. The baseball hat is the same. So are the sunglasses.

He looks kind of abandoned. I can't believe a private plane just dumps you at the door of a terminal and takes off, but I've never flown on a private plane, so . . .

"Hi." I walk up to him.

He smiles, picks up his bag. "Hi. Thanks for coming to get me."

An employee walks by and gives us an odd look. Maybe this isn't the way it usually works.

I can't act natural. I just can't. "What are you doing here? I mean, I'm definitely glad to see you, but where are you going? Why do you need a ride?" I stop talking before *What the hell?* or worse escapes my mouth.

We walk around the outside of the building toward my car. He lugs the duffel bag casually over one shoulder. Wherever he's headed, he hasn't packed much.

"Some of the people I work with are going skiing in Sun Valley and invited me to go with them. I wasn't doing anything, so I said yes. I don't ski, but it's important sometimes to hang out with the people in my business—you know, network and all that."

He reaches into his pocket and pulls out a pack of cigarettes. "I'm so sorry, but I have to smoke. I really need it. Filthy habit, I know. I never should've started. It's one of the vices I've yet to give up." He smokes, and we're almost to the parking lot. I'm still silent, still confused. "Anyway, the longer I sat on the flight with these people and listened to them, the more I knew I could not spend a weekend with them."

We're at my car. He hurriedly drops the cigarette and stomps it out. I pop the hatchback and silently cringe. We've got the dog's bed, two pool noodles, and a bag of clothes destined for Goodwill in the back. It's a total mess.

He tosses his bag in without a second glance and shuts the door. I don't even get an opportunity to sheepishly apologize. He's talking too fast.

"So then suddenly we're landing, and I realize we aren't landing in Sun Valley, we're landing in Boise—some nonsense about wind shears in Hailey, who knows, and we're on the ground, waiting it out."

He's climbed in the passenger side and now scoots the seat way back. Of course it's up too far because no one ever rides in the front seat. The boys are too young. He's still talking. "I'm really pissed now, really dreading the weekend, and as I fidget and look through my contacts on my cell, I see your number. And to be totally frank, the sudden idea of seeing you sounded immeasurably more appealing than being with those idiots."

Now, finally, he is quiet. I sit in my seat, keys poised to turn in the ignition, but I'm stuck. I think what he just said is still bouncing around the inside of my head, waiting for the neurons to fire and make meaning.

Stuff comes out of my mouth that I hope resembles sentences. "So you called because you want to hang out with me? Like, for the weekend?" I'm staring at him, I'm pretty sure.

"Kind of? I don't know. It was a whim. If it's a bad whim, just tell me." His brow crinkles a little above those very blue eyes.

I wake up. "Oh, shit! I have to get my kids." I start the car and gun it a little, rushing now to get across town.

It's ten minutes to three—the bell at school will be ringing, and Hunter and Beau will be standing on the curb waiting for me. I need to get my kids, but there's no way I can do that with a man in my car. Fabulous movie star or no, the boys haven't seen me with a guy since their dad. I haven't had coffee with anyone, I haven't done a single thing with anyone of the opposite sex who was not related to me or one of my friends, and I certainly haven't dated anyone since their dad. Not that I am dating *this* person, but still, what will the boys think when they meet him? Will they freak out? How badly will they freak out?

My hands shake all of a sudden. Andrew is still looking at me.

"Okay, I have to drop you somewhere."

Now he looks really confused. "What?"

"I have to drop you somewhere. I can't think straight, and I have to pick my kids up, and you can't be in the car when I get them. Then I have to think of something to say to them about you . . ." I trail off. We drive through downtown, headed toward the school.

"You didn't tell them you met me?"

"I didn't tell anyone about you. I didn't think I'd ever see you again." Now I'm blushing.

"I got your number, and you didn't tell a soul about me?"

"I thought you were just being polite. I didn't think you'd actually call. Or show up in my town. So, no."

"Geez. I appreciate you being discreet, but really . . ."

We're about to pass my house when inspiration strikes. I turn the car hard into the alley, throwing Andrew against the passenger-side door.

"What are you doing?" He looks a little panicked now.

I brake hard and stop the car behind our garage. It used to be a stand-alone one-car, but the owners before us built it out with a loft above, which is connected to the house by a catwalk to the second-story deck. Peter used it as his man cave—watched TV and tuned skis in it. Since he's gone, I put a bed in there so guests can stay, but it's not a place I can spend much time in yet. It's still Peter's room.

"Wait here." I grip the steering wheel and smile at him, take a deep breath and blow my bangs out of my face. I'm kind of proud of myself for thinking of a solution.

"In an alley?"

I nod.

"You're ditching me in an alley." He chews on his lip.

"No, no, this is the back of my house. It's our garage—a guest room, not just a garage. There's a guest room over the garage. It connects to the house. Just wait here. I'll get the boys, and I'll figure out a way to introduce you. We can hide you in the guest room while you stay for the weekend."

"You do know I'm not wanted by the law, right?" He smiles a little.

Thank God, because I'm pretty sure this is the worst hostess behavior I've ever exhibited in my life. There have to be thousands of Andy Pettigrew devotees who would skin me alive at this moment. Or offer to take my guest off my hands in a heartbeat.

"I just don't know about you staying in the house. Since my husband died, I just . . ." I seem to be running out of words a lot with this man.

He breathes in. "No, I understand. Your boys might jump to conclusions. You don't want to weird them out. I get what you're thinking." He swings the door open and nods. "Go get your boys. I'm fine. I'll hang out back here and try not to look felonious."

"I do want to hang out with you. I think you'll like Boise. I just need to figure it out."

"Go get them."

"I'll text you when we get back to the house."

So I pull away, leaving my apparent friend, the international movie star, in an alley while I drive to the grade school of my two children. Life has officially become completely absurd. Maybe this is some French movie.

And there they are. They're fighting about something—I can see that as I pull to the front of the line to pick them up. Both are loaded down with coats and lunch bags and backpacks. I stop, and the door by the curb swings open.

Maybe they can tell I've been behaving like a maniac for the last fifteen minutes or so, because they get quiet as they enter the car.

"Hi, guys." I may sound a little out of breath. Good lord.

"Mom, tell Hunter the orange thermos is my thermos. He keeps taking it, and then I have to pack the green one with the crack in it, and by the end of the day the bottom of my backpack is soaked."

I want to kiss Beau for being so normal. "I will buy you both a new thermos if that would help. Listen, guys, I need your help with something."

Hunter looks at me in the rearview mirror. He's gotten so tall. When did that happen? "With what?"

"I need you to make a swing through the house and straighten up when we get home. We're having someone over for dinner tonight."

A plan forms in the frenzied recesses of my brain. I can feed Andrew dinner, and then we can find a place for him to stay, or I can hide him in the guesthouse, but it will all be good.

"Who?" Beau's curious.

"A friend of mine from Indio."

"Who do you know in Indio? We just see Granddad and Gran."

"Well, Mr. Know-It-All, I met a friend down there last time we visited. We met at the coffee shop."

Which is partly true.

Hunter's already lost interest. "Fine. I'll help, but I'm not doing laundry. I just did mine on Sunday, and Beau won't put his in the hamper, so I shouldn't have to handle it."

"No laundry. Just straighten up a little. And he flew in early, so he may be there pretty soon after we get home."

Or not. Since he's standing in back of the garage where I ditched him. Andrew's never going to speak to me again. I'm an idiot of epic proportions.

We get home, and both boys whine a little more about the unforeseen straightening. I turn in circles, trying to get my bearings. I text Andrew:

We're home. Come knock on the front door.

Then I try to practice breathing like a normal human being.

There's a knock. Ditto the dog goes crazy, barking and jumping. The boys materialize from upstairs.

I take the deepest breath I can. "He's here. Come and meet my friend, you guys." I grab Ditto's collar.

The boys actually do as I say. They realize there's a stranger at the door. I swing it open.

Andrew stands there, smiling. "Hi, Kelly."

"Hi. Come on in." This is odd beyond odd. Andrew has to pretend he came from somewhere when in reality he's been stuck waiting for me by the garbage cans out back. Good thing he's an actor.

He walks in, and Ditto breaks away from me to try to get a lick. Andrew bends down to pet the dog for a minute. I realize he's not wearing his sunglasses and remember that extra thing here: he's a new friend of Mom's, but he's also a movie star.

"This is my friend Andrew from Los Angeles. I met him in Indio on our last trip."

There is quiet. I can feel panic rising in my throat. This is a terrible idea.

"It's nice to meet you, boys. You're Hunter, is that right?" Andrew stands and reaches out to shake Hunter's hand.

"You're Andy Pettigrew! No way!"

Andrew smiles. "Yep."

Beau looks confused. "Why would you want to come to Boise? How did you ever meet my mom?"

"She and I ran into each other at the coffee shop by your grandma's house. She told me how great Boise was, so I thought I'd come see for myself."

Beau speaks up. "Boise."

"What?" Andrew looks confused.

"Boy-see. You said *boy-zee*. It's pronounced *boy-see*."

Andrew smiles at me. "Well, your mom said you two might show me around Boy-see a bit."

Beau looks satisfied. He and Hunter elbow each other. Hunter adopts a very hip sound to his voice all of a sudden, kind of SoCal skateboarder by way of eleven-year-old. "Yeah, we can show you lots of stuff."

I'm worried. "Now, guys, Andrew's stay is not something to tell everyone about. He won't have a lot of privacy if the news gets out that he's in town."

Beau speaks up. "Are you staying with us?"

I panic. "No, he's not."

Beau looks perplexed. "Why not?"

That's not the reaction I expected. "Well . . ." I can't think of anything to say.

Hunter speaks up. "Because he can rent out the whole top of a hotel or something. And besides, our house is a mess. You should stay somewhere swanky."

Andrew shoots me a look and stifles a grin. "Well, I want to keep a low profile this go-around, so I won't be renting out a penthouse."

"We've got a guest room. Over the garage. You could stay there." Beau's a problem solver.

Hunter brightens. "Nobody would ever think to look for you at a house like ours."

Beau's got a better idea. "You could stay in our room if you don't want to be by yourself. We've got bunk beds."

The entire conversation is a runaway train. I'm not in any sort of control. Andrew's smile keeps getting bigger and bigger.

I must speak up. "You both need to slow down. Andrew doesn't need to stay in your room. The guest room would be fine. Andrew, would you like to stay with us while you're in town?" I can't believe this is happening.

Andrew looks at me, and his eyes twinkle. "Thanks, I'd appreciate that. Thanks, boys, for the idea."

Hunter, my perceptive one, speaks up again. "Mom, you call him Andrew. Is that what he goes by?"

I don't even know.

Andrew smiles very broadly. "Andy's my acting name. You can call me Andrew. Your mom could tell I prefer that right from the start."

So the short story gets a bit longer. Maybe this *is* the beginning of something. But what?

A Little Dose of Reality Would Make Sense Right About Now

It's so weird having him in the house, I kind of freeze. It's exciting. I mean, he's this amazing guy—at least that's how he comes off in his films. I haven't said anything about that yet, not out loud, but he does tend to play the kind of character who makes an entrance in slow motion accompanied by lots of power chords. He's good looking, though standing here in the kitchen, near the pot that still has the burned chili in it, that might be tempered a bit.

It's odd how relaxed the kids are. Beau brought in his rock collection to show Andrew, but Hunter reflexively turned on the TV and opened up his notebook to start his homework. Andrew now sits next to him at the kitchen table.

"So what's the job for tonight?" Andrew seems content to be here.

"Math. We're doing factors." He glances up at Andrew, then at the TV, and back at his paper.

"How many problems?" Andrew leans over the paper with Hunter.

"Just ten. I got most of it done in homeroom at the end of the day. Mr. McAllister was distracted by Robby, so we had extra time."

Beau loves hearing about the trials and tribulations of students in Hunter's class. "Oh, Robby. What did he do today?" He wants nothing more than to fit into his older brother's world. Hunter used to have no patience for it, but since Peter died, he seems to have softened. Or he's gotten used to the attention telling stories brings.

He launches into some story about Robby sharpening pencils down to the nub in homeroom. I take the opportunity to make a wild swing through the house. There's no way I will get to vacuum. It's not a chore done in secret. I do take a minute to pull off the bedspread in the guest bedroom, put a clean blanket on, and run the bedspread down to the laundry room. Then I'm back up to the boys' bathroom to wipe the pee from the toilet seat. We have three bathrooms in the house, and I have surrendered one to the destruction that is the male gender. If I can help it, I usually don't even go in there.

I come back downstairs. Hunter's done and has his feet up on the chair across from him at the table. He and Andrew are watching some annoying sitcom rerun.

Beau stands at the fridge, staring into it. Letting all the cold air out.

"Beau. Shut the door." I'm annoyed.

"Mom, I'm hungry!"

Hunter perks up at this. "Me too. What are we eating?" I groan inwardly. I haven't gotten that far. And we have a guest. I told the boys we were having him over for dinner, but we have no dinner. We don't even have milk in the house.

"I wasn't sure what Andrew would like, so he and I are going to pick up something for dinner. Can you two stay here while we run out?" My brain can't process all this quickly enough. I turn to Andrew. "I guess we'll risk the grocery store. Someone will recognize you, I bet."

"I doubt it. Grocery stores are a relatively easy place to keep a low profile. And I've got skills."

"Okay. Boys, you stay here."

Both boys are busy watching the TV now. They don't even turn their heads as they comment, "Yes, Mom." They sound faintly robotic.

It strikes me as odd that the boys are so normal, so unimpressed. I keep waiting for the shit to hit the fan. Maybe they're trying to be cool. Who knows? It's puzzling.

In the car, I worry more about the store. People will spot him, and then he'll be mobbed. "What if people freak out over you? Doesn't that happen?"

Andrew is back in the passenger seat. He's scooted it all the way back, but his long legs are still not able to fully extend. My car is too tiny. Peter never rode in it either. His car was the family-trip car. Mine was the I-drive-myself-and-the-boys-around car. I sold Peter's car. Way too many memories in there. It smelled like him. I couldn't climb into it without wanting to faint from his sheer presence. It was worse than his clothes in the closet or his razor on the bathroom sink.

"If we act normal—you'll see. People might do a double take, but they'll talk themselves out of it. We just keep moving and act normal, and it'll be fine."

"What do you want to eat? I'm a lousy cook. If I want to make something more than just edible, I have to come with a recipe. Peter used to be able to shop without one. Not me."

"Is that your husband?"

I realize it's the first time I've said his name out loud in front of Andrew. "Yeah."

"I like that name."

I guess he said that because, really, what do you say when a widow brings up her husband?

He puts his hand on mine for just a second when I shift into third gear. It's a pat, or a touch, just an *it's okay* kind of checking-in gesture. I like it.

I'm insane. None of this is going to work. Why is he here?

"Why are you here?" Oh, it just came out of my mouth. We pull into the store parking lot. This should be interesting.

He smiles, kind of closes his eyes for a minute, and then looks right at me. "To be honest, it just feels like the place I'm supposed to be right now. Beyond that, I have no idea."

"Me too." I smile at him and park. "I mean, it feels like this is the right thing. You feel like the right thing. No, not that. Oh, you know what I'm saying, don't you?"

He squints a little, still smiling. Maybe not.

I try again. "Look at Hunter, at Beau. They're so relaxed. They don't seem fazed by you at all. *At all.* Like you're supposed to be here. That's all I mean."

He nods and opens his door. "Let's find food."

We get out of the car. In the parking lot, he's got his sunglasses on, and I try not to fidget too much. He walks next to me. I don't know—maybe it's because Peter was average height, but I keep noticing how tall Andrew is. He's got a long stride, obviously, but he's also got a smooth way about him. He moves through space at an almost languorous pace.

We go inside. The shades come off. He grabs a cart and pushes it along, elbows resting on the handle. So far, we're down the first aisle, and no one has even looked in our direction. He isn't hurried, and he seems completely at ease. I'm impressed.

"What do the boys like to eat?" We're in the produce section.

"Nothing within a five-mile radius of these vegetables, I'll tell you that much."

He chuckles. "Men I have something in common with."

I pick up a head of romaine and a bag of spinach. "We'll do a salad, and they can drench it in ranch. It's still a vegetable, I guess."

We pass the beer and wine aisle. I ignore the regular knot in my stomach and act like a good host. "Do you want to get a bottle of wine or something?"

"Naw, I'm good. I'd rather save my calories for MoonPies. And I have a shoot coming up, so I can't go too crazy."

"I guess that's an occupational hazard."

"If you want something, don't let me stop you, though."

I'm relieved. "I don't drink, really. It's a long story from long ago. Nothing you want to hear about in the grocery store, trust me."

He looks curious but seems to respect the tone in my voice. "Maybe you'll want to tell me another time. But it means you're a good influence on me. The producers thank you for keeping me beer-gut free before the movie." He smiles. "When I retire from acting, though, I plan to let myself go, Elvis style. It's PBR and deep-fried peanut butter and banana samiches all the way."

He slows the cart a little to check out the apples.

The guy restocking the bananas looks at us. For longer than normal.

Andrew doesn't miss a beat. He stands up a little taller, turns his body to face me. He motions with his eyebrows. I was right. He whispers conspiratorially as he steers the cart toward the deli case. "The produce guy has made a positive ID. Time to move along."

I follow his lead. He doesn't speed up, and he doesn't look at the guy again. He just continues to amble along. We get a chicken without further incident.

We use the self-checkout and make for the parking lot without another sideways glance.

"That was impressive. It's a little like a Jedi mind trick or something. No one noticed you except that one clerk."

He bumps my shoulder as he steers the cart. "I told you I had the ninja skills. Pushing the cart is very un-movie-star-like. It works every time." He takes the keys from me and unlocks the back to toss everything in. He flashes all of his gorgeously white teeth. "Buying deli chicken isn't glamorous either. I don't think people want to meet their favorite hero while he's buying dinner or cat litter or something. Too normal. Ruins the mystique."

"I saw the governor in Target one time. He was looking at dishes. I played it cool."

"Good move." He tosses the keys back to me.

As I turn to get in the car I hear her.

"Kelly!" It's a yell—a bark, really. But it's a bark I usually love. It's Tessa, my friend. Right now I'd run her over with my car if it meant avoiding what's about to happen.

"Oh, God, Andrew, no Jedi trick in the world is going to save us from this. You better get in the car."

"What?"

"You should get in the car. This is my friend Tessa. You'll want to take cover. Trust me."

She's trying to steer an overloaded cart straight at us. She's sporting a shiny Patagonia down coat zipped up over her doctor's wife figure, and by the way she's walking, I can tell her antennae are up. She's always had a keenly honed sense of curiosity about anyone else's life. Her zest and candor are two things I usually love about her, but presently, I can't think of anyone I'd like to avoid more.

Andrew has his hands full of grocery bags, and he's clearly trying to decide if fight or flight is appropriate.

I try a preemptive strike. I trot over to Tessa, who's luckily having a heck of a time getting her cart moving. Part of this is due to the three insanely cute black-haired girls in it. And all the groceries piled in around them.

"Girlfriend!" Tessa's not even looking at me. She's got her eyes on Andrew. She's going to roll the cart over my toes in a second.

"Hey, Tessa. Hi, girls."

The triplets chime in. "Kelleee!" They are almost two, and they are little chubby-knuckled queens of the walk. Joe and Tessa tried for five years to get pregnant. They spent thousands on IVF to bring children into their lives. The month they found out they were having triplets, Peter and I found out he was sick.

"Who's with you?" Tessa doesn't mince words.

"A friend from Indio. He's on his way to Sun Valley."

"You don't have any friends in Indio. You have your parents. And they don't count." Tessa tries to look past me to check out Andrew more fully.

Why does everyone feel compelled to remind me that I have no friends in Indio? "Thanks. Thanks for that."

The girls are into the groceries. Josie has a box of graham crackers and has torn the top off. Genevieve and Jasmine pull Twizzlers from a hole they've made through the bottom of the grocery bag straight into the package. Tessa hasn't noticed yet.

Andrew's stowed the groceries in the car and has come to stand next to me. He puts his hand out. "Hi, I'm Andrew."

I can't believe his bold gesture is a good idea.

Tessa shakes his hand. Just as she lets go, she figures it out. Her big sunglasses can't hide the top of her eyes as they go wide in recognition. Silly me, I didn't recognize him with his sunglasses on, but she sure did.

"Pleased to meet you. I'm Tessa."

She might actually be at a loss here. I'm stunned that she's stunned.

"Andrew and I are friends from Indio." I have a moment where I'd like to tell her I told you so, that I do have friends from Indio—this one friend, at least. I love her, but she's the bossy sister I never had, and sometimes I like to be right. She and Joe are right 90 percent of the time, and I may claim a half percent or so. The rest is too nebulous or trivial to matter.

"What're you doing here?" She looks right at him.

"Buying groceries," I answer. "The boys are waiting at home, so we better get going."

"Okay." Her mouth may be open a little. Her keys dangle from her hand. The girls aren't even trying to be sneaky anymore: they've pulled an entire baguette out of the bag and are gnawing on it like little raven-haired scavengers.

"It was nice to meet you." Andrew gives her a wave and goes to the car.

I'm about to follow when she grabs my wrist.

"Oh no you don't. Do you know who that is?"

"God, Tessa, I'm not that dense. Yes, I do."

"How'd you meet him?"

"In Indio. I told you."

"Well, you might get away from me right now, but don't think I'm not tweeting about this as soon as I get in the car. I should've taken a picture! Damn, why didn't I do that?"

I poke her arm, hard. "Because. That's why."

"What?" She fumbles around in her purse.

"You will *not* ruin this for me. He's my new friend."

"Oh, come on! This is too amazing!"

"Tessa. Please." Now I'm quiet.

Tessa suddenly notices the girls. "Girls! How many times do I have to tell you, stay out of the groceries!"

"Yeah, stay out of it." I give Tessa my best pleading smile with lots of nervous teeth.

She sighs. "Whatever. If you don't text me this weekend, I'm coming over and breaking in."

She might actually do that.

"I promise. I have to go." I kiss her on the cheek, pat each little monster on the head, and hustle back to the car.

"That's your friend?" Andrew looks at me as I start the car as fast as I can and pull out.

"Tessa. She and her husband are my best friends. They've put up with a lot." I wonder if he can feel how her thumbs are itching to tweet about him. "Let's go."

We head home. Andrew brings his stuff in along with the groceries, and I realize in a moment of horror that his bag was in the back of the car all afternoon. But the boys must not have noticed.

After a very pieced-together dinner, the boys go to bed. Tomorrow is Friday, and they will go to school.

I will be left with a guest to entertain. What I would like to do is press Pause and spend the day cleaning the house so I can then relax and hang out with my new friend without trying to steer him around messes all day.

We sit at the kitchen table. He seems fidgety. Now I'm worried. Here it comes, the part where he has second thoughts and tries to escape.

He looks up at me, sheepish. Oh, God, I'm right.

"This is so embarrassing. I've got to have a smoke. I've been good all day, but to be honest, I'm dying right now. Do you mind?" He stands.

I'm so relieved it's not about me, I practically jump up too. "We can go up on the deck. I'll grab a blanket."

We step out. The night is clear. The inversion has lifted. The moon has a haze around it, and there's a slight stir of wind.

He stands at the railing and lights up. I can see his shoulders visibly lift and release, the tension going out of them. I sit on the chaise longue, the one Peter liked to sun himself on when he was sick. He used to joke that he was cooking himself with vitamin D. I shiver. I think it's less from the cold than from the memory, but I pull the blanket over me just in case. Sometimes it feels like Peter is in my skin. I shake at the strength of his impression, still so strong, sitting here on this chaise.

Andrew hasn't turned around yet. He looks out over the valley, bathed in the hazy moonlight. In fall and winter we have a clear view. In summer the trees obscure it.

"This is different. Not at all like my hometown. It's so open here; the view just goes on."

"Where are you from?" I'm curious. With my limited Googling, I don't know that much about him.

"Harrisburg. State capital of Pennsylvania; did you know that?

A little town outside it, actually. Lots different from here. Very lush and green, but with a working-class, rust-belt vibe."

He turns around and shivers. He's cold. The man is wearing a hoodie, either because he's from LA or because he's twenty-nine. A sweatshirt does not cut it in Boise in November.

"You're freezing. Come sit down."

"I smell like smoke." He stubs out his cigarette, looks for a place to put it.

I have a mom-ish moment, but I resist. I want to say something about the smoking. It's bad for you, stinky habit, people who care about you don't want you to get sick . . . But this is a grown man. It would be a welcome change to relate to someone in my life as an equal. It's been two years. Plus, I've been around enough to know that people don't quit things like smoking because of someone else. That thought threatens to open a door I don't want to walk through tonight, memories I don't need to recall in the presence of a new person.

Anyway, he has to make a decision to quit on his own, so I shrug all of those thoughts off in the cold night air. Now's not the time for any of that.

I lift the edge of the blanket. Andrew comes and sits next to me. We are shoulder to shoulder, sitting on the chaise with our backs to the wall. I have my feet pulled up under me to stay warm. He stretches his legs out, and for a minute I have an impression of him as a thoroughbred. No one would ever mistake me for anything coltish. I'm run-of-the-mill average height. Run-of-the-mill average everything, actually.

"Tell me about acting." I feel good. I'm having a normal conversation. I'm not behaving like a total doofus. For once.

He settles in under the blanket. I try not to notice that his leg and mine touch. He doesn't seem to notice at all. "I started in high school. I was a runner, in track, hurdles, but I got shin splints spring of my junior year. A girl I liked was in drama, so I tried out for the end of the year production of *Heidi*. I was the grandfather. Got to wear a gray wig and beard, use lots of spirit gum. It was awesome."

"After that?"

"I got lead parts in all the productions my senior year, and my shin splints hadn't really healed, so I stuck with drama. When I graduated, I went to LA and stayed with a friend of my mom's from high school. I was lucky, I guess, because I started getting commercials right off the bat. And I was sleeping on her couch, so I didn't have to pay rent."

He's finally decided to put the cigarette butt in a planter with a dead geranium next to the chaise. He grins a little. "The rest you can look up on IMDb. That's kind of weird. Just Google me."

I blush. Been there, done that. It's good that it's dark out here. "Uh-huh." I clear my throat. "You still like acting a lot?"

He's up again, walking around the deck, looking at the odds and ends on the potting bench, picking at the dead flowers in the planters on the railing. "Mostly. The movies with big sets are the best. You know, like it's 1918, and there's a whole train yard full of extras in uniforms. And I like the drama. The angst or the tragedy, and reacting in a situation the way someone totally different from me would. It's a whole world to disappear into. It's a great distraction from my life."

"You don't need to be distracted from anything."

"Oh, you'd be surprised. It's complicated. Left to my own devices, I don't do very well."

I try to picture him working. But I am really *cold*. "Let's go in. I'll make you some tea."

As I stand and pull the blanket around me to walk inside, he's behind me. He steadies me, putting his hands on my shoulders. It feels warm, familiar, kind.

And here we are in another kitchen, having another cup of tea. It's late, but I'm in no mood to get to bed. "It's good to talk to somebody. I mean, I've got Tessa, but I don't know, it's just like I've been asleep, you know? Or absent." It feels awkward, giving voice to the loneliness.

He sits across from me. His blue eyes take on a warm, smoky gray look. "I'm sure."

We don't talk any more about it. I'm grateful for that. When some of my friends come over or visit from out of town, I have to re-visit the concept that is widowhood with each one of them. It's not that I blame them, but they need the orientation to what it's like to be left alone when someone dies. They're just visiting, but I live in this land. Still, they all want to know what it feels like. It sucks being the there-but-for-the-grace-of-God person. They get to go home and hug a husband or a lover, and part of me knows it's because they're glad they aren't me.

I steer my brain in a different direction. "So what do you want to do tomorrow?"

"I have no idea." He shrugs.

"The boys'll be in school, so we have the day to do whatever we want." I'm not trying to sound suggestive, except to suggest that we can do adult-directed and grown-up stuff without two boys whining about everything or sullenly playing on their Nintendo DSes when they should be enjoying the beautiful day.

"Show me around Boise. Distract me."

This'll be a chance to be competent, to be more than a spaz who cries at the drop of a hat or who lives in a total disaster zone of a house or who is just me. "I can do that."

He stands up. "I'll get to bed. What time do the boys wake up for school?"

I can't help it. I get a little choked up. Someone else will be in the house in the morning. I know he's not a husband, or even a boyfriend, or . . . I wipe at the edge of my eyes with the knuckle of my index finger. I guess I'm almost crying.

He's very close to me all of a sudden. His hand is on my cheek. And he kisses me, softly, on the mouth.

"See you in the morning."

"Okay."

He walks out of the kitchen and upstairs. The night is over. I try not to scream out loud.

Things Come Together

When the first light comes into my bedroom the next morning, I'm up and out of bed in a new world's record. I move as noiselessly as I can. I don't want to wake the boys. The early morning is my time.

Ditto the dog stirs, and I immediately find the closest fleece available. I pull it over my head and grope around for my running shoes. I check on the boys upstairs—their room is still dark. I peek out across the deck, and the light in the bedroom above the garage isn't on either. Everyone is still asleep. I think I'm safe to get a run in before anyone else gets up.

To say that I feel like a rock star when I get out on my run is the understatement of the century. I've chosen what I like to call my Jesus-God-Sunrise route: out the back door and up the spine of the foothill behind our house. Usually about five to ten minutes into the run, depending on the time of year, the sun starts to crest over Table Rock and the Boise Front to the east, and it's spectacular. Today in particular, I can't help but think that if someone looked up here? Damn, I would look badass.

No one is looking up here, of course, because it's kind of chilly and everybody else is keeping warm under the covers with a significant other or getting clean in a hot shower to get to work before too long.

I think about Andrew. Andy Pettigrew, world-famous actor, sleeping in the guest bedroom over my garage. Is Andrew a good sleeper? Does he snore? Is he a drooler?

I talk in my sleep. Less now than when I was younger. I think. Of course, now that I've been alone in my bed for two years, who knows. Hairy Ditto doesn't complain about my nocturnal dialogues, and there's no one else to comment.

I must be burning it up this morning, because Ditto has given up running with me. He knows the path—when I get to the top of the foothill, I'll turn around and come blazing back down, ultimately ending back in the yard—but in the last year or so he's gotten lazy. If I'm going too fast, he sits his furry white butt down and waits for me about midway up the hill, then gallops down ahead of me to the house, ready for a morning scoop of kibble.

I can't help it. Last night has left me in a state of frenzied euphoria. Life is good. Hell, life is freaking awesome.

I make the top of the hill and stop for a moment. The sky is bluing up, going from a faint robin's egg to strong, crisp poplin blue. No inversion today. The sun will shine down, and I will take my new friend out for a very good day in a very good place.

I tear down the hill as best I can. My knees aren't quite as strong as they once were, so the bounding is limited a bit by the wish to not blow any anterior cruciate ligaments in the near future.

Peter always said the difference between men and women

when they skied was only noticeable at the top of a run. "A man drops down into the chute without question. A woman wonders which turn might turn into a fall. That possibility never occurs to a man until it literally occurs." We would debate the merits of each tendency.

Right now I wish for a little of the downhill plunge. I want to jump in and stop the constantly worrying nagging in my head. Fear is always right there for me. Anxiety? It's the what-if. When the boys were little, they often climbed up on the countertops. My first thought was always what it would look like when I found them with cracked-open skulls. The what-if still gets me constantly. I hate it. A lot.

Just this once I want to assume that things are going to be awesome. Or assume nothing, but also think about nothing but the present. Worry about the future when the future comes, and right now breathe in deep and love life and the possibility of great things.

I give my best war whoop as I run down the hill into the backyard. And you know what? I don't fall. I don't gouge my eye out on a low-hanging branch. Nothing bad happens to me. The drop into the chute doesn't bring any fall, not this time.

The house is still quiet when I return. The boys need to be up. They'll need to get to school soon. Neither of them showers in the morning, although Hunter is going to have to get into the habit soon, I suspect. Soon he'll be a teenager, and teen means stinky boy odor. His childhood habit of a nightly bath or shower isn't going to cut it anymore.

I go upstairs to rouse them. They sleep in one room. They have since they were little, in bunk beds now. Hunter has grumbled about moving into the game room. It's the bedroom next to theirs, which has been their playroom forever. Of course, both of them are too old for that now, so it has to be a *game* room.

I'm living in a foreign country. It strikes me hard for a minute. Peter was supposed to help navigate this territory. Puberty looms on the horizon, and this was not supposed to be my job. This was his job. He was the one who would have the "talks" and help the boys through all of this.

"Boys!" I begin the wake-up routine. "Time to report for duty."

There are groans from each level of the bunks. Some days they roll out of their own accord. Other days it takes tickling, full lights on, and all manner of wake-up maneuvers to raise these two.

Beau is up. His is the bottom bunk. He rubs his eyes and orients himself. "Hey, is Andrew still here?"

It's a good point. The whole thing felt very possibly like a dream. "I'm pretty sure. Yes, hon."

He's on his feet. "Good. I'm going to go get him up."

He's out the door and dashes toward the catwalk—I'm not fast enough to stop him. Oh, lord, he's going to go wake Andrew up. Beau doesn't know any better; the people who usually stay with us are family or friends who held him when he was born. They're willing to tolerate very early wake-up calls because they know him and love him.

I brace for the awkwardness, prepare an apology as I go after Beau. Hunter gets out of bed behind me and goes to the scary boy bathroom to get ready. He distracts me for a moment, and when I look back, Beau's already made it across the catwalk.

"Beau, it's not a good idea—" I get to the guest room door, which is ajar. I push it open a bit more.

Beau sits on the bed, spreading Pokémon cards across the comforter and explaining them in detail. Andrew is awake, reclined against the headboard, his hands clasped behind his head.

"So if this one evolves, which one does it turn into?"

Andy Pettigrew is in my guest bed discussing Japanese trading cards with my youngest son. I have to back out of the room. I almost feel faint. If I don't go make breakfast now, I will dissolve into a ball of noodley tears. Too many emotions and associations and possibilities for things to come swirl in my head, my blood pounding loudly in my ears. I have to get over it. I believe this man is a good man, and for some reason he's here. I'm not going to fuck this up by overreacting.

I go make breakfast and keep the facade of sane-girl behavior intact.

After breakfast I run the boys down to school. When I open the door to the house upon my return, I'm somehow surprised to hear Andrew in the bathroom. He's still here, and thankfully he's bypassed the boys' bathroom for the larger one downstairs. He is really here. Unbelievable.

The bathroom door swings open, and he sticks his head out. A waft of shampoo and shaving cream comes to my nose. Another detail I hadn't realized I've missed: shaving cream. I take a deep breath.

He speaks. "The boys make it okay?"

"Yep. Miraculously, no one forgot a lunch or homework or anything. And they didn't fight this morning."

He's brushing his teeth now, still standing partly out of the bathroom to talk to me. He's so relaxed. He wears a T-shirt and jeans. He turns back to the sink to spit, and then I hear him again.

"I have two older sisters. They didn't fight with me, they just never acknowledged my existence. I would've liked to have a brother."

"I have a brother, but I was a bossy old nag of an older sister, so I can't tell you. I pounded on my brother, and then when he was big enough he pounded on me in retaliation. We didn't get along until I moved out for college."

Andrew comes out of the bathroom, tucking his T-shirt into his jeans, now with a flannel long-sleeved shirt over it. The span of his chest is smooth and wide. He's a good-looking man, no doubt about it. I, as usual for this relationship (if that's what it is), am in running clothes and have questionable hair.

"What are we doing today?" he asks.

This is really happening. A day with Andrew.

Suddenly, my phone hops all over the kitchen table. Someone is texting me. My stomach lurches. I can bet who it is.

"Aw, crap." I grab the phone.

"What?" Andrew comes to my side.

"It's Tessa. My friend you met in the parking lot."

"Oh, yeah, the one who IDed me. Good thing it's not witness protection, or I'd be whacked next." He chuckles.

"Yeah, that one." I look at her text.

> Spill, girl. What's he like in bed?

Jee-zus. I snap the phone shut. "I hope you didn't read that."

"She wants to know how I am in bed." He smiles slyly. "I don't have to see to know that."

My face feels hot. Ugh. "I apologize in advance for anything she ever does to you. I better text her." I reply:

Shut. Up. HE'S HERE!

"I'd turn the phone off, but I always have it in case the boys need me."

"Did you tell her I was amazing?" He smirks.

"Are you amazing?" I smirk back.

"Getting sassy now, are we? Go get ready. You've got a tour to give."

Tour Guide Extraordinaire

I take a shower. I even shave my legs. I try to think when I last shaved my legs in the wintertime. It could possibly have been in the time of dinosaurs.

Even when Peter was alive, I could never claim to be a girly girl. He loved me, and he didn't seem to notice whether I was dolled up or in one of his crew T-shirts from college that had a hole in the armpit. We always had a good relationship—you know, *relations* relationship—whether my legs were shaved or not.

I don't think we ever took each other for granted, but we had very few secrets, to be sure. That many years together is too long to pretend. We learned that lesson.

But today I make an effort. I put on a clean pair of jeans, and I actually apply some lip gloss. My hair is pointless. No one ever showed me how to do anything with it when I was younger, so I keep it cut in a long bob and call it good. I think watching my cousin's curling iron fall apart and down the back of her prom dress when I was six probably scarred me for life. No big beauty routine for me.

My teeth are brushed, and I look casually decent. We get in the car.

"Where are we going?" He's curious. He smells a little of smoke. He must have had a cigarette while I was getting ready. I appreciate that he hasn't smoked in front of the kids. I understand addiction, so I know he's making an effort there.

"I'm showing you Boise, the West. And distracting you. I'm totally doing that."

I shift into fifth and hit the highway on-ramp. We're headed east, out into the middle of nowhere.

He looks out the window, watching the sagebrush and the wide sky. We see an antelope when we're about fifteen minutes out of town. He looks through my iPod, picks out a few songs. One is Coldplay.

"I like this." He sits back. He seems at peace, content. I wonder if he means the song or being here. I don't ask.

"I love Coldplay," I tell him. "I really love eighties music, though. It's the onset of middle age. I can't help but like cheesy music."

"Middle age?"

Uh-oh. We haven't done the full-disclosure thing on age. Now the cougar will be out of the bag. He's hanging out with a fossil.

"Um, I'm thirty-six."

He scoffs. "That's being cynical, isn't it? You're planning to die before you turn eighty?"

I roll my eyes. "Come on, you know what I mean. I'm not young. Not like you, for instance. How old are you?"

"I'm twenty-nine."

"For the love of Mike. You're a babe in the woods." I'm a little nauseated.

"It's not young."

"I was a total dumbass until my thirties. Twenty-nine is young."

He narrows his eyes. "Are you calling me a dumbass?" I'm about to protest/apologize when he laughs, hard. "Listen, it all depends on the amount of living you've done with your years. Now, you might have been a choir girl, but I got an early start on everything, trust me."

"You weren't a choir girl?"

"Not even close. Don't dig too deep on the interwebz. I've done some dumb, dumb stuff."

"So you *were* a dumbass, then."

"Touché. I like to think I'm a work in progress. I've learned a tremendous amount from my mistakes. I'd venture to say I'm quite wise, even."

I like the verbal repartee. "Am I blessed by the presence of an old soul, then?"

"Ancient. Like Yoda, I am."

"Were you alive when they made that movie?"

He punches me in the shoulder.

And no, he wasn't alive when they made that movie.

We're way out of town now. It doesn't take long. I pull off the highway and drive toward the fringe of hills in the distance. There's nothing but sagebrush. I know what I'm looking for . . . When I see the turnout, I guide the car off the road and stop. Dust swirls up around us. Andrew swings his door open, gets out.

"It's so quiet." He stands still, breathes in. "I'd give my firstborn for this kind of peace on a regular basis. In LA, sometimes I can't even think straight."

But he doesn't fully get it yet.

"Walk with me a little. I'll show you why we're out here." I find the narrow path between the sagebrush.

He comes up behind me. We walk silently for a bit. The highway whispers in the distance. The wind blows over the desert scrub, and we are utterly alone.

"Out here reminds me of the earth and how big it is and how tiny I am. Everyday life is too noisy for me to remember that." I wonder if he understands me. He nods.

I go on. "But here's the really awesome part." The path has just widened. We stand in front of two ruts in the desert floor. Running parallel with the highway, they stretch in both directions as far as I can see. To the east, the land slopes up gently, and the ruts meet with the horizon. To the west, the trail seems to curve to the left and thins into a point in the distance.

He's perplexed. "What's this? A Jeep trail?"

Here's the part where I feel cool. "These aren't tire tracks. They're ruts from wagon wheels. It's the Oregon Trail."

"Really?" He looks at me.

"Really."

He stands for a minute, then walks forward, faces west, and puts one foot in each wheel rut. He is still for a minute. Then he steps forward a few feet, bends down, and picks up a little of the dust, smoothing it between his fingers.

He stays crouched. He's looking for something. Then he stands up.

"What'd you find?" I come over to look.

He opens his palm—it's a smooth black rock. "I want to take this back."

I smile. I think I did good.

After a bit more exploring, we head back into town. I'm still nervous about public outings with him, but I've figured out lunch. We hit the Basque Block, walk around and look at the old sheepherder's boardinghouse, the wagon parked out front, the handball court.

We sit on the patio at a Basque grill for lunch. His sunglasses never even have to come off. The waitress is so distracted, she doesn't look either of us in the eye anyway. No one else is outside, even though the day is what I expected it to be: unseasonably warm and bright.

I'm almost through my lamb sandwich when he pushes back from his burger and sighs, contented. "That was good."

"I still say you should've had the beef tongue. If you were a risk taker, you would have." I smile at him and take another bite.

He steals a French fry out of my basket. "I'm not good at risk taking."

"Really? I would've taken you for a daredevil."

He exhales loudly, takes another drink of his Coke. "I'm not afraid of risk. It's just better for me to be conservative. There's some switch missing in me. I tend to have a hard time finding a balance."

"I don't understand."

"All things in moderation, right?"

I'm not following. "Yeah. So?"

"So, very often I can't do that. I don't know how to do that. Some things I can't do at all. Some risks I can't back away from once I jump in. It's complicated."

"What kind of risks?"

"Let's just say I'm at my best when I'm working. If I'm not busy, I tend to brood."

"Really?"

"I've been known to blow off steam in not-so-healthy ways." He eats another fry.

My stomach knots up. This new information doesn't feel good. I fight off the urge to worry by looking for something to distract me, a way to escape this conversation.

A large group of women are coming down the sidewalk in our direction. They're loud, laughing. "We should go before those girls walk by. If anyone's going to spot you, a herd of single women will."

He smiles, scoops up his Coke, and waits for me to walk with him down the street. "Lead on, tour director."

"Our next stop took me a while to choose. If it were summer, we'd go fly-fishing. But the river's frigid now. They release trout this time of year, but I don't like suffering. Plus, I never catch anything anyway. We could go up to Sun Valley like you were supposed to and see Hemingway's grave, fly-fish in Silver Creek. But it's too snowy up there now. In Boise, if it were full-on winter, we'd go skiing. Do you ski?"

He shakes his head. "This weekend was supposed to have been my first time—though I was going to snowboard."

"Well, skiing takes a while to get into, from my experience. I did *not* have fun the first couple of times." We're at the car. "Plus, I would hate it if you got hurt or anything. Someone would probably sue me. And skiing's hard to love after you get hurt, take my word for it. It took me more than a few seasons after I broke my leg to get back into it. And it's never been quite the same, to be honest."

We're in the car now. He raises his eyebrows at me. "You still ski?"

"Well, the boys like it. It's a good family thing to do. And Peter was amazing, so it was fun to ski with him."

He looks at me closely. It feels like he's trying to put something together. "Do you sometimes feel like you do a lot of stuff you don't really want to do?"

I don't know where he's going with this. "Sure. Having a family is about that sometimes."

He sits back. "Huh."

I start the car. "Huh, what?"

"Well, I just wonder if I'd be good at that." He smiles at me.

I shake my head. "You don't have to be good at it. It just happens. It's called compromise."

His phone vibrates, and he jumps a little. He pulls it out of his coat pocket in surprise. He stares at the screen for a second before silencing it.

My heart sinks. "Was that important?" I can't help but think it's the real world calling—they want their movie star back.

He sighs. "Naw. It's my agent. He's probably put two and two together about me not being in Sun Valley. He worries a lot."

"Do you need to call him? Should you call him?"

He stares down at the phone. I can't read the expression on his face. I have this weird feeling he's in trouble, that we're in trouble—like ditching-class trouble or something. "Did you have to do something this weekend?"

"No. I don't need to call. I'll text and tell him I'm visiting a friend. That's all he needs to know. And no, I wasn't contractually obligated to appear in Sun Valley." There's a bitterness to his voice in that last sentence.

I shrink a little. I hope I haven't upset him. "Sorry. Sorry I brought it up."

He shakes himself out of it, tucks the phone back in his coat pocket. "No. It's no big deal. I promise. Now, tell me what's next."

I bring a little pep to the whole tour director shtick. "Like I said, it was hard to decide. But we've got a little while before the boys come home. You've seen the wagon trail, you've done the Basque thing. Next is a sacred spot for a lot of Idahoans."

He adjusts his ball cap like he's readying for battle. His smile returns, and he looks at me mischievously. "Okay. Take me there."

I cross my fingers that my friend Barb got my text this morning. We pull into the east end of campus at Boise State. I park in the lot facing the river.

"I thought you said the river was too cold to do anything."

We're out of the car. "Oh, we aren't going there." I take him by the elbows and turn him to face the other way. "We're going there." Boise State University's stadium looms large above us.

"What?" He looks confused.

"The blue turf is hallowed ground around here. But even if you don't follow football, it's cool. You'll see." I walk with him toward a gray service door on the back side of the end-zone bleachers.

Now he just looks kind of nervous. "Is there something going on today?"

I wonder if he thinks I'm selling him out—using him for something.

The door swings open right about then. Barb pokes her head out, blinking a little in the sunshine.

She spots me and calls, "Hey, girl! Come on in!"

Andrew and I go inside, and the gray door swings shut behind us. Barb gives me a huge hug. She's in her best Boise State blue and orange.

"Barb, this is my friend Andrew." Barb shakes his hand. "Barb's the director of development for the Athletic Association. Andrew's my friend from Indio. He's in town for the weekend. He's never been to Boise."

Barb nods and smiles her big, wide smile. She's sixty-five and, bless her heart, has no idea who this man across from her is. She's not his target demographic.

She puts out her hand. "Pleased to meet you. Kelly brought you to the right place if you've never been to Boise. No trip to the Treasure Valley is complete without a walk on the Smurf turf. But we'll go up into the Sky Club too. Kelly hasn't even gotten a chance to see that."

He looks at me. She turns around and heads toward another door. She swings a big set of keys around on a bright orange lanyard. She's chatting away now.

Andrew whispers to me, "She has no clue who I am."

I nod. "True."

He smiles. "That hasn't happened in a while."

Barb has opened the door and ushers us through it. We emerge on the north side of the end zone. The whole stadium of forty thousand seats towers above. We are the only three people in it. The blue field stretches out before us.

Barb is done with the official tour talk. She smiles encouragingly at Andrew. "Go ahead, hon. You can walk on out."

He takes my hand and walks out on the turf. It makes me grin uncontrollably to have his hand on mine. I am apparently ten years old.

"I feel like someone should be cheering for us right now." He smiles. I think he's getting a kick out of this.

"I like how springy it is." I show him what I mean: I let go of his hand and do a couple of high skips down the field.

He follows me at a dead run. I take off even faster, running hard now. I may be giggling as he pursues me. I'm too fast, though, and am able to loop around to meet Barb back at the sidelines.

He gives up and walks back to us, laughing. He's still some distance off when Barb elbows me in the side.

"You've been holding out on me, Miss Kelly. You have a new flame."

I grimace. "Oh, Barb, he's just in town for the weekend. We've only met one other time. He never comes to Boise. It's nothing."

Andrew has just attempted a ridiculous-looking cartwheel as he approaches us. I laugh out loud. He yells at me, "That was just for you. Count yourself lucky!" He jogs toward us.

Barb jabs me again. "Nothing, huh? Whatever you say."

Required Reading

Barb takes us up to the Sky Club after that. The view is a knock-out. I'm *ooh*ing and *aah*ing as much as Andrew. I've never been much for football, and I'm certainly not on the who's who list of Boise movers and shakers, so I've had no reason to come up here.

But, man, what a view. The focus of this building perched at the top of the stadium is the blue football field, obviously, but the spectacular bank of floor-to-ceiling windows faces downtown and the foothills too. The hills are dusty white, and the buildings glitter a little in the afternoon sun.

We stand for a while, and I'm proud of myself. I enjoy the moment, and I don't chatter, don't try to fill up the quiet.

"It makes everything seem easier when it's calm like this, doesn't it?" He puts an arm around me.

I don't exactly know which *everything* he's referring to, but I do know the feeling. "Yeah."

He turns and walks back to the elevator where Barb is waiting. Back at the stadium entrance, we say good-bye to her and head home. Andrew's quiet in the car.

We're in the drive-through for Fancee Freeze milk shakes, and I'm eager to hear how I've done. "Well? What do you think?"

He smiles as I hand him a chocolate shake. "I like Boise. It's cool."

I slurp my shake as we drive off, headed home. "I love it. Did you like the tour? Did you have a good day?"

He closes his eyes for a minute. "Definitely. Your tour goes beyond passing muster. You might consider doing this for a living."

I grin as I steer. "Good. So we'll go home. You can relax, and I'll go get the boys." I think ahead for a second.

And gasp. "Oh!"

He pauses, mid-drink. "What?"

"How're you going to get home? You're leaving on Sunday, right? Do we need to get you a flight?" My mind is suddenly calculating how much a very last-minute fare is going to be.

He crinkles up his eyes, embarrassed. "Um, I have a ride."

I'm not following. There's a surprise. I seem to be the last to figure out anything around here lately. "What do you mean?"

"Private jet. It's coming for me. On its way back to LA."

"Oh. Well, of course." I try to sound like I know. I don't.

He chuckles.

We're quiet for the last few minutes of the ride. I wonder what he's thinking about. I try not to think about what I'm thinking about right now. It's not appropriate, to be honest.

Okay, it's not that terrible, but I haven't thought about anything remotely like this in probably two and a half years. I want to kiss him again.

I almost run into the mailbox as I pull in the driveway. I probably need to stay away from the daydreaming while operating a motor vehicle.

Then we're home. It's quiet. The boys are due to be picked up in forty-five minutes. I'm happy to have Andrew here, but I'm tired. I look at the dishes in the kitchen sink, contemplating how to avoid cleaning up.

He comes into the kitchen. "Leave them."

"Okay." He doesn't have to twist my arm on that one. I turn around to face him.

"Come sit in the living room. Relax for a minute." He takes my hand and leads me in.

There is a stack of books next to the couch. I put them there probably three weeks ago, hopeful that I would plow through them. I think I'm twenty pages into the one on top.

Andrew flops down on the couch, and I cringe, because in the fading afternoon light, I can see the dog hair flutter up in the air.

"Andrew, there's dog hair all over. Ditto rules the roost when we're gone. I also think he uses my toothbrush when I'm not looking." I try to pull him up off the couch, guide him to a less-hairy perch.

"Sit down. I want to look at your books." He pulls me down to the couch with him.

"At least you're not wearing black." I sit, trying to relax about it. He ignores my reaction; his attention is on the pile.

"Have you read all of these?" He trails a fingertip down the spines of the books.

"Some of them. I may be a few pages into the one on top. I buy books. The joke was that Peter would read everything in the house. I bought 'em, he read 'em."

Andrew smiles. "He suffered through a lot of chick lit, then."

"Hey, you may recall I said I was a teacher. Mixed into the girl crap was always some good stuff. Then I could have him tell me what they were about while I was grading the hundred-millionth essay."

He plucks the bottom book from the stack. It's an old, thin copy of *In Our Time*. He thumbs through it. "What's this one?"

"The first Hemingway I ever read. It's a collection of short stories. My junior year in high school, my English teacher assigned it to us. I remember reading a lot of it and not getting it. Then I came back to it in college and fell in love with it. Now I read it every so often for fun. I wanted to read it again this fall, so I pulled it back out."

He looks at the worn-out binding. "You've read it a lot."

"Hemingway is my man. I've been inside his house in Sun Valley. I bet even Mr. I-Fly-in-Private-Jets can't lay claim to that."

"How'd you manage it?"

"Two of my friends and I crashed a reception on the property. I crept in the back door behind the caterers."

"What was it like?"

"Eerie. I don't think it's changed since his last wife died. There was a stack of mail on top of the fridge, even. Very normal and lived in, but like it was frozen in the 1960s."

"You're a daredevil, then? Breaking and entering?"

"Only entering. The caterers had the door open, and my friends dared me. And no, usually I hate taking risks. But it was Hemingway. Totally an exception."

"Why do you like him so much? I thought he was a terrible womanizer."

"For his writing. It's clean. A lot of what's important goes unsaid, but it's in there. And he loved Idaho, so I give him a lot of points for that."

He looks at the book again. "Can I borrow this?"

If he wants me to fall completely in love, he's on the right track. "I would love it if you borrowed it."

He stretches back on the couch, swings his legs up to rest on my lap. "What's your favorite story in here?"

"'Big Two-Hearted River,' both parts. The first time I read it I thought it was the most boring thing in my life. But then I reread it, and it definitely grew on me. I won't say anything more about it—you read it and report back."

"Okay, Professor McBossy." He looks for the table of contents.

"I'll just be curious as to how you see it. Since you're such an old soul and all." I like sitting here with him. I like the weight of his legs on my legs. I like that he appears to be at total ease.

"How I see it?"

"It's one that's especially up for debate—what it's about."

He pulls me to lie down with him. I rest in the crook of his arm, reading along as he starts the story. We're quiet and still. My mind leaves the print in front of me. What's going to happen? In two days he will board a plane. Then what?

But I resist. I'm in the chute. Now is not the time to pull up and try to see the end of the run. To do so would mean a slip, a tumble, and a disastrous crash. Worrying about what lies ahead is pointless. It is unknowable, and for once I want it to remain that way.

Family Home Evening

The boys are excited that Andrew's still here. It cracks me up that they've completely claimed him as *their* guest, not mine, and they seem sure he regards me the way they do. Moms do not hang out with cool people, and they were certain a boring day with their mom would send him packing. Part of me is with them on that one. Although I still think they have a picture of him buying a hotel downtown, renting a gigantic Hummer, and rolling through Boise in said Hummer playing rap music really loudly. I see more of a complete evaporation into thin air, followed by the moment when I wake up and realize I've been institutionalized for delusions.

But he's here. And he helps me clean up the kitchen, in fact. And when he asks Hunter if he wants to go with him to buy a take-and-bake pizza, Hunter is all over it. (Later Andrew reports that Hunter asked if he could drive home. So maybe Hunter just thinks this is a new adult to try to scam or that movie stars are so cool they've turned into permissive idiots.)

Beau and I vacuum and use our magic hair-away sponge on the

living room. Maybe we can all hang out there and actually relax in a dog-hair-free environment.

Hunter and Andrew come back with pizzas and movies, and the rest of my night is bliss. We sit on the couch, and the boys drag in all manner of sleeping bags and comforters to crash on the floor. We eat pizza, watch movies, and laugh at the boys' silliness.

It's time for the last movie. Hunter picks up the case and announces, "Ladies and gentlemen, our last selection is *HMS Furious.*"

This is one of Andrew's first hits, about World War I—a very epic action movie with lots of epic, emotion-filled speeches and epic explosions and just epically big stuff, you name it.

Andrew groans.

"What?"

"There's a lot of lip gloss in this one." He sighs.

Beau's interested. He takes the bait. "What do you mean? The girls you had to kiss had gross lips?"

I'm relieved to hear that kissing still grosses Beau out.

"Naw. Watch me in the scenes where I give the big speeches, especially. I totally have lip gloss on."

The movie starts, and watching it with *the* Andy Pettigrew sitting next to me is the most hysterical and surreal thing I have ever experienced. It's like having the DVD commentary in person, only funnier. He is viciously self-deprecating. Hunter and Beau are eating it up. They even join in. I know they're bonding when they give Andrew a lip-gloss rating for every scene in which he appears.

Then the movie is over. Hunter stands up and stretches. "That was so funny, Andrew. Thanks for hanging out with us." He gives him a chest-bumpish hug and heads upstairs.

Beau's asleep. His mouth is open. His head is soaked—this is a trait from my side of the family: head sweating at night when little. I don't know why, but I've always loved it.

"Beau." He is totally out. I look at Andrew. "Brace yourself. I'm gonna have to wake him up, and he's not going to be happy about it."

Andrew pulls himself up off the couch. "I'll carry him."

"Andrew, he's eight. And our stairs are scary and narrow. And he's a sweaty little beast."

He looks right at me. His eyes are soft, vulnerable. I'm not sure what it means.

"Let me, Kelly. Let me help."

"Okay." I feel like I'm going to melt into a puddle of warm candle wax. Seriously.

He hoists him up, makes a funny face at me like Beau's really heavy, and carries him almost effortlessly. I guess his taut physique probably involves the routine lifting of heavy things. Silly me.

He comes back downstairs.

I stand very still.

He takes my hand. I feel like I should say something, but it's not there. He kisses me.

This time, I kiss back. I put my arms around his waist. He has a hand at the nape of my neck, playing with the twisty tendrils of hair there.

He pulls away and looks at me. "This was a good day."

"I like this part especially." I kiss him again, softly. We stand in the middle of the living room.

I feel suspended, floating in an in-between world. Part of me definitely wants to move this along. It's the part of me that's making my palms sweat.

The other part of me wants to call it a night. This has come along so fast. I'm mostly convinced it's a delusion. But if it's real, I want to do it right. No rushing.

Andrew kisses me again, and I feel the buzz of warring voices quiet in my head. Maybe he can sense my reluctance. He seems to kiss me without great urgency. He pulls away again, wraps his arms around me in a tight embrace instead.

"I should hit the sack." He doesn't make any move to let go after he says this.

"Okay."

Finally he steps out of our hug. He grabs the Hemingway, uses it to give me a minisalute. "I'm off to do my assigned reading." He kisses me one more time and heads to the guest room. As I watch him walk away, I feel myself flush again. He is heavenly.

I wander around for a minute, picking up a little, trying to regain my composure. I've never been much for cleaning up, and I do it now only to keep from completely overanalyzing what's going on.

I finally stop puttering around and decide to go to bed. I brush my teeth and get ready to sleep.

I can't find Ditto. I realize this as I am at my door. He's not in my bedroom. He's not on the couch in the living room. I go upstairs. He's not in the boys' room. I slip out to the catwalk, tiptoe to the door of the room above the garage. The light's still on, so I peek in the window. Ditto is in the guest room, all right. He's asleep on the bed, at the feet of my guest. Andrew is also asleep, still halfway propped up on the pillows. The Hemingway book is splayed out at whatever page he's left off, turned over on his chest.

I look up at the moon. The night is quiet and beautiful. I go to bed knowing sometimes it shouldn't be as hard as I make it. Right now might be one of those times.

Rolling on the River

The next day, I decide we're driving to Swan Falls. The boys groan.

"Mom, Jack was supposed to come over and play Mario Kart with me." Beau is put out.

"We have a guest. We're going to do something fun."

"You mean something tourists think is fun but turns into a big headache?"

"What? Tourists don't even know about Swan Falls."

Andrew walks into the kitchen. "Are we plotting our day?"

Hunter snorts. "Mom's trying to bore us to death. Or freeze us to death."

I get a little defensive. "It was sixty-five degrees yesterday. We're not going to freeze to death. Now, everybody go get your shoes on. And bring a coat. And, Beau, find Ditto's leash."

Hunter takes this as the last straw. "Aw, Mom, he stinks! Do we have to bring him?"

Andrew jumps in. "I did shower."

"I was talking about the dog." Hunter looks at Andrew. "Are you saying you actually want to go do this?"

Again, I think this is probably an activity that goes counter to the image Hunter and Beau have of a Hummer-driving, bling-wearing, rap-playing Andy Pettigrew.

"Well, what's it like?" Andrew winks at me. He knows he's got some pull here.

"It's actually not that bad," Beau chimes in. "It's not a big waterfall, but it's the Snake River, and there's a cool old-fashioned dam. Sometimes you can find arrowheads on the other side of the river."

Andrew looks thoughtful. "Sounds decent. Why don't we go and humor your mother?"

I appreciate his ability to get the boys to comply. "Let's go, shall we?" I get the keys.

Everyone piles in the car, dog included—who is, incidentally, pretty smelly. I have a moment where I wonder if this whole thing *is* going to turn out to have been a terrible idea.

But the boys are in command of the iPod, and they're playing all the songs they like for Andrew. Of course he knows most of them and has something to say in response. The boys especially like when he mentions the artist and what he or she was like when he met them. Movie-star cheater. A normal mom can't compete with street cred like that.

Finally we drop down off the rocky plain into the Snake River Canyon. Hawks twirl above us in the sky. The river is low, and though it's warm, there's a cold autumn wind coming up.

We have the place to ourselves except for one pack of mountain bikers.

The boys let Ditto loose. He runs for the green lawn around the old white farmhouses. They stand tall with sharply arched Victorian roofs.

"What are all these houses?" Andrew asks.

"The caretaker's house, offices, a house for the workers. This wasn't an easy spot to get to at the turn of the last century."

Hunter rolls his eyes. "Watch out, Andrew. Mom's preparing to go all tour guide on you."

I roll my eyes back. "I already did the tour guide thing with him yesterday. Why don't you tell him something about it, then?"

This seems to surprise Hunter, but in true tween fashion, he never misses an opportunity to be the one who knows it all. In his humble opinion, he does know more than anyone. This is one of the side effects of approaching adolescence.

"This was one of the early dams in the West. Silver City had electricity because of it. It was a mining town." He pauses and looks down at his feet. "That's what I know."

That'll probably be the most we hear from Hunter all day. He slips in his earbuds and begins to walk big circles around us, like a moon in orbit.

Beau chases Ditto down and puts him on the leash. Together they bound around from one object to the next, whipped into a frenzy by the new location. Beau yells at us from the edge of the road. "Are we taking the dam road or what?"

Andrew looks at me. "What did he say?"

I roll my eyes. "Expect several 'dam' jokes out of Beau. It's one of his favorite parts of a trip out here."

Andrew walks alongside me. We make our way slowly to the dam itself, which stands atop the old stone of a real waterfall in the riverbed. The powerhouse is actually perched on the metal walkways of the dam. It's another Victorian structure, this one hewed out of sandstone. The old paned windows are whitewashed, as is all the equipment and the small outbuildings that squeeze onto the wide metal walkways.

"You guys want to walk across the dam?" I hope there isn't a mutiny brewing.

"We're running! Ditto hates the way this dam grating feels on his paws!" Beau yells, mostly at Andrew, as he flies past in a full sprint. Even though he's being silly, he's right. The dog hates the metal grating. He'll be glad to get across quickly.

"Hunter?" I look around for the older. He's right behind me.

"Geez, Mom, I'm right here." He passes us in exasperation, still listening to his music, but I can tell he's formulated some game about where he's stepping on the grates. Looks like it has something to do with avoiding the welded spots.

Andrew watches them get farther ahead. "They're good kids."

"I think so." It's reassuring to hear it from someone else.

"They have a good mom." Andrew smiles.

"Oh, stop." I elbow him.

"Okay."

I smile. "Keep it up. I was just pretending to protest. Flattery will get you everywhere."

He raises an eyebrow. "I knew it. I like the humble act, though."

As we come around the corner of the powerhouse, the breeze picks up. Both boys have made it across and now scour the river-bank for special rocks and arrowheads.

"Now it's a little chilly." I can feel the wind cut through the arms of my jacket.

"This is a great place." Andrew puts his arm around my shoulders.

"Keep your eyes peeled. This is a good time of year to see bald eagles." I look to the bare cottonwood trees that line the river for signs of nests.

"When I go back tomorrow, what do you think's going to happen?" Andrew asks me. He hasn't stopped walking with me; we're still in a rhythm. His voice has changed, though. It sounds tentative.

"I thought I was supposed to ask that."

He stops. He scans the cliffs above us, as if looking for an answer there. His lips form a tight line. Then he's shaking his head a little.

"See, that's where I just don't know. Your life has a rhythm to it, a purpose. I like how grounded you are. You've got the boys. You've got a home here. With me, I just don't know. Sometimes I don't know how to slow it all down. I used to do some stupid stuff instead of putting the brakes on . . . Now I think I'm better at it, but when I go back to LA, things get . . ." His voice trails off, and the wind whistles in the emptiness that's left.

"My life feels crazy from the inside a lot of the time," I offer. "Yes, I have the boys. But look at Hunter—soon they'll both grow up and be gone. They're already starting to distance themselves, which they should be. I don't want them to live with their mom forever. But then what? Then what's my purpose? Then what's my routine? I feel like I'll go from mother to nothing."

I take a deep breath of the clean river air. "But anyway. Here's what I hope happens. You go back to LA, back to work, I presume. We do this crazy thing where we call each other on the phone. As often as we want. Just like the people in the phone commercials. And then . . ."

I can see some sort of idea spring to life in his eyes. When he speaks, he sounds a lot more certain: "And then, when I'm filming my next job, you'll come see me."

"I don't know . . . The boys can't be—"

"No, here's where it's perfect. My next job is in Ventura County. It's doubling for Colorado. That's the magic of movies. You and the boys fly down to see your parents, and you come and visit. Or you could come to the premiere of the movie I just finished. It's about World War Two. I get to make dramatic speeches and pound the table with my fist a lot. It'd be great."

I'm trying to think about our next few months, the boys' school holidays. "There are teacher training days . . . Thanksgiving's only a few days, but we do get two weeks around Christmas."

"That'd work out. You'll be down to see your mom and dad at Christmastime anyway, right?"

I take a very deep breath.

"What?" He looks at me, measuring my reaction.

"You want me to see you in LA?"

"Why not?"

"Frankly, I keep trying to figure out what you see in me."

"Because why?"

"Because you are a world-famous, handsome movie star. I am a widow with two kids and a very hairy dog."

"Now, just because I've mostly seen you in running clothes with a liberal coating of dog fur—"

"Don't forget—I haven't had a good hair day in your presence yet."

"True. But you're missing the point. You have your eyes open to the stuff that matters to me too."

Right now, for whatever reason, I feel overwhelmed. Suddenly I see this for what it is: I'm standing at the top of another chute, another steep run. I can almost hear Peter. *Well, what's it going to be? Stand up here and think about all the ways you're going to crash, or jump in and ski already?*

"Ski already."

"What?" Andrew heard that. I must have said it out loud.

"Nothing. I'd love to see you work, and the boys would love it if they got to visit with you again. Maybe you could . . ." I leave off. I was going to say *meet my parents* but the words totally freaked me out and stuck in my throat.

"Maybe I could meet your folks." He said it. Wow.

"Yeah, that too." I need to be pinched.

"What?" He's looking at me. I must be wearing a weird expression.

"I just keep waiting for the other shoe to drop. Or to wake up. Or for you to turn into Ike Turner."

"Who?"

Exasperated, I'm about to respond, but he elbows me. "I know who he is. You're too easy." He chuckles and jogs ahead to catch the boys.

I stay on the dam's walkway for a moment and turn to face downriver. The wind pushes me from behind. I see a flash in the corner of my eye and look up to see a bald eagle swoop down from the canyon rim. He cruises past me, flying downriver to who knows where. He doesn't seem too worried about his destination. I wish I could say the same.

You Just Got Here

When we get home, both boys must be done with the whole bonding thing because they disappear upstairs. There are many TV shows to watch and other boy things to be done, apparently.

Andrew paces in the kitchen. "Can Hunter and Beau stay here tonight for a while if we want to go out for a bit?"

Red flags wave. "If we go out, you'll get recognized, won't you?" I don't want the weekend spoiled.

Andrew puts on the teakettle. "If we went through the McDonald's drive-through, I bet no one would notice."

"That sounds fun." I watch his face for a clue about what's brewing.

"I'm just saying, there are ways for us to go out without, you know, *going out*." He pulls out two mugs for tea.

"I'll let the boys know they aren't to pound on each other for a couple of hours tonight. If we hook them up with Chinese takeout, it'll buy us some time."

He nods. He's up to something.

A few hours later, we say good-bye to the boys after outfitting them with provisions and movies. As we walk out the door, he takes the keys.

"You're the driver tonight?" I ask.

"If it's okay with you. I've got a plan."

I'm at a loss. This is supposed to be my turf. "I have to say I'm intrigued. Where're we going?"

He hustles around to the passenger side and lets me in. Only then does he answer. "We're just going on a drive. Go with it." Then he's in the car.

He smiles devilishly. I'm in for it. It doesn't matter where we're going; with a smile like that, it's got to be trouble.

"All right. I'm in."

He pulls out of the driveway and turns north. Then we head into the foothills.

The road winds its way up through the sage. I look out over the city as the dusk deepens. Boise is a flat, twinkling blanket. The Owyhee Mountains are turning pink in the distance, their tips frosted with snowfall.

"It's so pretty." I have been known from time to time to say really deep things, but now is not one of those times.

Andrew puts his hand on mine for a moment. "You picked a great place to live, Kelly. I like it here. It suits me more than LA, I think."

This makes me happy. I'm not sure why it's important, but if someone doesn't get Boise, chances are he might not get me.

By now we've climbed far enough up the Boise Front that our options for destinations are narrowing.

"There aren't a lot of restaurants up this way, you know." I look at him suspiciously.

"Another demonstration of your lack of faith in me. Trust me." He slows the car and pulls off on a logging road.

I stay quiet for a minute. How does he know his way around up here? Has he been doing reconnaissance? When? "I'm very impressed, Mr. Pettigrew. How are you doing this? Or are you totally lost and just a really good actor?"

He doesn't look at me, just keeps driving. "I have friends. And I am a really good actor, but I don't need that right now, thank you very much."

The car comes to a stop. We've come in the back way on Mores Mountain. We're sitting in front of the Nordic Lodge at the ski resort. It's not open for the season yet. But the lights are on.

"Andrew, what did you do?"

He turns off the car. "I asked the boys to tell me about a cool place you liked. They said you liked the mountain. I did some calling around. And then I had a friend call and set this up for me."

We're standing at the front porch. "I smell food."

"You're an observant one, you are." He takes my hand and pulls me up the steps. "It's cold out here. Let's go in."

The door is open. I've always liked this lodge. It sits at the trailhead of the very unassuming cross-country area above Boise. It's a small log building, but the main floor has a huge A-frame main room. The windows open to a sparkly view of forest and the valley below.

The river-rock fireplace is lit. Most of the tables are still turned on their sides and pushed to the back wall. One is out, set with a white tablecloth and candles.

"This is awesome. I'm impressed." It's been a long time since I've had a fuss made over me. I remember now that it feels good.

"You might want to reserve judgment until you try the food." He pulls out a chair for me, another thing I'm not used to at all.

The meal makes me smile. It's from one of our favorite restaurants downtown. Included are plenty of mashed potatoes, which Hunter and Beau eat by the bucketful when we go there. "The boys helped, didn't they?"

"They said it was your favorite. You'll recall that I don't cook much."

I feel a warm lump in my throat. I don't want to cry. I may not have a choice. "You guys . . ."

"Well, you showed me a good time in Boise when I appeared unannounced. It's the least I could do. Plus, tomorrow I go back."

Ugh. Reality again. "What time?"

He grimaces. "Painfully early. I guess the group in Sun Valley didn't have the best time together, and they're ready to get home."

"You called it. You said you didn't want to spend a weekend with them."

He nods. "I knew *I* didn't want to be with them, but seems they realized they didn't want to be with each other either."

I sigh. It comes out before I even realize it. "I'm bummed that you're going back."

He stops eating and looks straight at me. "Me too."

We don't talk for a while.

He breaks the silence first. "Can I take your plate?" He stands.

"I can get it. You did everything else." I'm on my feet.

"I didn't. I paid someone very well to handle it for me. One of the perks."

I have both plates in hand. "So does someone know the fabulously famous Andy Pettigrew was in Boise this weekend?"

He shakes his head. "Nope. The beauty of Hollywood is that the I-have-people thing is true. I called a very accommodating production assistant I know in LA, and she made some calls, so as far as anyone knows, someone with a lot of money from somewhere put this together. Nice and vague all the way around."

We clear the table together, and he leads the way out to the deck. It's another cold, clear night.

"Well, I guess good-byes are in order." I try to sound like it's not a big deal, but it kind of breaks my heart.

"Geez, good-byes? That sounds so terribly final. I'm just going back to LA."

"Yeah, but, Andrew . . ." I leave off. I think he knows what I mean.

"But nothing. I like you. I had a good time. Did you?"

"Well, yeah, but . . ."

"Honestly, will you stop doing that? We've decided we're going to call each other, and we're going to see each other again. Doesn't that sound good?"

It sounds amazing. But I still don't buy it. Really, at some point he's going to recover from whatever brain injury has caused this inexplicable attraction to me. "I don't know what to say."

He puts his arms around me. "How about, 'That sounds good.' Or 'Yes, let's do call each other and see each other again.' Generally that's how people do it."

I smile. "Let's do."

He rolls his eyes. "Come on, you need to give me a little credit. I'm not going to fall off the face of the earth."

I hear a voice inside say something to the effect of *I'll believe it when I see it*. But I don't tell him that. Not when he holds me close in the November chill on the top of the mountain and kisses the spot where my earlobe meets my neck. At that moment, I'd like to give him a lot of credit.

I shiver, and his lips travel from my neck to my lips. His kisses are soft, then strong, and I feel myself pressing closer. Every muscle in his body seems tense. I let my hands wander. Despite the temperature dropping, his skin feels electric under my touch. I can hear my breath. It comes in sharp, deep inhalations, and I can feel how shaky I am as I exhale.

He stops. "Are you okay?"

I must admit, I may be hyperventilating, but really . . . "I'm beyond okay. You are driving me crazy."

He kisses me again, his lips parting into a smile. "The feeling's mutual, but don't pass out on me." He stays close, our foreheads touching, and I can feel his hot breath on me. It's a delicious sensation.

I want him to kiss me again. I snake my hands into his coat, feel his warm back against my cold hands.

"You're freezing!" He shudders. "We should go."

This was not what I was thinking. Not even close. "I'm fine."

"No, hypothermia's not fine. I can't freeze you to death on our first real date."

"But—" I try to protest. He kisses me again, and now I'm shivering uncontrollably. I can't tell if it's the weather, to be honest. It could be pure physical exultation. But he's made up his mind.

"We're going. You're an ice cube." He kisses me one more time. Then he takes my hand and takes me home.

Short Good-byes and Long Distances

The road in front of us twists just in front of the headlights. There are banks of snow on both sides, and tall pines climb into the pitch-black night. Peter pushes the tiny sports car through the curves, revving the engine to a high whine.

We don't night-ski. I don't recognize this road. I can't tell where we are, and it feels like with each curve, Peter races faster. The tires squeal and skid.

I look at him, but he looks out at the road, oblivious to me in the passenger seat. I open my mouth, and no sound comes out, but noise explodes outside the car—a deer comes up on the hood. The front windshield shatters, and everything goes black.

I sit up. I'm somewhere near the car, still in the cold night, still on the mountain road. My legs are splayed out in front of me. They won't move.

I see the wheels of the car over the side of the road, downslope. One wheel is still turning, and smoke rises from the car.

Andrew is at my side. He picks me up, carrying me in his arms, carrying me away from the crash.

I start to cry. I yell as loudly as I can, "No! Peter's still in the car! Peter's in the car!"

Andrew can't hear me. He keeps walking.

I wake up, startled. I'm clutching my pillow for dear life. I sit up, listen to see if I've woken the kids. It's quiet. I can't help but look at the picture of Peter and me on my nightstand. I don't know what to do, and my heart pounds. I lie down and cover my head with the pillow, closing my eyes as tightly as I can. I don't know how long I stay frozen like that, but I finally fall asleep again.

The next morning, I'm up and dressed before it's light out. After the nightmare, I slept terribly, convinced I would oversleep and Andrew would leave without me. I think part of that comes from an underlying disbelief that he actually exists.

I'm sitting at the kitchen table, trying to focus on the newspaper, when he shuffles in. His hair's messy and sticking up in the back. He looks tired.

"Good morning."

He nods a little. "Morning."

"Did you sleep okay?" I don't know why I'm asking—it's clear he didn't. I'm an expert at ignoring the obvious.

"Okay, I guess. I started thinking about work, and then it was hard to get settled."

I have a hard time imagining what he could be troubled by. "What's worrying you?"

He's into the cereal, pulling out a box and looking for a bowl. "Aw, nothing big. I have a ton of stuff to do to get ready for my next role. I'm worried about the way my last project is getting handled in post-production. There are a lot of hands on a movie before it's done, and sometimes it doesn't end up looking anything like how it felt when you shot it."

"What do you like least about acting?"

"Doing press. It's three or five minutes at a time with people you don't know who ask the same questions over and over. And some of them are out for blood, or a scoop, or some sort of slip-up from you." He pours milk into the cereal and almost overdoes it—this subject distracts him. "But it's not a hard day's work at all. I hate to say anything bad about it because one summer in high school I helped my uncle with his roofing business. And I can tell you I would much rather have to talk about a movie with a lot of people than strip shingles off a Pennsylvania roof in one hundred percent humidity in the middle of July." He plops down next to me and eats his cereal.

"Are the people nice?"

He's midbite but answers anyway. "Mostly. I dunno—there do seem to be more egomaniacal people in the business. And shallow. Lots and lots of worries about looks and stuff you have and stuff you need to get. I guess it's partly the subject. I mean, it's the movies. We're all about creating a false impression. I guess you can't expect people to be very honest when they lie for a living."

"Except for you."

He's done eating and dumps his bowl in the sink. "Of course. I remain unchanged, the same humble, kind boy I've always been." He coughs sarcastically.

"Uh-huh." I smile. "Saint Andrew." I look at the clock. "We better go." I hop up to find shoes and a coat. The boys decided to say good-bye last night. Andrew might be a world-famous movie star, but they weren't willing to give up sleep to take him to the airport this morning.

He sighs. "Maybe everyone'll be too tired to talk on the way back."

"You can hope."

He walks out of the kitchen. "I'm going to find my headphones right now so I can put them on at the first sign of an attempt to make conversation."

We pack his stuff into the car and sneak out before Ditto realizes a car ride is happening. The boys don't even stir.

As I drive Andrew to the terminal, I start to chatter. I guess I'm nervous about saying good-bye. "What was your favorite part of the trip?"

"I liked the part where I kissed you." He has a sly grin.

I feel myself blush hotly. I hate the blushing, but I love what he said.

"No, really, what'd you like best about Boise?"

"No, really, I'm serious. The part I liked best was hanging out with you and the boys."

One thing he has in common with Peter is his honesty. Peter never played coy about how he felt about me. Andrew's apparently not a game player either. I'm thankful, because I suck at games. All kinds. "Me too."

We pull up to the terminal.

"Okay, you need to drop me. If the plane's here, I don't want any of those creeps anywhere near you."

I don't think he's joking. But I hope he's exaggerating a little. I don't like the thought of him having to work with people like that all the time. It can't be good for a person.

I set the parking brake and get out on the pretense of helping him with his luggage. Which is one bag, so the pretense is a stupid one. But I'm just not ready to wave and drive off.

He closes the back and slings his bag over his shoulder. "Okay."

"Okay." We stand there. This is going smoothly. Or not.

"Come here." He pulls me close and kisses me briefly. I step back, happy but also worried someone might see. "Kelly, I'm confident no one is going to spot me kissing you good-bye at six a.m. on Sunday morning in front of the Western Air terminal in Boise, Idaho. If anyone does, he deserves an award as the most brilliant paparazzo of our time." He dances around a little. It's biting cold.

"Next time you come we're buying you a decent jacket. You can't run around Boise in a hoodie, I swear." I realize I just said that he was coming back here. Well, I'm going with it. He can be the one to burst the bubble of my delusion.

He hugs me again and kisses me, a strong, deep kiss. "I better get going. I had an awesome time. I'll call you this week." He kisses the tip of my nose playfully. Then Andy Pettigrew slings his bag over his shoulder and strides away.

I don't stand there and watch the takeoff, though I'm tempted. I'm trying to shake the feeling that I've fallen into a movie, so I avoid the *Casablanca*-esque plane-taxiing moment. I will admit to thinking that when he walked away, it would've been the right moment to hear some power chords or a Shins song, though. I can't help it.

Working Vacations

Again the boys and I go back to our lives. This time it's a little easier—at least the boys were witnesses to this last encounter in Fantasy Land. The fact that Hunter and Beau remember Andrew's visit helps me brush off the feeling that this is a weird *X-Files* episode. David Duchovny is waiting around a corner, I just know it.

I worry a lot at first that the boys have bragged at school, or that they're getting a lot of guff for making up shit about Mom's new friend. But it becomes clear that Andrew's request to "keep it on the QT" (which doesn't help to debunk his secret gangsta thug persona with the boys, language like that) hit home with both of them. I honestly think they've kept it to themselves. Maybe they enjoy sharing a secret with each other. They don't count me because I'm old, and how could I possibly appreciate how cool my new friend is anyway?

He is cool, though. Starting the first week, I get little texts each day: Here I am in LA. How're the boys? Or: Development meeting in 90210. Lady across from me has taken "bee stung" lips to a horrifying new level.

And at night, he calls. He actually calls, and we chat about what Hunter did in soccer practice, how my last run went, the crush Beau has on his teacher. He tells me about diva directors and scripts he wants to make into movies—the usual details of a ho-hum movie-star life.

The boys ask after him, and I keep them up to date on Andrew's latest Hollywood adventures. They seem interested.

But they stay quiet. And I am too. Barb from Boise State emails to ask me how my new "friend" is (heavy on the quotation marks), but I reiterate that he was just visiting and, as predicted, he's back in California. Of course, I neglect to mention to her that he's back in Los Angeles getting ready to shoot his next movie.

Then there's Tessa. She texts me constantly: the morning he leaves, the next day, the day after that. She asks again how he is in bed. The last time she does it, I send her this text: He's gay. Get over it.

We'll see how long that shuts her up. I've been trying to avoid her since, but I promise coffee in the near future in the hopes of stalling her for a while longer.

And I'm trying to get back into my rhythm here in Boise. I don't even want to imagine how wonderful being with Andrew at Christmas might be. Each time I think of it, I try to shut my brain down before I start spinning *It's a Wonderful Life* scenes with the two of us in them and Beau playing the part of ZuZu.

The other time I shut off my brain is when I start to go down the jealousy road. Let's see . . . The guy I'm dating is surrounded twenty-four/seven by women younger, richer, and more beautiful than I am. I don't even know where to begin with that one.

There's a strong possibility that I could turn into a bathrobe-wearing crazy lady: forever reminiscing about my seventy-two-hour relationship, not washing my hair, eating too much takeout and saving the boxes, so eventually I show up on *Hoarders*. Or a crazy cat-lady show. Though we haven't had a cat since before Peter was sick.

Peter. So far I've had that same nightmare two more times in the weeks since Andrew's visit. I keep waiting for my subconscious to finish processing this new relationship, but apparently it's got more to do. I find myself in a weird world, dating again, and when I have a self-aware moment, it often brings that ache back, the one under my collarbone. I'm thrilled to be dating Andrew, or whatever this relationship is, but I miss Peter, and if he were here, none of this would be happening. Bitter and sweet. A paradox.

Relationship. Silly Kelly, using that word. *Relationcation*, maybe—it's a little vacation romance. At the school where I taught, kids used to call them CTRs: choir trip romances. Many of these romances blossomed and shriveled within the distance from Boise to Elko and back. That's where I should be categorizing this experience.

That's what I think until I get the call. The call that's more than just an idle chat. I'm in Albertsons, staring at the five million different toothbrush choices, when my cell rings. I answer it without looking, fully expecting it to be one of the boys.

"So, there are only teal and magenta in the kind of toothbrush you and your brother like. Can one of you live with a pink toothbrush so you don't use the other's?"

"I would sooner die than brush my teeth with a pink toothbrush. Brushing with that would mean the end of my social life as I know it. Or turn me into a nun."

It's Andrew. "Andrew! What are you doing?"

"Talking with you about toothbrushes, apparently."

"You see, this is why my life is so immensely gratifying. These are the life-or-death decisions I'm dealing with here."

"What are you doing?"

"You mean besides shopping? We're going over to Tessa's for Thanksgiving tomorrow. I promised to bring the canned cranberry gel, so here I am. And the boys are keeping me busy driving them all over for all of their stuff."

"You told Tessa about me yet?" He sounds like he's teasing me.

"I told her you were gay. That's shut her up so far."

"Ouch!" He laughs. "Well, you're not the first person to think so. I'll have to work on proving that wrong to you."

I grin involuntarily. And try to change the subject. "Where are you? Out in Ventura County now?"

"Yep. We've been filming since last week. It's going fine so far. I'm busy, and busy is good."

He's shared a few details about his project with me. It's a Western—*The Last Drive*—and it's one of those "end of an era" kind of Westerns where the range is getting all fenced in, and the sheriff in town has to make peace between the greenhorn homesteaders and the longtime cowboys who like their range open and their horses trusty and their little dogies running free. Something like that. He's playing the sheriff.

It sounds interesting enough, but I've resisted the urge to go online and research to sound more "with it." If I were dating a real estate guy, I might look at some of his houses so I could talk about them with him, but I wouldn't feel obligated to go get my broker's license. Likewise, I'm trying not to nerd out on movie stuff just to entertain him or sound smarter than I really am. Not that I'm not interested, but I figure I'm his friend, not his biggest fan. I don't know. It just feels important that I have a line there and stay on this side of it. Kathy Bates waits on the other side of that line.

Consequently, I didn't venture into the who's-playing-your-love-interest conversation with him, and I haven't heard, so I am assuming it's not a big part of the movie. And if it is, I'd rather not know. This is coming from the same place that prevents me from doing a lot of research into his former real-life loves. He dated that one girl from *Redcoats Rising*, and I do recall a few pictures in the tabloids of him with dates—a model once, I think, and a tennis player. But I'm hoping he's not been a player, à la the young Warren Beatty, and I don't remember him ever being part of a hyphenate. You know, Andralina, or Pamdrew. So I'm going with the ignorance-is-bliss coping mechanism for now.

I come back to our conversation. "Have you met your horse yet?" Last time we talked, he was excited to meet his horse.

"Yes, and she loves me dearly already."

"How can you tell?" There's something goofy coming, but I play the straight man.

"Today when she stepped on my toe I only had to have two grips help me get her to move. Last time four of them had to haul her off me."

The grips are the sturdiest members of the film crew, from what Andrew's told me.

"What's her name?"

"Petunia. But in the movie she's Querido."

"Ooh, what's that mean?"

He laughs over the phone. He sounds happy. I like that. "It means *my love* or *my dear*. Pretty, no?"

"I miss you." Well, I said it. Chalk one up for the nonsubtle lonely girl. Great.

"I miss you, which is why I'm calling. Do you want to wait until Christmas?"

He's talking about our planned Christmas visit. "Don't I have to wait?"

"Do you?"

"Are you going to answer each of my questions with another question?"

"Am I?" He laughs again. "No, really. I think I can swing it for you to come down next week. Do you have anyone who could look after the boys for a few days?"

My brain is racing. Who? "Mom's always offering to come up and give me a break. It would probably involve me telling her about you, though."

There's an exasperated *fuff* of air on the other side of the phone. "Honest to God, you still haven't told your folks about me?" He sounds annoyed, but it's fake annoyed. I think.

"Umm, I was going to tell them when we got down there for Christmas. That way I would have proof on hand—you know, you'd be there so they couldn't institutionalize me."

He's quiet for a minute. It sounds like he's muffled the phone. "I'm back. Listen, I'm due on set. Here's the plan. Call your mom. Tell her I'll have someone pick her up in Indio or LA—where are she and your dad right now?"

"In LA."

"Okay, I'll have someone pick her up and get her to you in Boise. Then you'll switch places. You'll fly down here. A quick visit. Now, go make the phone calls. Make it so."

"I will see what I can do, Jean-Luc Picard. You're a huge nerd."

"You're the one who knows the name of the captain. Of course, I'm sheriff of a town and ride a horse named Petunia, with whom I have a hot date right now. We're in a dead heat for nerd supremacy. Call me tonight, and we'll finish plotting."

"Okay. Talk to you soon."

The line goes dead. This'll take some doing, but I'm totally game. I'm going to see him again.

There's One in Every Bunch

I can't avoid her anymore. Tessa's my friend, and I'd like to keep my friend, and after a while, people won't be friends with other people if they are constantly avoiding them.

Thanksgiving at Tessa's is a tradition. It was even before Peter died. I have to take the boys to Thanksgiving, I have to speak to Tessa, and it looks like I'll have to tell her what's up. If I take that trip before I tell her about him, she'll disown me.

I decide to tell her pre-turkey. We usually do something in the morning, just the two of us. Sometimes we bake the pies together (she bakes them, I watch) or go on a walk with Ditto. I suggest a run today. She agrees, which is impressive. Tessa is constantly trying to get me to go work out with *her*, but she never wants to run on the trail with me. For her, working out without an audience is without a point. There's a reason she goes to the Y. It's to be seen. Working out is secondary. Probably tertiary—she also likes to see who she can spy, and so seeing is almost as important as being seen.

For that reason, running on the trails is never very appealing to her, and it speaks volumes about her curiosity that she's agreed to go out with me now. That she insists on it, actually.

So here we are, running up the Corrals Trail, the path muddy and the air wet and cold. Ditto is with us, and he's already a lovely shade of mud from the tops of his legs down. Yuck. But I owe Tessa an explanation, and I need to placate her too.

"Let's stop, can we? Please?" Tessa's got her arms akimbo, and she's walking already. We've run for maybe twenty minutes. Maybe. Ditto's thrilled. He wanders off trail to sniff for critters.

I pull up and walk back to her. "You need to walk?" She's fit, so I know it's not that she's tired.

"What I need is for you to dish on the movie star you were so casually hanging out with in the grocery store parking lot three weeks ago, that's what I need. And yeah, I don't feel like running anymore." She turns around to walk toward the trailhead, so I follow.

"What do you want to know?" I don't know how this is going to work.

"Have you slept with him?"

"For the millionth time, no. I haven't."

"Why the hell not?"

"Because, that's why."

"Because is not an answer."

"Can we start with something easier, like how he and I met?"

"Oh no, he *is* gay, isn't he?"

"What makes you say that?"

"Because you're avoiding the sex discussion, and 'because' isn't a good enough reason to avoid having sex with a gorgeous specimen like Andy Pettigrew."

"Maybe he doesn't want to sleep with me. Maybe he doesn't like me like that."

"Is that true? He's not into you?"

"I don't know."

"Has he at least kissed you?"

"Yes."

"Was it a gay kiss?"

"I don't know. What the hell is a gay kiss like? Is this some weird homophobic streak in you?"

"No, it's not that. Gay as in he's not thrilled to kiss a girl. No tongue. You know, he closed-mouth kisses you like he's kissing his grandmother, like he's Mr. Darcy in *Pride and Prejudice*."

"So if a guy doesn't French-kiss a girl, that makes him automatically gay, does it? And have you even read that book?"

"You're making it sound so dumb, but yeah. And no, I haven't read it. I saw the movie."

"Mr. Darcy is not gay, and I'm not having this conversation with you anymore."

"Okay, listen. Do you like him?"

"Yes."

"Did you really meet him in Indio?"

"Yes."

"Are you really not going to say anything more than that?"

"Probably not. The French-kissing line of conversation was kind of off-putting. You've made me crabby. Plus, you said you were going to tweet about him, so that makes me suspicious."

"You're not ever allowed to say *tweet* as a verb again. It doesn't suit you." She kicks the dirt in front of her. "But listen, I think it's great that you've got a new friend. Just promise me you won't get too tied up in it, okay? I'd rather see you have a little meaningless sex."

"What do you mean?"

"It's your first foray into the world since Peter. And, man, you took 'go big or go home' to heart, didn't you? This guy is not an easing-back-into-things guy, Kelly Jo."

I don't answer, so she keeps going.

"I just mean, look at the world he lives in. Women throw themselves at him. How can he possibly resist all of that?"

I take offense. "Because I'm such a loser, how can he not sleep with other women? Is that where you're going with this?"

She shakes her head vehemently. "Of course not. Kelly, put your brain in your head for a second. He's a Hollywood movie star. They're not famous for their fidelity. I don't want to see you get hurt."

"He's not like that."

"How do you know?"

"I just know."

"What if I told you I researched him a little?"

"I would tell you I don't care. I've spent time with him. We know each other. How is it fair that I can do a full background check on him courtesy of the Internet? I wouldn't do that with a normal guy. And half of what you read is lies anyway. I'll find out about him like I would any person I'm getting to know."

"This is happening pretty quickly, though. Are you sure about him? What have you told him about you and Peter?"

"He's my new guy, not my new counselor. But he's great with the boys."

"I'm just saying. He was pretty wild when he first went out to LA."

"I've stopped listening to you."

"Okay, so let's assume for a minute he's not into cheating with other women. He's not gay, or at least you don't think he is. Has it ever crossed your mind that he might just be looking for a diversion, a distraction?"

I hesitate. I hate it, but I feel doubt creeping in. "No."

"Could he be goofing around?"

"Do you mean screwing around? Sleeping around?"

"I thought you said you hadn't slept with him."

"I haven't, so why would he bother with me? I didn't jump him the second we met, and you know he's probably got plenty of women who'll do that, so why has he stuck around?"

She throws up her hands in surrender. "Listen, Counsel, I'm not getting into a legal debate with you. The point is, he lives in a different world from you and me, sister. Don't be naive about that. Okay?"

I feel pouty. Of course she has a point. Tessa's right. She's always right—surprise, surprise.

But no, on second thought . . . "You know what?"

She's not even pretending to exercise now. She's just strolling. She stops and looks at me. "What?"

"I'm not being naive. I want to trust my gut on this one. This is a good man, Tessa."

She smiles at me gently, or condescendingly. "Okay, okay. Maybe I'm wrong. It happens."

I feel better that I stuck up for Andrew. "It doesn't happen very often, but maybe this time."

I try not to hesitate. I'm not telling her about my trip to see him, though. I don't want to hear something cynical about it, not right now. I want to trust, to risk, to take a chance with Andrew. And not have to take a tumble because of it. Sometimes the reward is worth the risk. Let this be one of those times.

Tessa points to the car at the trailhead. "C'mon, let's go stuff ourselves with white flour and starch and turkey that I'll have to work off in spinning class later." She breaks into a brisk run.

Time Together

I could start this discussion with the obvious, which is to say it's been a very long time since I've had a weekend with a man I'm interested in without the boys being in on it—like, before they were born. And that's just a distant memory.

Or I could start with how Mom was impressed with the car Andrew sent around for her (a black Mercedes coupe with tinted windows), a little disappointed by the flight (first class commercial—no friend with a private jet to lend this weekend), but thrilled to hear who I was dating (mostly because he exists, with the bonus of being someone exciting).

Or I could discuss the talk my dad had with me over the phone about not losing my head, knowing what I was doing, considering the boys, etc., etc. I sort of expected him to give me a curfew too, but I guess I should be touched that part of him still thinks of me as a little girl.

Instead, though, I'll start with one of my favorite parts of the trip so far: riding shotgun in a convertible, heading out to Ventura County, listening to Florence + the Machine loud on the stereo with my head tilted back to see the blue sky and clouds racing by overhead. If I had the *To Catch a Thief* long scarf trailing out behind me, it would've been totally perfect, but I did have the Cary Grant-esque leading man at the wheel next to me, so I was good.

And then we arrive. Andrew has already assured me that on set I'm Kelly, the friend from Indio, and he's given most people the impression that our families have known each other forever and there's a wedding in Ojai I'm going to this weekend. We will keep the PDA to a minimum. He may or may not also be attending said fictional wedding. He's apparently saving that in case we need it for some other diversion or excuse. Who knows.

The sun is setting over a dusty old rodeo arena. I'm up in the bleachers, which did not exist before yesterday but were constructed to match the old arena for the purpose of the movie. I sit behind the crew, safely out of the shot. This is my only objective this weekend, movie-set-wise: keep the hell out of the way and lie low.

Though it is quite fun to watch. It's warm. The sun soaks into my shoulders and back, and I was right: watching Andrew work is fascinating.

Every once in a while, in a long stretch of setting up a take, I'll catch him looking up into the stands at me. He'll toss his sun-bleached (actually bleach-bleached, but that's the movies for you) mop of hair toward me and smile.

Most of the time, though, he's intent on his work. Occasionally he confers with the script supervisor, reviewing the scene's dialogue, I assume. After most takes he stands behind the director with the producer and gets a look at the scene on the playback.

That's about the extent of moviemaking that I can figure out. The rest of it seems to involve a *lot* of standing around as cameras are moved, big lighting setups are fussed with, or some other mystery of a delay is created.

The director is Logan VanderSmoot. He's a Dutch filmmaker, and this is his first foray into American movies. He's got quite a reputation, apparently, as an eccentric. Word has it he puts the *Oh!* in OCD. He keeps his socks on those tiny hangers they hang on in the stores, installed fans in the back of his closets to keep the air moving through his clothes, has a nanny for his pet Maltese. But he's a fan of Westerns, Andrew seems to like him, and he's very warm when we meet, so I like him.

He paces a lot. He fiddles with the video screen he wears like a fanny pack in front of him on his belly (maybe more like a Baby-Björn), and when he gives Andrew direction, he always seems to pull him into what looks suspiciously like a football huddle with either the writer (on set today), the producer, or both. Then they break, and I half-expect him to pat Andrew on the butt as he gets back out on the field to execute the play.

And have I said anything about the execution of those plays? Andrew has a gift. When the fussing of all the people stills and they roll, when it's quiet and focused on him, he's in another dimension. I swear the air shimmers around him like a mirage. His intensity is palpable.

He's beautiful to watch. Besides the gift of his craft, he's been groomed into full-on matinee-idol form. His hair, as I mentioned, has been bleached a golden brown/blond. He's wearing a cowboy shirt, cut to move with him closely, and his boots and riding pants are equally well fitted. He's broad at the shoulders, slim at the waist, noble. Now I understand more fully why he has approximately nine bazillion Facebook fans. He's a man who deserves followers, devotees, just for the look and charisma of him.

I'm trying hard not to be too starstruck. I'm glad I get to be at a distance from all of this, because there's a small possibility that I would, as the fangirls say, make a sound that closely resembles *squeee* if I were closer to him right now.

In the middle of my reverie, there's suddenly a lot more activity down in the arena than there has been all afternoon. The light is waning—Logan prefers to shoot during the "golden hour," when the afternoon sun illuminates his scenes with a warm glow—so the shoot must be winding down.

I look for Andrew. He's giving me the all done sign, waving at me to come down. I meet him at the fence of the arena, climb up on it to look down at him.

"We're done. What'd you think?"

"I didn't understand everything you had to stand around and wait for, but it's cool, Andrew. It's really cool. And you're really good."

He scoffs. "You couldn't even hear."

I wave him off. "No, seriously. From up there—hell, from up in a blimp—I could still see it. You command the scene. You light the place up."

This seems to please him. "Thanks."

I'm starting to sound like a suck-up. "But enough about you. I want to meet Petunia."

He fake frowns. "That bitch is always crowding me out of the shot. She's a total diva."

"Speaking of divas, we haven't touched on your leading lady. You have one, I assume?" I try to sound completely nonthreatened. Totally lying, but you know.

"Franca? She's fine. She's not on set today—mostly just me and Petunia and a little of Gerry."

Gerry Turner plays the old, retired sheriff Andrew's character turns to for fatherly advice when the chips are proverbially down in the movie. I've seen him in quite a lot of movies, but meeting him was like meeting an accountant your dad uses. Just a normal guy.

I'm glad Franca's not on set. Maybe I can avoid a direct side-by-side comparison all weekend and escape before Andrew realizes he's been shortchanged.

He breaks my wishful thinking. "I'm starving. Let's go back to my apartment. I want to cook you dinner."

"You can't cook." I smile at him.

"Neither can you." He climbs up on the fence and sits next to me for a second.

"Point taken."

"Well, let's go back to my place and do a bad job preparing something for dinner together."

He swings a leg over and hops to the ground, out of the arena. I worry about achieving a similarly nimble dismount, but Andrew reaches up for my hand and helps me. The set has cleared rapidly. An armada of golf carts and ATVs hauled equipment and crew away, and a wrangler took Petunia and walked her back to the stables. Andrew and I walk down the dusty road to the parking lot. I rode in to the set with one of the production assistants in our continuing attempt to keep things appearing mellow.

"Boy, y'all close up shop quick around here." I'm enjoying the soft pink light of approaching dusk, and the birds flitting from the trees and calling to one another.

"Y'all?"

I didn't notice I'd said it. "Yeah. Holdover from my past."

"Where?" He likes to walk a little ahead of me, turning and

keeping eye contact more than I think a normal guy would. Okay, maybe more than Peter would. He was a side talker. Big conversations often took place sitting next to each other on the back stoop at night, watching the dog wander around the backyard.

"I lived in Tennessee when I was a kid. Went to college in Virginia. That's where I met Peter." Oh, yes, Kelly, let's bring Peter up again. Score another one for the girl who has no brain.

"Did you guys get married right out of college?"

"No. We dated some at school. He was too wild for me. When I'd been out in the real world for a couple of years, I ran into him again. He was living in the same town as me; he was in grad school. I went to dinner at a friend's house, and there he was."

I skip the vivid memories that rise to the top with the story. I've found that if I dive into them, I can get lost in a deep lake of grief. For some reason the early stuff hurts the worst. Maybe because it feels like we were so far away from anything bad happening. I look back at my younger self and think, *Poor girl, she has no idea what's coming,* while I watch her falling in love with Peter over dinner. That's one interesting thing about me then: I was never waiting for the other shoe to drop like I always seem to be now.

"Hello?" Andrew's voice startles me. It doesn't sound a thing like Peter's.

"Hi. Sorry." I try to refocus. I'm back in the present, on the dusty road, walking with a new man.

He stops. He puts his hands in his pockets and faces me. He smiles gently. "Don't apologize. You've got things you remember. That's good, right?"

"I guess so. Some things hurt to remember."

He takes a step forward and puts both hands on my shoulders.

"This is when I should say something helpful, and preferably deep. For now, all I can say is that sucks, and I hope it stops soon."

"You're making me look bad, getting all wise and stuff."

He throws his arm around my shoulder, and we continue walking down the trail. "I told you I was good. I won't charge you for that bit of wisdom. Soon, though. Soon."

We've Got Tonight

At the end of the road, I follow Andrew into one of the many tents the film crew has put up in the fields around the farmhouse they're using as a location. It's like a huge traveling circus. White tents dot the field, each one with a different purpose: mess, makeup, costumes. Andrew goes back to his trailer to change. The plan is to share a ride to his place. Although Andrew drove us to Ventura County, apparently being famous and on location means not being trusted to ferry yourself around—no convertible ride this time. Someone else is driving us home.

A plain-looking minivan with dark windows is parked just inside one of the wider entrances of the tent. When Andrew returns, we get in, and a guy I'm told is named Tucker drives us out. As we leave the set, another van pulls through the gates and out of the camp at the same time. At first I figure it's just other people leaving the set for the day.

Then I realize it's a decoy. And I realize we were parked inside the tent so no one could see who got in the van. This is a little disconcerting. When Andrew and I were together in Boise, it felt normal. In this world, it's a different story. Things appear normal at first glance, but I'm beginning to think that takes a lot of careful orchestration.

We arrive at the block of condominiums where Andrew's staying. It's a little mixed-use development—one of those old-time town square fabrications. There are restaurants and shops on the bottom story, and buildings of various heights to make the whole thing look organic, when in fact it probably all went up in a couple of months during the last building boom.

Tucker drives us into the underground parking garage. Again, this seems to be just part of the way Andrew's life works. No one sees him arrive. I wonder if anyone has figured out he's staying here. Now I know why the top on his convertible went up a couple miles out of town when we drove here from LA. It wasn't the weather.

In the garage Tucker gets out. He comes around to the door. Andrew steps out first, and suddenly, I feel like the wind's been knocked out of me. Tucker isn't a production assistant like the scrawny but very amiable college boy who drove me to the set today. Now that he's out of the car, I can see that Tucker is huge. He's as tall as Andrew, and he's solid muscle. Tucker is a bodyguard.

I sit in the van for a second, letting this sink in. How do I feel about this? For some reason, I'm afraid for my boys. What am I getting them into? Could I be placing them in danger by hanging out with this man—a man who needs a bodyguard like that?

Andrew pokes his head inside. "You coming?"

I take a deep breath. Just because it's new doesn't mean it's bad. People live lots of different kinds of lives, right? This is just a little different. "I'm coming."

He helps me step out, taking my hand in a very chivalrous way. But what really helps me relax is the way he continues to hold my hand as we walk to the elevator. Tucker walks ahead of us, but he ambles. He doesn't act as though we're in any danger.

We get in the elevator alone. Tucker stands at the doors and waves, smiling. "Have a good night, Andrew."

Did I notice a slight eyebrow raise with that good-bye?

"You too, Tucker. See you in the morning." The elevator doors close.

"So you don't drive your car when you're here?" I'm wrapping my brain around this.

"No. Tucker does the driving." Andrew's still holding my hand, still relaxed. I don't think he's picked up on the state of alarm over here next to him.

"Does that bug you?" I look up at him.

He looks at me. "No, not really. It's easier if he drives."

"He's your bodyguard." I say it like it's a secret.

"Yeah. I like him. He's cool."

"Is it weird?" I hold his hand a little tighter for a minute.

"I don't think so. When I'm working, Tucker usually is working too. People know where the sets are, so it's better to have someone around in case a crowd forms. And if I do press, or a premiere, sometimes it's Tucker and Dean too."

"Two?"

He grins. "I'm kind of a big deal, you know."

The elevator stops at the top floor, and I take a step forward, ready to get off.

"Wait." He pulls a small key out of his pocket and sticks it into the elevator panel. It turns, and then the elevator resumes its climb.

"How very James Bond of you."

The elevator stops again, and this time the doors open on to a foyer. There's a hotel-looking fake orchid sitting on a little table.

"Is this your place?"

He nods. I step off the elevator and around the corner.

It has high ceilings and a very open, loft-style floor plan. It must be the penthouse. I guess that's a no-brainer. I face a wall of tall windows and French doors and a large deck that runs the length of the room.

Lights of the town twinkle outside. Inside, it's austere. There's a guitar and a piano over by the windows. A sleek dining room table has piles of mail and other paper on it. The kitchen hardly looks touched, though I do notice a rather sizable collection of cereal boxes lined up on the counter by the fridge.

"I like this—do you like it?" I turn around. He's been standing behind me. I guess he's been watching my reaction.

"I do. It's just what they rented for the shoot, but if I had a style, I guess it'd be like this."

"Do you have a house in LA?"

"I'm renting one. Buying something seems so permanent. Plus, I'm gone so much, I don't think it matters. I'm not into accumulating stuff yet. Maybe when there's more to it than just me."

This is interesting. For me, there's been more to it than just me for a lot of years now. It's different to look through his eyes.

"I can't remember what that feels like. And kids grow stuff, I swear. They're born, and their stuff starts multiplying everywhere. Is it lonely or does the freedom feel good?"

He walks over to the fridge to inspect the contents. He has a lot of take-out cartons. "Oh, you know, sometimes I feel at loose ends. I envy you your boys. I miss my family, but they have their own lives. My sisters are both married, and my mom turned my room into a craft room fifteen minutes after I came out to LA. If I'm working, I'm fine. If I have time to think about it, I guess loneliness is one thing I feel."

He reaches in and grabs a handful of cereal straight out of one of the boxes on the counter.

"Are you feeding me cereal for dinner?" I poke the box.

He shakes his head, breaking whatever thought he was lost in. "Sorry, reflex. Cereal is man's greatest triumph, but I do have a plan for dinner. You need to camp out in my bedroom for a while."

I raise an eyebrow. "Really?"

"It's all very innocent. I just want to attempt to surprise you. And I'm not going to oversell it, so don't get any pictures of nine thousand candles in your head." He takes me by the elbows and steers me through one of three doors off the great room.

It's again a Spartan scene. There's a king-size bed dressed out in basic khaki sheets and blankets. There are some generic-looking oversize black-and-white photographs of trees on the walls. They must be from the same decorator as the fake orchid in the foyer.

"Is any of this stuff yours?" I circle the bed.

"Nope."

I stop. On the nightstand is *In Our Time*. He's reading it.

"Hey!" I'm so pleased, I can't keep it out of my voice.

"Are you proud of me?"

I put my arms around his neck. "That you're reading it makes me very, very happy. I'm proud of my star pupil."

He gives me a peck on the lips. "Wait before you call me a star, because we haven't actually discussed it yet. My insights may bring tears to your eyes, but not in a good way."

He unlocks my fingers from behind his neck and turns on the gigantic TV. "You park it in here while I get things going."

"I may be blind when you come back. No one needs a TV this big."

He chuckles. "Especially when you watch the crap I do." He closes the door behind him.

I sit on the edge of the bed for a second. I'm tempted to see how far he's gotten in *In Our Time*, but that seems invasive. I get up and wander, and something catches my eye on the top of his dresser.

It's the black rock he found on the Oregon Trail. I pick it up and rub it between my fingers. My face hurts, I'm smiling so big. He is perfectly adorable—heck, he's just perfect. I want to do a little dance.

Next I peek into the master bath, 'cause, you know, that's not snoopy at all. There's a fancy tub with lots of rolled towels stacked on the shelf next to it. None of it appears to have been touched. In the shower there's a bottle of grocery store shampoo and a bar of soap. Shaving cream, a razor, and Old Spice deodorant sit by the sink. And a toothbrush.

I'm not sure what I thought I'd find, but his normalcy in grooming products is a relief. Not a lot of movie-star preening going on in here.

I wander back out and try to watch *Dirty Jobs* on the Gigundo-tron. Poor Mike Rowe is up to his waist in sludge of some sort or another.

Andrew peeks back in after a half hour or so. "Let the magic begin!" He swings the door wide with a goofy flourish.

There's a slight breeze, because the doors are open to the patio. He's plugged in lots of Christmas lights, and the deck twinkles. There are several potted palm trees, and the lights on them are charming. He's also set the table.

"I'd offer you a glass of wine, but I don't know whether red or white would work better with our meal, and I know you're not much of an imbiber." He ushers me out onto the patio.

It's warm. It's probably freezing cold back in Boise right now. I try not to get distracted by a thought of the boys and how Mom's doing with them.

"Okay, sit."

I do as he says. There's no food on the table. My curiosity is piqued. "What're we having?"

"Patience, patience. I'll be right back." He hustles off to the kitchen.

I can smell something savory. I hate to admit it, but I was the person in my marriage who ate whatever was put in front of her. Thankfully, Peter was a good cook. I hope somehow my boys won't be as useless as I am in the kitchen.

Andrew walks out and sets a plate down in front of me with a waiterly bow.

It's bacon, eggs, and pancakes. I laugh out loud.

"Madam, may I present? Breakfast for dinner." He sits down next to me and hands me my napkin.

"And you were fretting about red or white wine. What a faker."

He grins. "I actually don't drink at all when I'm on a movie. Too many empty calories, and I want to stay focused." He takes a bite of his eggs.

"If we're going to keep doing this, one of us needs to learn how to cook."

He looks right at me. "If we're going to keep doing what?"

Uh-oh. Panic city. "I don't know." I swallow hard.

"You mean dating?" He talks with his mouth full.

"Are we dating?"

He stops chewing for a minute this time. "Umm, you flew down to see me for the weekend. Yes, we're dating. I have so decreed it. End of story."

I sit there and spin my fork a few times. "I like to hear you say it."

"Well, good. Now eat your pancakes."

Juke Box Hero

Dinner puts me in a very good mood—the kind of good mood I get in when I run a lot and feel like I'm twenty, except smarter than when I was twenty. These are the times when I'm almost successful at quelling the worry in my head. I'm almost normal in these spaces of my life.

The air is cooling, but we've stayed out on the patio to talk. Andrew smokes. I'm restless, ready to explore his place a little more. It's too bad it's not really his house—I could glean a lot more clues that way.

"Let's go in." I take his hand.

I think he likes that I'm taking the lead. "Okay. Are you cold?"

"Well, yeah, but I also want to snoop. You've seen my house, met my kids, seen me crying my guts out—I need more dirt on you."

"You don't want the dirt on me. Trust me."

"Oh, come on. You can't have too many skeletons."

"Let's say I have enough that I'm changing the subject. Maybe we can listen to music."

We go inside. The air still smells like bacon. The stereo's on, but I can't make out the music, it's so soft.

"What's playing?" I spy his iPhone docked on the stereo over by the piano.

"I have no idea. But I do have some songs on there for you." He grins.

"Oh yeah? Which ones?" As I look at it, he scoots between me and the stereo.

"Listen. Tell me if I'm on target." He fiddles with it for a moment and presses Play as I sit on the couch. It's Duran Duran's "Rio."

"Oh, I do love this song."

He comes over and sits next to me. He puts his arm around me, and we listen for a minute. Then I get up and wander over to the piano for more clues. While Simon Le Bon serenades us, I try to decipher the notes and scribbling on the staffs in front of me.

"You write songs?" I can distantly remember how to read music from high school band.

"Nothing of substance. But it's fun. My sisters are both good singers. They stick mostly to church choirs, but we play a lot of music when we get together. I'm always the one who accompanies."

Of course he can play the piano. Would it be too much for him to be sucky at more than just cooking? He's too impressive.

He's up at the stereo for the next song. "How about this one?"

It's Journey's "Don't Stop Believin'."

"You just know this from *Glee*. Suddenly you young 'uns know all the good eighties music." I go to the stereo this time. "What else?"

He stands behind me. "Well, I like this one a lot. It might be cheesy, but it speaks to me." He reaches around me to pick the song, and I feel the hair on my arms prickle from his energy. I love feeling him close to me.

I recognize it as soon as he plays it. "Juke Box Hero."

He wanders around the kitchen, picks up a wooden spoon. He sings the first verse into it. Then he speaks up to be heard over the music. "The story song. That's why this song's cool. Same with 'Don't Stop Believin'.'"

I walk over to him so I don't have to yell. "They're both about small town boys who turn out to be rock stars. Is this your secret? You really want to be a rock star, don't you?" I jab him in the ribs for emphasis.

"Now you've gone and done it. Don't you know every actor's a closet rock-and-roll god?"

"You're not going to pull a Bruce Willis on me, are you?" I make a terrible face.

He still has the spoon in hand, and it looks like he's going to swat me with it. "You'll pay for that."

I take off around the kitchen island, but he's in hot pursuit. I grab the nearest utensil in self-defense.

He stops. "Not the whisk!" He's laughing so hard, he can't finish talking.

"It's not that funny. You forced me to find a weapon." I bop him on the head with the whisk.

He's ready for me. He ducks under and grabs me around the waist in one swift movement. Now I'm over his shoulder in the fireman's carry. And I'm yelling. I hope his neighbors aren't too close, because we're definitely making a ruckus.

"Juke Box Hero" is almost over—the rocking with one guitar is at full tilt. Andrew hauls me over to the couch and flips me off his shoulder. I land with a plop, but I have a decent hold on his arm, so he comes down with me.

He kisses me. The release, the emotion of it rushes through me, and I kiss back, hard. I have him by both arms and pull him to me without hesitation.

He, on the other hand, pulls back. "Wait, I want to play another song for you." He gets up off the couch, pulls me up too. I try not to appear petulant.

He presses Play again. It's one of my favorite songs of all time: "Don't Dream It's Over." "Your boys said it's on your top-ten list."

"You asked the boys?" This is interesting.

"You mentioned you liked eighties music. Last time I called, the boys checked the iPod for me. A little reconnaissance. I played a spy in a movie once."

"Did you play a stalker ever?"

"Ha, ha. Let's dance."

The song's decidedly down tempo from the last one. He pulls me into his arms.

"Okay, this is nice too." I hum as he leads me around the great room in large, slow circles. I listen to the lyrics. "This song seems kind of appropriate."

He listens for a second. "Which part?"

I stand close to him, rest my head on his chest, listen to the music and feel him against me. "The title, mainly because I keep waiting to wake up from all of this."

We sway together as our orbit around the room tightens to a small spot.

"Well, stop. Don't look for reasons why this shouldn't be, or why this shouldn't work."

He's right, I know, but my brain whirls for a minute, clouded with images from nightmares, worries about the boys, a fleeting grip of pain when I think of nights spent with Peter. I take a deep breath, try to stay in the moment.

The song is over. He slips out of our dance to change the music. "Last song for real."

He pushes Play and comes close to me, waiting. I feel my heart rev up. I think something is about to happen that hasn't happened in a long time. It's terrifying and exhilarating. Though for a moment I toy with the idea of running for the door, I really want him to kiss me, hold me, put his hands on me.

The song starts. It's Beck's "Let's Get Lost." As Andrew kisses me, his hands move down my back. I tug at his shirt, pulling him even closer.

We kiss with urgency. Then he stops for a moment and looks into my eyes. He wants me, but he's waiting. He's waiting for me. For me to say yes.

I want this. I want this, and I want it to be right. I'm taking the plunge. I close my eyes and feel the pain under my collarbone release me from its grip. It's replaced by desire blooming in my blood. Peter would ski the chute, take the risk, get lost in the moment. I know what to do. I am bold. This is right.

I take Andrew by the hand and lead him to the bedroom.

Well, Then

Utter bliss is a wonderful, wonderful place to be. When I wake up in the morning, I'm there. I'd forgotten what it feels like.

My heart has been pumping at two-thirds capacity for a very long time. Now someone has opened a floodgate, and I just got a transfusion of fresh, clean, joyously happy red blood. Every cell in my body is getting a boost.

I wake up snuggled into a broad, tan, gorgeous back. I examine the freckles for a minute before I move up to the neck and nuzzle the cowlick of hair at the nape.

"Andrew. Andrew Pettigrew." I don't know his middle name.

He turns over, a marvelously sleepy smile on his face. "Good morning."

"What's your middle name?" I kiss him.

He kisses back. "Ummm, Fleming. It's a family name." He stretches, twists his legs around mine. It feels glorious.

"Andrew Fleming Pettigrew. I like it."

"I don't. Kids in junior high called me Flem. What's yours?"

"Jo. As in, 'Kelly Jo Harrison, you're in trouble, young lady. I'm going to tan your backside.'"

"Is that how your mom talks?"

"No, but my grandma sounded suspiciously like that. She was from Tennessee. She also called me a *pantywaist*."

Andrew puts his arms around me. "That's awful. You aren't a pantywaist."

"I think it was a term of endearment, coming from her. She was a tough old lady. She ran the volunteer fire department. When I broke my arm at Skateworld in fifth grade, she threatened to ground me if I passed out."

He can't help it. "Well, passing out is a little pantywaistish. It's just a broken arm."

"I was ten! And it hurt!"

He kisses me again. I was thinking about getting up, but now I'm totally lost.

He's the one who sits up abruptly. "What time is it anyway?"

"I have no idea."

He pulls his cell phone from the nightstand. "Christ. Tucker'll be here in half an hour."

"Wait."

"Yes?" He's up on one elbow. He smiles that crazy high-wattage smile.

"No fair. That's an acting face, isn't it?"

"That's not an acting face. *This* is an acting face." He smiles again, and there's just a little too much cheese this time.

"Anyway, I had a fabulous time last night." There. I said it.

"Me too." He hops up and goes to the bathroom. It's too much to watch him walk away. I have to cover my face with a pillow to hide the blush. Lord, he's beautiful.

Today I'm not meeting him until later. We're going to have lunch together and then meet back up when he's done shooting tonight. Tomorrow morning we have to head back to LA so I can go home.

Right now, though, I lie in bed and listen to the water from the shower. I want to stay in this moment, savor it.

Drowsing, I almost don't hear his phone buzz. It skitters across the glass of the nightstand table.

He comes into the room, towel wrapped around his waist. "Was that my phone?"

"Yep."

He picks it up and checks it. "It's Franca. She wants to know who you are."

"Why is she asking about me? We didn't do anything."

He's texting her back. "She heard you were on set. I'm sticking to the old family friend story. And we did do something, just nothing she knows about." He arches an eyebrow at me.

Seconds later, the phone vibrates again. "Oh. She wants to meet us for lunch."

Well, yay. That's exactly what I think of when I imagine a superfun time with my new lover. Hang out with his insanely gorgeous, rich, and famous costar. "Why?"

He snorts. "'Cause she's a snoop. That, and she's bored. Franca's famous for being difficult on location. She's not good at keeping herself occupied. She's looking for a diversion."

"Great, and I'm it?" This is not a good idea. I can feel it.

"I promise not to leave you alone with her. Truly." He texts her back.

You know, I should at least feel superior to her in one way. I'm older. Yes, she's older than Andrew, but not by much. And I'm definitely taller than she is. And I know a little about her. She's divorced, and she's impossibly blond and tiny.

Andrew returns to the bathroom, hustling to get ready. I hear a ding. Oh my God. It's the elevator.

"Andrew, someone's at the door! Andrew!" We're about to be totally outed. Exposed in literal and figurative ways.

Andrew's got jeans on now, and he walks out to the great room. "Stay put. You're fine."

"Andy!" This is a voice I don't know. We're doomed.

He closes the bedroom door behind him. I'm grateful for that. And I'm trying to find my jeans as quickly as I can, as silently as I can.

I can hear the conversation, and I can hear this person clomping. Whoever it is, he's loud and wears cowboy boots.

"What's up? How's my man this morning?" Loud, loud talker.

"Pissed that you let yourself into my place." Andrew's voice is different. This is man talk. This is the sound of guys circling, snarling, marking territory.

"Seriously? I get no love from you? I brought you a tea. I even got Tucker his Frappuccino fix. Is he not up here yet?" The boots are on the move again, and they seem to be coming dangerously close to the bedroom door. Is he scoping out the place?

"Jeremy, you know he's not. He's the one you forced to hand over the elevator key five minutes ago before you shamelessly barged in on my peaceful morning." Andrew's voice is moving away. He's in the kitchen. Maybe he's trying to lead this Jeremy away from me.

"How was your night last night? You do anything?"

Now *I* want to growl at this guy. He's fishing. Why? Is there something I don't know about?

"Stayed in." Andrew's not biting.

"With who?" Now Jeremy sounds a little more aggressive too.

"I was here at home. Why do you care? You're my agent, Jeremy. The last time I checked, Mom was still living in Pennsylvania."

"We're working on the whole package here, Andy. Just remember that." Jeremy's walking away from the door. I want to sneak a peek at his face so badly. Who is this guy? But I've seen enough movies to know that the villain finds the girl snooping behind the door and there's a big ruckus, so I resist the urge.

I hear another voice. "Andrew? Everything all right?" It's Tucker. He knows I came home with Andrew last night. This should be interesting.

"Hey, Tuck. Jeremy was just breaking and entering—you know, doing what he does best."

Tucker's voice is relaxed. "You all ready?"

"I was on my way out when Jeremy stopped in. Let's go."

But this Jeremy is not done. "Is this all of us?"

Does he know I'm here or just suspect something? And besides the fact that we want to keep it a secret, why should he care if Andrew brought someone home with him? What's going on?

Tucker answers. "Did you bring someone else with you, Jeremy?" His tone is one of total confusion. So he's an actor *and* a bodyguard.

"Never mind. I'm driving. I'll meet you out there." Jeremy's boots clomp in the direction of the elevator.

I do peek now. Andrew just about gives me a heart attack—he's standing right in front of me.

"What the hell?" I'm utterly lost.

"Long, long story. I'll catch you up when we get a minute

alone. Enjoy your spa thingy." He kisses me. "Tucker'll swing by later to pick you up for lunch. Be sure to wear a disguise."

My head is spinning. I have no idea—

"Kelly, I'm kidding. See you." Another kiss, and he's off to the elevator.

Tucker calls from the great room. "See you later, Kelly!" He doesn't seem fazed.

I answer him, still standing just inside the bedroom door, afraid to come out. "Okay!"

Why are we hiding from Andrew's agent?

The only thing I can remember is the text Andrew got from him in Boise and the bitterness in his voice when he discussed it.

Something is up.

Lunch with Sharks

I get ready and spend the better part of the morning fretting. I'm not excited to have lunch with the skeletal leading lady, Franca. Especially if I'm pretending to be an old family friend. I've never enjoyed lying.

Once, my freshman year in college, I was hanging out in the dorm with my friends when these boys showed up in the main lounge. The poor souls were fraternity pledges from a neighboring college. Part of their hazing involved their fall formal. These guys weren't allowed to ask out any girl at their school. They were dropped in front of our dorm and had twenty minutes to pick up dates to take to this dance.

Three of us agreed to go with them, but in self-defense, we decided to lie about our names and our lives. In the first hours of the date it felt fun, liberating. But when my very sweet date asked if he could call me and profusely thanked me for being such a good sport, I felt like crap as I tried to explain that my real name was not Alexis and that my daddy was not Greek shipping magnate Aristotle Onassis's younger brother.

Anyway. The point is, I suck at lying, and when I do lie, the universe always finds some way to make me feel absolutely atrocious. My karma comes on strong, and often comes on immediately. Luckily, I stay out of trouble (or maybe *because of that* I stay out of trouble) most of the time.

Besides anticipating doing a poor job at staying incognito at lunch, I'm also worried about this whole agent thing. No, I don't want to take my relationship with Andrew public right now. I haven't thought anything through beyond not wanting to expose Hunter and Beau to any attention. But why was Jeremy ready to toss the whole apartment looking for contraband girls? I mean, I get that I don't fit with a Hollywood image, but that was about any girl. Did Andrew take a vow of celibacy for the movie? The whole thing makes me uneasy.

Finally, after I get a massage in the spa downstairs, the morning drags by and Tucker is due to pick me up. I'm having another moment. I have no idea what to wear. I'm in jeans, because that's what I packed, but I worry that this is a fancy restaurant. And I'm looking plain. I've learned from experience that trying to doll myself up under pressure often leads to weird and unfortunate makeup issues—smudged mascara, uneven eyeliner, and odd foundation lines under my chin—so when nervous, it's best to stick to the tried and true. But it's pretty spare. I put the basic lip gloss on, add a little liner under the eyes only, and cross my fingers that some sort of unlikely facial fungus or rash has befallen the lovely actress who will sit next to me at lunch and inevitably invite comparison.

My phone rings. It's Andrew.

"Hello?"

"It's me. Tucker's on his way up."

I ignore the panicky adrenaline starting to flow in my veins. "How was your morning?"

"Good. Lots of big drama today."

"Were you 'ACTING!'?" I'm trying to be funny.

"What?" He's too young to remember that *SNL* bit, probably.

"Never mind. I'll see you in a bit."

"Okay." He ends the call. This isn't boding well.

The elevator dings. I jump, even though I've been warned to expect Tucker.

"Kelly?"

I grab my coat. Here goes nothing.

After a few minutes I feel a little less stressed about lunch because as we drive through town, I don't see a single intimidating place to eat here in Santa Paula. Maybe that's why Franca's so unhappy. There's no place for her to be in her element.

That's why I've always loved the West. I came from a high school in Tennessee where your purse and your shoes should match your skirt. In Boise, the kids wear T-shirts and flip-flops most of the time. Beau and Hunter have avoided any real pressure to look a certain way. Santa Paula seems to have that laid-back vibe too.

Tucker drops me right outside the restaurant. It's a cute little place in a brick house. I am buoyed by the setting. I can handle this.

Then I walk inside. I give my name to the hostess, and she takes me to the back of the place, around a little shuttered door, into a garden room. Of course, a private room. How silly of me.

That's when I stop short. Andrew's there, of course, and Franca is there with an enormous Birkin bag at her side—maybe it's her date—but there's another guest at the table.

Jeremy. It has to be him. This man is wearing cowboy boots and a Cheshire cat grin a mile wide. I'm reminded vaguely of Tommy Lee Jones in *The Fugitive*. He's gotten his man, except this time it's his woman.

Andrew stands as I come to the table. Franca doesn't. Jeremy doesn't just stand, he bounds over to me.

Oh. My. God. I smile as broadly as I can.

"This must be the old family friend! Kelly!" He gives me a big hug. I am paralyzed. I think I know what the mouse feels like right before the boa constrictor swallows her whole. Yikes.

"And you are?" I'm not going down without a fight, damn it.

He smiles slyly. He was trying to trip me up. If I said I knew who he was, he'd know I was up in the apartment earlier. No chance, buster.

"Oh, I thought Andy told you about me. I'm Jeremy. Jeremy King."

"Kelly Reynolds. Good to meet you."

Andrew's come over to my side. "Jeremy's my agent. Kelly, I want you to meet Franca Delaney, my costar."

Franca doesn't get up. She turns a little in her chair and offers her hand. Okay, not all of her hand. She's one of those creepy from-the-knuckles-down hand shakers. I hate her already.

"Hi, Franca." I shake her half hand.

I think both of these people know who I am, in truth. I sit down between Franca and Andrew. He shoots me a look for one millisecond. I try not to burst out laughing. This is ridiculous.

Jeremy pulls himself up to the table. "This is a pleasant surprise. What brings you into town?"

Andrew jumps in. "Kelly's going up to Ojai for a wedding this weekend. I wanted her to see the set, since she's here."

"So you're from Pennsylvania too?" Franca has spoken.

"No, my folks knew Andrew's from a trip they took to Florida one summer. They met there while they were golfing." I'm totally ad-libbing here. What the hell.

"Aren't your parents older?" Franca asks. She's got the claws out already, I see.

Andrew looks surprised. I want to tell him girls are lethal when they're mean. He should be glad he lives in the land of men, because girls fight dirty.

I ignore the comment. "How was the morning's filming?"

"It was great. Your friend here was in fine form. One of the many reasons I love having him as a client." Jeremy winks at Andrew. Andrew rolls his eyes.

"What're you doing this afternoon?" Franca's participating, but I can't tell why she's bothered to ask.

I don't get a chance to answer, as the waiter comes to take orders. Jeremy has the Reuben, Andrew orders a hamburger, and then there's Franca.

"I would like a Cobb salad with no dressing and no yolks in the hard-boiled eggs. And no croutons. And no bacon. And a Pellegrino."

Oh, I want to say something catty soooo badly. Instead, I just order. "I'll have the BLT. And an iced tea, please." If we were being a little more transparent, I would now duck under the table to wait for the next missile Franca or Jeremy will lob in my direction.

"Wow." That's all that Franca can say. I want to smack her.

Andrew sits up a little taller as he hands the menus back to the waiter. "Thanks," he tells him, then comments under his breath: "You might come back in a while to see if everyone's still standing."

"Andy." It's Jeremy.

"Jeremy." Andrew smiles. Just barely.

"Oh, Jesus, let's cut the shit. You're dating this woman." He points at me with a bread stick.

Andrew tosses his napkin on the table, pushes his chair away. "I'm done. Let's go, Kelly."

This is the part where I'm confused. I'm not sure why this is a deal breaker.

Jeremy puts a hand on Andrew's arm. "Wait, now. Wait there, big guy. Let's talk about this."

Andrew sits back down and looks right at me. "Jeremy did a great thing when he signed me on to this movie."

"You mean the insanely huge salary?" There's a bite to Jeremy's voice.

"No, I was talking about the language that says I can't date anybody until we finish the media push."

"Or until the end of the awards season, if you get a nod. Which I fully expect. This film has a magic to it."

"That's total bullshit. The whole thing is." Andrew appears to be gripping the side of the table in order not to hit someone.

"You signed it," Franca says, chiming in.

"Why?" I ask. Seems like a fair question in the middle of all of this.

Jeremy takes this one. "Well, my dear, perception is reality. And for this movie, the perception needs to be that Franca and your friend Andy here are dating. Or at least are secretly kissing and not telling."

"People love the are-they-or-aren't-they gossip. It sells a lot of tickets." Franca smiles a toothy grin at me. She's creepy.

"Oh."

Jeremy smiles. "So, friend-of-the-family Kelly, it'd be inconvenient to have the press find out Andy has a new pet."

"Pet? Jesus, Jeremy, show a little respect." Andrew grits his teeth.

"Lighten up, Andrew. Have a drink." Franca doesn't even look up from her phone to say this.

"You are a stone-cold bitch sometimes, Franca." Andrew is barely in control.

Franca doesn't care. She doesn't even lift an eyebrow. "I know."

Jeremy puts up his hands. "Slow down, everybody. No offense, Andy, but I just don't want any problems on a film this big."

I don't know what's next. Dumbfounded, I wonder if we're going to get to eat, or if everyone is just going to yell at everyone else until someone storms out. I'd like to eat something.

"There's not a problem here." Andrew's voice is ice cold. I wonder if he's going to punch Jeremy. He still has a pretty tight grip on the edge of the table.

"What do you mean?" Franca's intrigued. Intrigued enough to set her phone down and stop texting.

"No one's going to find out because there's nothing to find out. Kelly's a good friend, and when I happen to have someone come to visit, and she's attractive, you all freak out and overreact."

I think I hear Franca say "mildly attractive" under her breath, but since I'm not sure, I skip jumping on her and beating her into the carpet. For now.

"Give me a break, Andy. I saw the way you looked at her when she walked in." I like Jeremy a little more than Franca.

"Until the press has proof of a relationship, there is no relationship. And I'm in compliance with my contract."

The waiter approaches the table with a tray of food, but even he looks afraid to get too close to the action.

Andrew snaps his napkin out of its folds and smooths it into his lap. "Let's eat."

It's the oddest lunch date I've ever had in my life. Bar none.

Glutton for Punishment

Because that was so much fun, Andrew suggests we take a little walk down to the shops near the restaurant. Franca wants to come along. And Andrew doesn't tell her no. Why, I have no idea. Jeremy seems to have decided his point has been made, so he leaves, promising to return to the set that afternoon, presumably to get back to spying on his client.

We walk with Franca ten steps ahead of us, her head buried in her cell phone, thumbs all atwitter with texting. I'm still waiting to learn why we didn't just go back to his place or part ways until after the afternoon's shooting.

It could be that we're blowing off steam. Andrew's brow is a dark line, and his hands are buried in his pockets. His shoulders and his hood are up. Everything about him right now says hostile. I feel a knot forming sympathetically between my shoulder blades.

He smokes too, and for the first time he seems to be doing it without thinking. He finally speaks, through gritted teeth. "I told you I like structure, but there comes a point when even the most docile farm animal strains against the yoke. I usually do what I'm told, but this sucks."

"I don't know how you handle that." I truly don't. No one has ever told me who I could or couldn't be seen with. My dad expressed displeasure over a few college or high school boyfriend picks, but nothing more than that.

Franca stops a few feet in front of us. She's spotted something in a store window. Suddenly she acknowledges our presence again.

"I want to go in here." We come alongside her, and she pulls me by the sleeve into the store. Andrew waves me in—his phone is ringing—and in a swift move, I've been separated from the herd. I'm alone with the toothy predator, and my one defender, who promised not to leave me alone with this woman, just left me alone with this woman.

It's a boutique. I shop at Old Navy. When I'm feeling insanely extravagant, I go to LOFT. This place has me in hives, and I haven't touched a thing.

Franca holds a blouse up to herself. Does she really worry if it'll fit? Maybe she recognizes the hanger as a cousin, because she bears a striking resemblance to it.

Oh, yes, I'm being mean, but it was only a matter of time.

"We should find something for you." She's talking to me. I notice that she checked to make sure Andrew's not in the store. Excellent.

"I'm not much into clothes." I'm going to make an effort to stay on the sidelines here.

A salesperson has wandered over. If the colossal Birkin bag and the colossal sunglasses still on in the store didn't give Franca away as a movie star, the salesgirl will have a chance to ID her now.

Franca pokes her on the shoulder and pulls her shades down

enough to look patronizingly over them. "Do you have anything for her?" Franca points at me.

"Oh my gawd, you're Franca Delaney!" The salesgirl sounds Valley Girl circa 1985.

Franca nods shyly. She's quite the actress. "She needs something. What might you have?"

This is going downhill fast. I do need something. I need a way to avoid bolting out of the shop screaming in terror.

"You mean, that would fit her?"

Oh boy. Here we go.

Look, I'm not fat, but I'm not skinny either. I run, but I eat too. I'm five feet seven, and I'm a steady size ten. I'm an eight when I take better care of myself. There you have it. Total truth telling. I'm not a twig—never have been, never will be. I sprouted boobs when I was in sixth grade, and that's all she wrote.

The salesgirl is done giving me the up and down. "Size six is the largest we go. In the quality brands, it's size four."

I purse my lips, looking for the choice words that might kill these women on the spot. I unfortunately know no such words, but I can't help but say something. "I'm sorry, I missed it. Did the sign above the door say 'Big Heads on a Toothpick R Us'?" I turn to go. "I'm going to wait outside with Andrew."

Skeletor has me by the shirtsleeve again. "You know this'll never work."

"What do you mean?" Why I ask this, I do not know. Am I actually interested in Franca's opinion?

"Look at you. He's way out of your league. You'll slow him down, you know. Nobody wants to see a guy like him with someone like you."

Franca suddenly lets go of my arm and flashes more teeth than one human should have in her head. This lends weight to a theory I'm developing that she's a wolverine.

Andrew touches me gently on the shoulder. "Are you done?"

And now I know why the fake smile. More done than you know, my friend. "Franca and I were just chatting. I'm ready to leave."

"Tucker's out front. You want to ride with us, Franca?" Andrew seems to have cooled off. I'm glad. I wish I felt better too. I feel worse.

Franca seems smug. I tried not to show weakness, but she seems to sense that one of her slings and/or arrows met its mark. That makes me even madder than the nagging feeling that she might be right.

She waves us on. "I think I'm getting a few things. I'll be along in a bit. I've got a PA coming to take me out to the set soon anyway."

So we're done with her. I check to see if I'm bleeding. In the car, Andrew seems tense, still distracted by lunch. I decide against sharing Franca's thoughts with him. He has to work with her, and he doesn't need drama to get in the way of the drama. Plus, I'm feeling more and more like a complication. Franca's little talk is just more of that, even if it hadn't bothered me.

We're back in the garage of his place.

"Here we are." Tucker kind of announces it. I think he's trying to snap Andrew out of whatever distracted place he's in. I think he's trying to tell him to pay attention to me for a second before he boots me out of the car and goes back to his Hollywood world where no woman is over twenty and no woman weighs over 120 pounds.

Andrew only kind of snaps out of it. Suddenly I'm paralyzed

with a new fear: It's finally sunk in, and he's regretting it. Sleeping with me. He's regretting it. I bet that's what's up.

"See you," I say and try to get out of the car as fast as I can.

"Hey." He touches my arm.

"Yeah?" I have a glimmer of hope.

"You need the key." He hands it to me, and his phone rings again before I can say anything else. I practically sprint to the elevator. We can talk later. Right now he's late to the set, has to take a phone call, and I need a good, long cry.

Oh, the Self-Doubt of It All

I sit on the edge of the bed. I know the tears are on my face, but all I can feel is the pain under my collarbone. This is familiar. After a while, I'm too tired to feel any punier, so I lie down.

I fall asleep.

The first thing I'm aware of is the crunch of leaves under our feet. Andrew holds my hand as we walk through a dark forest. Now I can see light beyond the tree trunks, and we come out into the clearing. We're on campus—at college, where Peter and I went to school. Andrew looks at me, and he leads us to the steps of a fraternity house. It's Peter's old frat. People mill around, red cups in hand. It's a party.

Then we're inside, weaving through the crowd. Andrew lets go of my hand, and I lose him in the crowd. My heart starts to pound. I climb narrow stairs up to the second floor, and I try one door after another. The music throbs in my ears, but I can't make out the song. Finally a door swings open. It's a dorm room, two beds and two desks. The air is smoky.

Andrew sits on one of the beds with a cigarette in his hand.

Next to him is Franca. Her lips are painted bright red. She smiles at me and then turns to Andrew and kisses him, wrapping her arms around his neck. I shout, but neither of them pays attention. I look around for the door to leave, but it's gone. Someone sleeps on the other bed under a thin quilt. I pull the covers back. It's Peter. I shake him, but he won't wake up. With no other way out, I go to the window, open it, and look down. It's too far to jump. Suddenly Andrew is behind me, and I turn around. I lose my balance and stumble backward, tripping. I feel myself slipping out of the window, falling.

I awake, startled, the sensation of falling still unsettling my stomach.

I grab a Kleenex and blow my nose. I'm shaky. I must have been crying in my sleep.

"Kelly?" Oh, no. Andrew's here, in the great room. I can't tell how long it's been, how long I slept. I jump up and turn on the TV, try to straighten out my clothes.

Then he's standing in the doorway. I turn away, ashamed of these tears. I don't like feeling so vulnerable, so shamed.

"Are you okay?"

"Hi. I was just watching this." *Storage Wars* is on. He looks at me, looks at the TV.

This would be a great time to not be stranded in his place several hours by plane away from my house. I am unwanted and stuck.

"You weren't asleep?"

"Nope."

"'Cause when I came home half an hour ago, I'm pretty sure you were asleep."

I give up. "I thought you just got home." I try to take a deep breath to stop shaking.

"Did you have a nightmare?"

"Yeah."

He comes over and sits on the edge of the bed. "Do you want to talk about it?"

"No, I have them a lot. It's nothing." I grab my shoes and put them on. I don't want to look him in the eye. What I really want to do is get out of here. "I thought I'd try to catch a ride back to LA in the morning."

"What the hell for?"

"Andrew."

"What?"

"None of this makes any sense. You don't belong with someone like me."

"You don't make any sense. What Jeremy wrote into my contract doesn't matter. We're going to keep doing what we're doing. We never wanted to go public right now anyway. The boys need their privacy, and the way it is now, we have Boise to ourselves."

"Franca—"

"Do not listen to a thing she says. Did she go after you in that shop?"

"I'm the definition of awkward. Beautiful, creepy Franca doesn't have to tell me that. I know it." I pull a pillow up in my arms. Maybe I can make myself small enough to hide behind it.

He looks mad. "Awkward? You're real! God, you have no idea how desperately I need someone like you in my life. I lie for a living. I'm surrounded by plastic. Then you come along."

I stand. "You don't know what real means. Real means that sometime in the next ten years, I will develop the Harrison chin, which is actually no chin at all. Real is outweighing that big-head-on-a-toothpick costar of yours by at least twenty pounds. Real is having things in your past that are ugly. Real is a mortgage and crow's-feet and sometimes getting sick and tired of driving kids and doing dishes and sometimes even getting sick of the person next to you every night." I flop down on the bed, covering my head with the pillow.

He scoots next to me, and I feel his hand on my shoulder. "In ten years? In ten years I may or may not still have a career. I may or may not still have my hair. And you don't think I've ever screwed up? God, let's not start in on that list. Despite what everyone in the world thinks, I'm real. I want a partner who's real. A real woman who's raised two boys alone for two years. I want you. I want you, flaws and all. I can only hope you'll want my very flawed self in your life too."

I roll over to look at him, stunned by his admission. He wants a partner? Like a girlfriend or a life partner or a wife partner or what? I didn't see that coming. "I'm speechless."

He hands me a tissue. "You're fine."

"Just once I'd like to look like a normal human being in front of you."

"You've got a bit of a wet face thing going, that's all."

"And everything's okay? You were so distant after lunch. You weren't having regrets?"

He frowns. "I was pissed at Jeremy, pissed at myself. And getting seven million calls from my publicist about totally unrelated stuff that distracted me. I didn't even notice Franca. She was trying to keelhaul you in that store, wasn't she?"

"It felt more predator than pirate, but yeah."

"If I were perfect, I would've had a clue about how you were feeling. I wouldn't have let Franca get you away from me. Are we agreed that I'm by no means perfect?"

I nod. I'm smiling a little now.

He grins too. "Except my teeth, they're perfect." I hit him with the pillow. "No, really, I paid a lot of money for these suckers. They're gorgeous."

I sit up and kiss him.

"Watch it. You may still be a little snotty."

I push him over on the bed.

Three for the Road

O h, the days between Ventura County and our Christmas visit
drag—so slowly that I think I'm going to lose my mind. I'm
worse than a kid the way I'm counting down. I'm almost ready to
make a paper chain like we used to in grade school, but I remind
myself that I'm an adult. But an adult who happens to know a small
boy who will make a chain with eleven rings on it for her . . .

I've enjoyed shopping for the boys and my folks, but shopping
for Andrew is at once insanely fun and acutely terrifying. I remember this from the early days with Peter. I want desperately to
pick something that'll tell him, "I'm cool. I'm amazing to be with.
If you love this gift, you'll love the giver even more." But at the
same time, if it looks like I'm trying too hard, I worry the gift will
scream, "This one's totally clingy! She wants to marry you
straightaway! Run!"

I think the boys are happy about the new developments in my
life. I hate to say I've been a nag, or overprotective, but I suspect
I'm less meddlesome to them now that I have a few things of my
own going on. And they do like Andrew. Anyway, they try to be

helpful and suggest gifts for him, but very often the discussions sound like this:

"Mom, he's totally cool. How can you possibly get him something cool?"

"Are you saying I'm not cool?"

"Mom. Of course I am. Get real."

"So what's cool?"

"You should totally get him . . ."

And this is usually followed by something that eight- and eleven-year-olds think is legit: a car, a sound system for a car, a game system, bling . . . Often things they would like to own themselves. Once in a while the suggestion is a puppy. That's a totally transparent one, but again, this is like Hunter hoping Andrew would let him drive. They're occasionally under the impression that adults have misplaced their brains altogether.

I waffle, I vacillate, I have no idea what to get him. Finally one day I give up. The perfect gift is going to have to wait. Instead, I buy him a warm coat for his next visit to Boise, whenever that might be.

I also shop for three little people who are a lot easier to please: Tessa's girls. Their birthday on December eighteenth (five days until LA, but who's counting?) is a nice diversion from the Christmas countdown. And having only boys, I enjoy shopping in the Barbie and pink-sequin sections of the store for them.

Beau, Hunter, and I pile in the car and head over to Tessa and Joe's for the girls' party. I can't even believe it. Genevieve, Jasmine, and Josie came into the world after Peter died, and here they are turning two. Life moves on mercilessly.

Another merciless event is the conversation I'm about to have with Tessa. I've been to Ventura County, and I've *been with* Andrew, and she'll see all of this coming from a mile away. Because I have no poker face. My only hope is she'll be too busy with the hoopla of the party to notice me.

We park down the street from the house. Joe and Tessa live on one of the "best" streets in Boise in one of the "best" neighborhoods. Tessa makes a house quite a home too. Their white house is rambling and shabbily chic, but definitely chic. She doesn't have dog hair on her couch, I can guarantee that. But she welcomes everyone in as her family.

The place is packed with her real and adopted families right now. All manner of friends, kids, grandmas, aunties—everyone crowds into the living room, the kitchen. The party spills out into the backyard, even though it's freezing. Kids howl with glee upstairs, probably jumping on beds judging by the barely perceptible swaying of the living room chandelier.

I take our presents into the living room. The boys have friends here, no doubt, and they've gone off in search of them. I wander to the kitchen in time to see a pony walk by in the backyard with Jasmine perched on it. She's bundled up in a parka and looks thrilled.

"I know, it's totally ridiculous. Pony rides for two-year-olds in the backyard in the middle of December." Tessa stands at the doorway, looking out at the line of tiny kids waiting for a ride. All of them hop up and down, either from excitement or the cold. The pony and the pony's handler look very blasé about the whole situation.

"I wouldn't expect anything less." I kiss Tessa on the cheek.

"How are you?" Tessa looks at me for a second, slips her arm around my waist, but turns to keep an eye on the toddlerpalooza out in the yard.

"Fine."

"I heard you took a trip." She shoots me a sideways look.

"How'd you hear that?" Tessa knows everything.

"Your mom answered your phone and told me. Come on." She pinches my side.

"What was that for?"

"I'm fully prepared to inflict physical pain here, Kelly Jo. And I have about fifteen minutes before Misty of Chincoteague out there leaves and the fits are thrown. So now would be the time to redeem yourself as a BFF and tell me what happened."

"I went to see him."

"On his movie set."

"Yeah."

"And you slept with him."

"Yeah." I blush. I can feel it. I hate that.

"And it was awesome."

"Yeah."

"You suck at this, telling me about your new romance."

"Yeah." I smile uncontrollably.

"I feel like this is a Choose Your Own Adventure. I'm just writing the story here."

I approach the fridge, looking for somewhere to hide. "I know. I just don't know what to say, or even where to start."

"I can't believe you. I'd be shouting it from the rooftops. You've been with a movie star."

Two of the neighbor kids walk through to the backyard at this point, and I elbow Tessa.

"What was *that* for?"

"This is completely top secret, Tessa."

"What the hell for? What's the point of dating someone like Andy Pettigrew if you can't brag about it?"

"Oh, I don't know, maybe to be with someone you like?" I

open a bag of Cheetos and start to mow through them. I will have orange hands and an upset stomach, but the occasion calls for some stress eating.

"Seriously, what are you so worried about?"

"The boys, for one. I don't know what kind of attention we'd get if anybody found out, and I'm not ready for that." I leave the part out where Jeremy has also forbidden it. That information would send Tessa into orbit.

Tessa has a handful of Cheetos now too. "I hadn't thought about that. Would you get stalked? How would that work?"

I think back to Tucker, to the decoy van in Ventura, to the underground parking garage. "Maybe you can get stalked by association, I don't know. I don't know where this is going."

Through the window, I can see Josie trying to feed the fat little pony old snow from the flower bed. The pony doesn't look amused.

"I'm impressed." Tessa's given up the Cheetos and now munches a celery stick. This is why she's a doctor's wife. She has the whole vegetable-eating thing going for her.

"Impressed by what?"

"Despite your best friend's cautions, and despite your inherent chickenness, you're in uncharted territory and going for it, my friend. Usually you'd be hyperventilating by now."

"I heard your cautions, but I'm ignoring them, remember? And no, I wouldn't usually be hyperventilating." I feel the need to defend my honor.

"Oh, yes, you would. You don't do change well. You know it."

"Give me one example."

Tessa twirls the celery stick in the kitchen air, thinking, and then points it at me. "Oil of Olaygate."

"What?" I know what. I've already lost this battle.

"Raise your hand if you went around town and bought up all of the old version of your favorite face scrub when you realized the formula was changing." Tessa pauses for a second. "Oh, that's right, it's you." She crunches her celery with authority.

"Okay. I don't like change. But I think I have reason enough to hate it, don't you?"

Tessa opens the sliding glass door. "Girls! Five-minute warning on Seabiscuit out there." As she slides the door shut, much groaning from the little people outside can be heard. She turns her attention to me. "No, you're missing the point. Girl who hates change and uncertainty is up to her eyeballs in the unknowable right now. Like I said, I'm impressed."

"Yeah, well. If I think too much about it, I completely freak out. So I'm trying not to think."

Tessa eyes me impishly. "Just keep thinking about what you'd like to do to him. That'll keep you distracted."

"Stop." I grab for a celery stick.

"Okay, if you don't want to think about it, I volunteer to think of all the things you could be doing to him. He's a tall drink of water, indeed."

"Who is? Are you girls talking about me? Stop, I'll blush." Joe comes in from the living room with his coat.

"Hi, babe." Tessa gives him a pat on the ass. "We're chatting about Andy."

"It's Andrew. And thanks for telling Joe about him." I'm starting to feel snappish.

Joe gives me a quick side hug and puts his coat on. "My lips are sealed. Tessa's, I don't know. Now I have to get out there and break some little girls' hearts."

Joe goes out back and closes the slider behind him. Tessa looks at me. "Yes, I told Joe, but I get it. I won't tell anyone else." She pauses. "I can still think up things for you to do to him, can't I? He's fine."

"Calm yourself. That's my boyfriend you're talking about." *Boyfriend* sounds like he loaned me his letterman's jacket to wear. I'm a complete dweeb.

"Okay, Sandy from *Grease*. I will keep my impure thoughts off your *boyfriend*."

There's a wail from the backyard. Joe and the pony handler must have just announced the end of the pony rides. Genevieve is heartbroken.

"I've got to get out there. Next time you see Andrew, I'm gonna need serious details. Take notes if you have to. Hell, you can borrow my video camera." She opens the slider, calling over her shoulder to me, "Intimate details!"

Christmastime Is Here

Finally, I'm done with the excruciating waiting. On December twenty-third, the boys and I fly to LA. When we arrive, my folks greet us, and we decamp to their main house in LA. We're following the plan as it has been for the past two years. My mom took over Christmas after Peter died. I couldn't stand the thought of hosting without my husband in the house, and it's proved a lot less painful to be in LA for the holidays than I think staying at home would be.

We get settled, but I'm distracted. I can't stand it, actually. It's as though I've been put back in the skin of a quivering teenage girl. I think about him. I wait for him to call, to text. At home, I've been my normal self, but here I behave like I'm fifteen.

Maybe he's mercifully psychic, because Andrew calls.

"Hello?"

"Did you make it in one piece?" He sounds like he has a cold.

"We're here. Beau is interrogating Mom about the gifts under the tree. Hunter is scoping out the fridge. Pretty typical."

My dad swings through the kitchen and eyes me suspiciously.

He's not sold on this dating thing yet. When I mentioned last week on the phone that I'd like to have Andrew over or that Andrew and I thought about doing a dinner at Andrew's house, Dad developed a very loud, dry, suspect cough. Mom even shushed him, which she never does.

"Is your dad frowning at you about this phone call yet?"

I grin. "I was right. You *are* psychic."

"I'm so going to win that man over. Doesn't he know I was voted *Cosmo*'s Yummiest Guy last year? There's no escaping my charm. Just you wait."

"Maybe if you clip out the *Cosmo* article, you'll convince him. He'd love that, I bet."

Dad's wandered out of the kitchen again, followed by Hunter, who has snacks.

"So are you guys coming over here tomorrow?"

"I'll be over around eleven. Mom and Dad'll bring the boys around four. They always take them out shopping for me when we get here."

"Thank you for that. I need to see you."

I think he's talking about what I'm thinking about, and I blush. "I need to see you too." Suddenly tomorrow's not fast enough, and the kitchen feels not private enough for this conversation. I clear my throat, embarrassed.

"I'll see you tomorrow, then. You've got the address?"

"You texted it to me. I'm good. Any secret passwords I need to know?"

"There's a gate, but it's not NORAD. What're you driving?"

"Dad's Ford Focus. You're jealous, I know."

"Sweet ride."

Beau comes into the kitchen and waves at me wildly. I gather quickly that Mom has announced he can open one present early.

"I've got to go. Beau's going to bust a gasket if I don't get off the phone."

"See you in the morning."

"Okay." I end the call, and Beau drags me into the living room. Things are back to the normal holiday routine for the evening.

The next morning, I sleep in, skipping my morning run. It feels liberating to let it go once in a while. When I get up, Mom's already in full grandson-spoiling mode. She's cooked them eggs to order and bacon. Dad's sketching out some plan for Hunter and him and the wood shop. The two of them usually concoct one or two outlandish birdhouses or something similar while we're here for this visit. Dad has been adamant about setting the boys up with manly experiences since Peter's been gone. It's one of the reasons I love him. He's looking out for them in his own way.

"Good morning." I survey the scene.

"Hi, Mom. Gran made breakfast."

"Smells awesome. What's the plan this morning?"

"You're leaving, we're shopping, and we're reconvening for dinner at Andrew's." Hunter says this with full authority. He has these moments of very adult behavior that surprise me. He's going to be a man. I'll turn around, and he'll be running the show.

"Well, I guess I better go get dressed then." I turn to Dad. "You sure you can find the house later?"

He shoots me a withering look. "Yes. I've lived here for twenty years. I think I can find my way to the Hollywood Hills."

"He can find the Hollywood sign, Mom," Beau says. "It's not hard from there." He doesn't know what he's talking about, but he's trying to capture the same acid tone as Dad. It's cute, the way he has his granddad's back.

I make sure to MapQuest it myself before I leave, in an effort to look at least as able as my dad. I drive into town from my folks' house, trying hard not to be totally rattled by the traffic. As I wind my way up Andrew's street, I feel my pulse revving. It's hard not to be embarrassed by the physical way I react to proximity.

The street number is literally plastered to a tall wall. I pull up to the gate and press the buzzer as instructed. The gate swings open, and I drive through.

The house isn't insanely big, but in California, this kind of big is an extravagance. In Boise it might be within a normal person's orbit. Here it's completely out of my league.

It's a Spanish-style older home, probably from the 1920s. The red tile roof is charmingly overgrown with bougainvillea. I like that it doesn't look like a frat boy's place. I don't know if part of me expected something out of *Animal House*, but I'm glad to find the front courtyard free of sofas, flamingos, and underwear.

The driveway's empty except for the black convertible we drove to Ventura County. I smile as I park Dad's car next to it and remember the drive and the rest of the trip.

Then, Andrew's out front.

Of course he looks good. He makes a living making an entrance. It's not very fair. The only time I made an entrance was in college when I accidentally had toilet paper trailing from one foot as I reentered a room at a party.

He smiles widely. "You found it."

"Yep."

He puts his arms around me, and it feels insanely good. Each time, a little part of me continues to be surprised. At some point, I guess I'll have to accept that this is actually happening, and it isn't a result of a mental breakdown on my part or a great misunderstanding on his.

"Let's go inside." His voice is husky with feeling. It takes my breath away. On this front of our relationship, I feel like a strong equal. And I like it very much for that—and a lot of other reasons. I follow him in.

He holds my hand, just by the fingertips, and leads me through the house. I notice little or none of the details of his living room, kitchen, stairs. All I can focus on is the tingle in my fingers and making sure I don't step on the back of his heels in my haste.

"Do you like it?" He turns around as we climb the stairs. He hasn't let go of my hand.

"Like what?"

"My house." He smiles. Does he know how distracting that smile is?

"Yes." I'm thinking about his lips, his shoulders, his hips, his back.

"Are you just saying that?"

"Yes." I sound breathless.

He laughs. "Thought so."

We're at the door of his bedroom. He kisses me, and my head spins.

"I don't want to be forward, but you need to cool it with the Parade of Homes tour." I push past and pull him into his bedroom.

"The master suite does have a lot of amenities." Now he's just being goofy.

"Shut up and kiss me."

He takes the hint. He does take direction well, I must say. On this occasion especially . . .

A little while later we lie in bed together. It's so warm, and most of the heat is coming off his body. I'm always cold. I don't get why guys are the ones with the internal combustion when I'd rather be the cozy one.

He tugs on the covers, turns over to look at me.

"Hey!" Now I'm really cold—without the covers, I'm bare.

His fingers trace my shoulder. "What's this?" He touches a straight, white scar.

"I got it crawling under a barbed-wire fence in fourth grade. We were playing Cold War."

He raises an eyebrow. "What kind of game was that?"

"*The* big game in my neighborhood. I was a Soviet, as I recall. *Red Dawn* was a very influential movie that summer. We ran amok in the woods."

"Sounds fun." He looks a little lost.

I realize why. "You're too young. You were probably three when it came out."

I lie back, cover my eyes with my arms. This young-guy stuff is painful. Sometimes I feel like an artifact.

Then I feel him kiss my stomach. I uncover my eyes. He's looking at another scar.

"What's this one?" He's languidly tracing a jagged-looking pucker of skin, right over my belly button. I think I'm starting to get goose bumps, and not from the chill in the room. I resist the urge to attack him and answer instead.

"That's a stretch mark. Thanks for pointing it out."

"From babies?" He sounds so naive sometimes.

"From baby number two. Beau was two weeks late, and I was all proud of how smooth my stomach was, but then my poor belly button couldn't handle it anymore, and the skin pulled. No *Sports Illustrated* swimsuit cover for me."

He kisses it again. "It's called Photoshop. Trust me. See this?" He tugs on his left ear, moving the hair away. There's a huge notch taken out of the top of his ear.

"What's that from?"

"When I was three, the neighbor's dog mistook me for a chew toy. I'm pretty sure if my sisters hadn't been there he would have torn my ear off."

"Then that's not so bad, considering, huh?" I trace the deep V chunked out of his ear. I think about kissing it.

"And, if you were to check most of the magazine covers featuring yours truly, I bet you won't see it."

"Really?"

"They want their movie star perfect. It takes a minute and a few clicks of the mouse, and it's done."

"That explains why you are totally homely in real life," I tease.

He rolls over on top of me and has me by the wrists. "You're so cruel." He kisses me. He leans over and kisses my shoulder, the one with the scar. Then he eases himself down, kisses my imperfect belly button again.

After that, I lose track of all the kisses and their locations. It's one of the best endings to a discussion of my flaws to date, though.

Later, the sun begins to slant a bit through the bedroom windows. I like this place. It has white walls, lots of warm wood trim. The ceilings have old wooden beams and fans that loop lazily in the warm afternoon air.

"I think we need to get up." I'm feeling sleepy, and I know my dad would have a coronary if he made it to the house and found me asleep in the arms of the dastardly movie star.

Andrew sits up reluctantly. "This means we have to tackle dinner, you know."

"We're two grown people. We have recipes. Surely we can do this."

"I don't know if we can, and don't call me Shirley."

"Please." I watch him get up, enjoying the lithe length of his back, and try to turn my focus to making dinner for my family.

Julia Child, We Aren't

It's sad. I like to think of myself as an intuitive person, but all that goes out the window when I enter a kitchen. I don't know how long it takes to bring a turkey up to 160 degrees on the inside, and I have no idea where the best place is to stick the thermometer to see if it's still cold or not.

Andrew's no better. He keeps saying things like, "These directions aren't very clear." And laughing to himself. We already decided the wallpaper-paste gravy will not be making it to the table. Then he spent some time showing me all the things he could stick straight into it that didn't move: forks, knives, chopsticks.

I focus on the pie. We've whipped up a pumpkin one, and it actually looks promising. It just needs to go in the oven.

I have it in my hands when I hear the doorbell. And I reflexively turn toward the sound. So does the pie filling. The pie shell doesn't move as quickly, and in the course of about two seconds, the most hopeful part of the meal sloshes on the kitchen floor. I'm left standing with an essentially empty pie shell.

"Andrew!" I can't help it. I sound totally panic-stricken.

He stepped out to open the door for the rest of my family, but he pokes his head around the corner and gets a look at the kitchen floor. "Well, maybe we'll go out for dessert."

I think of A *Christmas Story*, when they had Christmas dinner in the Chinese restaurant. This may just be Christmas Eve, but we should've called in some professional help.

Too late. I hear my dad's voice in the hall. "So you're the infamous Andy Pettigrew."

"Please, call me Andrew."

I resist the urge to run out to defend Andrew. I hear Hunter and Beau briefly, but I can tell they've run off to check out the house. I have a feeling they're going to be disappointed to find no bowling alley or screening room or garage full of Bentleys.

I wash the remains of the pie from my hands and go out to greet my folks.

Andrew holds the poinsettia my mom's given him. "This is so thoughtful. Thank you."

She pats him on the hand, and I'm happy to be out here. She sometimes needs me to rein her in. I credit her with a lot, but she's always been great at revealing way too much information about me, my family in general, everything.

Dad puts his hands in his pockets and looks around. Maybe he's also wondering about the bowling alley.

"Hi, Dad."

He smiles widely when he spots me, hugs me warmly. "Kelly."

"You found it fine?" I can't help but ask. I'm secretly hoping I found it more easily than he did.

"Your dad didn't even need me to navigate." Mom gives me a big hug too. I pull away before she can whisper something totally embarrassing too loud. She does that a lot.

"Come on in. Can I take your coats?" Andrew helps my mom out of hers. Dad keeps his on. He's being so silly. I can't figure it out.

We go into the kitchen. It's open to the living room with a fireplace and a flat screen over the mantel. There's a big, warm wood table in the adjoining dining room. The living room has French doors to the backyard.

"This is very nice, Andrew. Isn't it nice, Dan?" Mom's trying to soften Dad up. She needs to stop, because his tendency is to dig in even more deeply when prodded.

Dad nods. Andrew goes back to the oven and checks the turkey. I say many, many silent prayers that what's left of the dinner will not give my parents and children food poisoning.

"We're about fifteen minutes out."

I wish I could speed that along. I go to set the table, and I realize this is the moment Andrew's been waiting for.

"Kelly tells me you do some woodworking," he begins.

I didn't know this topic was going to come up. Andrew's swinging for the fence on this one. I hope he connects, for his sake mostly. It's sweet that he's making an effort.

"Yeah, I putter a bit."

"The guy I rent from is kind of a fanatic. You should see the workshop." Andrew motions out the French doors.

C'mon, Dad, take the bait. I'm sending him this psychic message as loudly as I can.

He bites. "I'd like to." Andrew walks him to the door, turns around slightly to shoot me a hopeful raise of the eyebrows. I cross my fingers for him.

With the boys gone, the men out in the workshop, Mom has me to herself. But she's going to have to wait for the girl talk.

"Mom, take the turkey's temperature. I'm terrified it's too cold. I don't want to kill you people."

She smiles at me, and we spend a good ten minutes reviewing the dishes that *will* make it to the dining room table. She has a good laugh at all the stuff Andrew stuck in the quick-set gravy.

Finally, content that we have a meal that won't kill anyone, I sit at the kitchen island with her.

"So, Kelly Jo . . ." Mom is gearing up. "Tell me what's going on."

I guess I should expect this. "Mom, I don't know."

"You like him a lot."

"Yes."

"He likes you."

"I think he really does. He makes me feel amazing, Mom."

Her eyes widen a bit. My mom was a fierce advocate for Peter. There were points when he and I were together that she liked him more than I did, it seemed. I wonder how she's going to take this. Am I being disloyal?

"Oh, honey, I'm so glad." She gives me a huge hug.

I'm sort of relieved that she approves.

"I really like him, Mom." This is a weird feeling. It occurs to me that I haven't talked to anyone about Andrew. Obviously not the boys. And Tessa's not been much help. She makes me too nervous to share much with her.

"Do you love him?" Mom looks at me. She's treated me very gently in the last two years. I wonder if it gets old, handling me like a cracked teacup.

I pause. "I think so. It came on quick, and it was really hard to believe. But it feels right. The boys took to him so fast. He's just . . ."

I leave off. I don't know how to describe it. I haven't thought about it. I've just been living it.

"What?"

"I overthink and worry about everything. There's been a lot less of that. It just feels right."

I'm done talking, and the boys come tearing back into the kitchen just in time. I don't know why, but talking about it feels like I'm going to jinx it.

Mom pats my hand and busies herself getting Beau to fill the water glasses. Hunter turns on the Discovery Channel and settles on the couch.

I turn around at the island in time to see my dad and Andrew walking across the backyard. As they come in the French doors, Dad gives Andrew a friendly clap on the shoulder.

"Granddad! Come look at this squid they found at the bottom of the ocean!" Hunter calls.

Andrew catches my attention from across the room, where he stands behind Hunter and Dad. He points at Dad, makes a heart sign, and points at himself, all while mouthing, "He hearts me."

I try not to guffaw, but Cosmo's Yummiest Guy apparently has added the ninety-one gazillionth fan to his Facebook page.

It's Better to Give, but It's Fun to Get Too

Christmas morning dawns colder than usual for LA. I wake up at Mom and Dad's and marvel that I'm up before the boys. This must be a sign that they're getting older. The way they're beginning to value sleep is decidedly adolescent.

I might as well run. Last night was fun, but I have to say I felt torn at the end of the evening. Obviously I wanted to spend Christmas Eve with my sons and my mom and dad, but it made me sad to leave Andrew in his rented house all alone. Yes, he talked to his mom and dad, and the phone rang as we were leaving, and I'm pretty sure it was one of his sisters, but still. I had to fight the urge to pull him into my camp and circle the wagons around all the people I love.

Yes, I said it. I love him. I haven't told him that in so many words, but I've said it to myself, and this is a big step for me.

Partly because of Peter. I just wasn't sure how it was going to be to love someone besides him. Maybe part of me wondered if I'd be struck by lightning for feeling it, let alone saying it. Sometimes I feel like there's an unwritten widow's code, and I'm never sure if

I'm following it or not. But when I stop worrying about what everybody thinks and follow my own plan for widowdom, things always seem to go more smoothly.

That's a big step too, because I don't feel like I'm on solid ground. I wish I felt more confident. I wish I could say hearing him say he wanted me settled all my doubts, but it didn't. If I give in to my natural tendency to fret, I still find way too many things about this relationship that make no sense or seem very precariously balanced. House of cards comes to mind often. I don't know.

So the run's good for me. It's a beautiful day, and I'm able to clear my head a bit.

When I get back, Mom is holding the boys at bay in the kitchen. They want desperately into the den, to get at the tree.

"Thank goodness you're back. This was getting ugly."

"Mom! Do not do that to us again!" Beau is irate. "This isn't the time for a run!"

Hunter's a little less rabid, probably because he's a little less awake. "Yeah, Mom. There are presents to open."

Dad strolls in. He's always had the best Christmas poker face. He could stroll in like that after putting together an entire bike from Santa in record time. He's probably been stuffing last-minute things into people's stockings.

"Hi, Dad."

He encircles my waist with an arm, pecks my cheek. "How was your run, sugar?"

"Good."

"When's Andrew coming over?"

Andrew works miracles. The man's charisma is unstoppable. A little time spent alone with Mr. Pettigrew, and my dad is a changed man. He almost sounds eager.

"I'm not sure. I told him he could come have breakfast, if he wanted."

There's a knock at the door. Andrew's actor's instincts are well-honed. He shows up on cue.

I get the door and find him with a shopping bag full of presents in one hand and my folks' newspaper in the other.

"Merry Christmas." He smiles at me and walks in. Now I feel content. Now everyone's where they should be.

The boys can't stand it any longer. Hunter yells from the den, "People! Come on, already!"

Andrew kisses me on the cheek. "No time to waste. Let the carnage begin." He carries the presents past me and into the other room.

I've always been a fascist about present opening, so it takes me a minute to relax. I insisted even when the boys were little that we open one present at a time. Everyone has to ooh and ahh a bit, and then we can move on to the next gift. Peter always teased me about it, because in his gigantic family, Christmas was a free-for-all.

Andrew gives Beau some very deluxe Legos, and there's a long break in the gift opening as Beau, Hunter, and Andrew do some serious building. It's not entirely clear who enjoys the Legos more, the boys or Andrew. Then Hunter opens two autographed CDs from his favorite band, and Andrew scores with that gift too.

Andrew opens his gift from me, and the coat fits. He seems to like it, so that's good. Of course, he's an actor, so he might really hate it. I'm just going to hope for the best.

The boys each get cash from assorted relatives, of course, and games for various gaming systems they've accumulated over the years. My dad always gives each boy something they'll use with him over summer vacations. This year it's rods for surf casting. This is a big deal, because the boys can tell this means they're regarded as mature enough to handle the big rods. Both disappear into the backyard with Dad to practice. I pray we don't have a Christmas visit to the ER. I still recall a vacation with Peter when he and I went fly-fishing and I put a hook through my finger.

Mom putters in the kitchen. Andrew sits on the couch, looking at the back of the book my dad gave him. I'm already thinking to later in the day, wondering how he and I might steal some time away. But for now I stand and start to straighten the piles of loot the boys have strewn around the den.

"You've got one more to open." He smiles and hands me a wrapped box.

"You already gave me the cookbook and the bracelet. I only got you your coat!" I try not to have present anxiety. He's giving me too much.

"Stop. Just open it." He takes my hand and pulls me down to sit next to him.

I unwrap the box and take the lid off. It's a book. It's *The Sun Also Rises*. It's an old copy. A really old copy. I have a feeling how old, and I start to tear up.

"It's a first edition, isn't it?"

He nods. "Do you like it?"

"Do you have to ask? I love it." I hug him.

"I found it in a store downtown. It's cool. I'll have to take you there."

"I love you." Well, that popped out, didn't it? It feels good that it's out there.

He pulls out of the hug and looks at me, clear-eyed. "I love you too." He looks a little surprised. He looks happy, though.

And I'm happy too.

No Sunglasses Necessary

If my life were a movie, this would be the part where the montage begins. You know, they'd play a kicky song like "Walking on Sunshine," and there'd be shots of Andrew and me getting ice cream, riding bicycles through the park, playfully doing lots of things as a happy couple.

And it's close to that. I don't know how many of those movies also include two young boys, but Andrew does an awesome job hanging out with Hunter and Beau. Christmas break is filled with my family and Andrew, and it makes me sad to go back to Boise so the boys can go back to school.

But then he comes to visit us. For MLK weekend he's flying in, catching a ride with someone on the way to Hailey again. Only this time it's planned.

And this time I'm ready for him. The house is spotless, first of all. I'm well-groomed, and there is nary a dog hair on my whole ensemble. He's coming in Saturday morning and leaving Sunday morning, so we have to make it count.

The boys come with me to pick him up from the Western Air

terminal. I feel kind of suave. I know where to go, I expect the lady at the desk in the office area to wave us by, and I let the boys know Andrew will be standing there while a private jet taxis away.

We're all glad to see each other, and we have a great afternoon. But after dinner is what I'm really excited about.

Andrew sits at the kitchen table, looking at the Boise newspaper. I'm finishing up the dishes when the boys, on cue, bring the ski gear in from the garage.

"What's this?" Andrew asks.

Beau's just plopped a large pile of coats, bibs, and other ski detritus in the middle of the kitchen. "We're going snowshoeing," he announces. Beau loves to be in on the plans.

Andrew looks out the window at the deepening purple night. "It's dark outside."

Hunter's impersonation of a SoCal Lord of Dogtown rears its head again. "Bro, that's the point. It's sick, trust me."

Okay, I have never heard him use *sick* to mean cool in his life. Maybe he's studying up on Andrew's movies for appropriate dialogue.

Andrew raises an eyebrow. "Night snowshoeing? This should be interesting. I'm down."

If the conversation gets any hipper, I'm going to have to go out and buy an urban slang dictionary.

We pack ourselves into the car and drive up to the ski resort. It snowed early in the morning today, but now the night has fallen clear and cold, with an almost-full moon to boot.

Once we park in the cross-country parking lot and get out, Andrew gives my hand a little squeeze. He looks across the lot to the lodge, where we had dinner on — hard to believe — a much warmer night than this a few months ago.

Beau's in heaven. We're all together, he's good at snowshoeing, and he loves the novelty of it being at night. We approach the trail-head, which glows with luminarias, and he stops and turns around.

"This is totally 'Silent Night.'" He starts singing just to make the point: "'All is calm, all is bright.'" He crunches ahead in his snowshoes.

He's right. The moon throws thin shadows from the branches. The trees are coated with snow, and the moonlight bounces off each frosted limb. There are also luminarias along the trail every so often, and the night is almost day. It could not be more perfect.

Andrew leans over and kisses me. "This is almost as gorgeous as you."

Okay, I was wrong. *Now* the night is perfect. Seriously, the man is good.

The boys get ahead of us. We crunch along for a while, our snowshoes breaking the crust of the frozen trail. I follow Andrew's steps, and I watch the smile on his face spread. He spots an owl in a bare aspen tree and points out the moon with the rainbow of haze around it.

Then he stops for a moment, and I come up even with him. "You see something?" I look off the trail to see what might have held him up.

"No. I just wanted a second with you." He smiles.

"Okay." I try to hold still and not fidget.

"Can I tell you something?" He speaks softly.

His face is lit with moon glow. The angles of his face are half in shadow, half in light. I can't read his expression well. "Sure." I don't know what's coming.

"I just want you to know that I love you. I know we said it on Christmas, but I want you to hear me say it, for real."

"I love you too."

"There's more than that." He glances down the trail at the boys. They've stopped to pull clumps of snow off the low boughs of a pine. He waves at them, and they wave back, return their attention to the tree.

"I'm listening." I try to quiet myself so I really can. It's not my strong suit.

"I'm not perfect. If we keep dating, you're going to hear about a lot of stuff and a lot from my past."

My mind winds up. "Like what?"

"When I first came to LA, I had a hard time keeping my head screwed on straight. The business is crazy—"

"I can see that. I met Franca, remember?"

"It made me a little crazy. And some stuff happened, when I was younger. I almost blew my career before it even got started."

"But you didn't. We all have a past, believe me." I don't really want to get into that discussion just now. Mine is full of Peter, and that hurts.

"Well, I just want you to hear it from me. Anytime you want to talk about it, I will. I work all the time to stay clearheaded now. I'm not perfect, but having you in my life, things feel right, I feel good. I think everything's going to be fine."

"I'm sure it will be. Don't worry so much."

"All things in moderation, right?"

"Exactly." I kiss him. "Except that. You can completely overdo the kissing thing. That's very allowed."

He kisses me one more time, slowly, and I feel a surge of emotion radiate through me. I want to hold him, protect him.

"Hey! Mom! Stop the smooching!" Beau comes back down the trail toward us.

Andrew gives me a quick squeeze. "We're coming!"

His face is different, the moment over. He jogs off to meet Beau.

I try to sort out what that moment was, but the boys call to me, and it slips away.

When the night comes to an end, I feel truly sad. It's not often that I have time with the boys, with Andrew, on such a beautiful night.

We get home, and the boys collapse into bed, exhausted from the exertions of the evening.

I get the house locked up and realize, suddenly, that this will be the first night Andrew is in my bed, here in my house.

He comes out of the kitchen and into the living room. He seems to pause.

"What?"

"Nothing."

I take his hand and lead him into my bedroom. I turn on the stereo, choose a song. "This is in honor of the holiday." It's "MLK" by U2.

"I love this." He kisses me.

"It reminds me of Indio." I think of Joshua Tree—the empty, bright blue sky above the red earth and the shimmering heated air. But the peace of the song, the calm, reminds me of tonight too.

Something about it makes me want to be as close as possible to Andrew. We're sitting together on the bed, the moonlight streaming in through the windows. I face him, kiss him on the lips, and pull back to take off my shirt. I want to be here with him, next to him, nothing between us. I move slowly, deliberately, and kiss him again before I pull his shirt over his head.

He seems hesitant, gentle. I'm not sure where that's coming from. I kiss him again, and then I feel tears come. Why am I crying? Everything was so good two seconds ago. "I'm sorry . . ." I sit back for a moment before he pulls me to him, holds me.

"This is your room. *Your room*, Kelly."

It's amazing how everything can turn so quickly, change in a breath. Pure joy is woven tightly together with grief, and suddenly here is the deep, deep sadness, ready to clobber me over the head. Andrew and I will be together in my bedroom, yes, but it was first my bedroom with Peter, our bedroom.

I shiver, not from my bare skin, but from the realization. Andrew kisses me, eyes open to the tears in mine. He leans back on a pillow. "Let's take a minute here." He strokes my hair.

"Okay." I'm quiet, trying to find my center. "I'm not sure what to say."

"Don't say anything. I'm happy to be here with you." He closes his eyes, a content smile on his lips.

I rest my head on his chest, listen to his heartbeat. I feel my mind quiet as I let my breath fall into rhythm with his. At some point, I must doze off.

I stand on a train platform with the boys. They're little. They cling to me, each drags me forward toward the station. It's cold and wet.

There's no train at first, but then I turn and the train is there, standing at the platform, steam coming from the undercarriage. It creaks, massive, black, and glistening in the rain.

The boys jump up and down with glee. Peter comes to us off the train: young, smiling, bundled up in a camel overcoat. He hugs each of the boys, stands to hold me.

I'm about to feel his arms around me when someone calls to him. He slips out of my embrace and walks to the station. He swings open a door, waves to us, and walks in.

I rush to the doors, and they're locked. I can't see inside the station. The boys hold on to me. I pull at the doors, calling out to Peter. He does not come back. We're locked out.

I feel a gentle brush on my shoulder. I come to the surface from sleep. Andrew's fingers trace a pattern on my shoulder blade. His blue eyes are on me. He smiles.

"Hi."

"Hi."

"You were talking in your sleep."

Uh-oh. "Did I order a Diet Coke? I do that sometimes."

He sits up on one elbow, tucks the hair that's fallen into my eyes behind my ear. "I think you were talking to Peter."

"I guess I do that sometimes too." He leans forward and kisses me.

He looks straight into my eyes. "I couldn't make all of it out, but it seemed like you were trying to get him to stay."

He's probably right. "I'm surprised I didn't wake myself up." I try to sound like it's not a big deal, but there's no disguising the twinge of pain in my voice.

He takes my hand and squeezes it. "I want to fix it for you. I wish I could."

"There's no fixing it. Just be here with me." I touch his cheek. He closes his eyes, turns to kiss my palm. I lean forward and brush his long eyelashes with a gentle kiss. "But I love you for trying."

I think back to the dream. I can almost feel Peter's arms around me. I do feel new tears on my face.

Andrew doesn't say anything.

Something occurs to me. "You know what? You know what the best part of tonight was?"

"What?" He traces the path of one of my tears with his finger.

"I had a moment where I really missed Peter. But I missed him because I wished he could be here to meet you."

Andrew pulls me close and holds me. I stay still, thinking.

After a moment I put my hands on his face and kiss him. "I love you."

Sticks and Stones

It seems like we do a lot of leaving each other, Andrew and I. I guess it's good—obviously he needs to work. And I need to keep pinching myself. I like the breaks so I can ensure that I remain connected to the real world.

After our weekend, the new semester begins for the boys, and I once again look ahead to the next time Andrew and I will be together. Our plan is a big, bold, daring one: he has a premiere to attend for his spy movie, *Churchill's Man*. I'll be attending too, under the radar. In the movie, he's a World War II intelligence officer—with an amazing life story, of course, and it's true, of course. This is the movie he was doing reshoots for when I first met him in Indio. For that reason, it will be a movie I like.

He's noncommittal about it, says he doesn't like to watch his own performances. Since I'm not in his business, I don't press it. I have no idea what that would feel like, beyond the fact that I never had a school picture turn out well, even in my years as a teacher. So if I had to watch two hours of myself on a forty-foot screen, I think I'd develop a rash. Maybe that's where he's coming from.

Filming on the sheriff movie with Franca is winding down. He won't have much of a break between that and the premiere. This is where we stand when I wheel my cart into the twelve items or less line at the grocery store and see Andrew. On a magazine cover, of course. With Franca.

It's a good thing I don't have a hot cup of tea in hand, because if a spit take were ever apropos, it's now. He's hugging her. It looks like that, at least. It's definitely him. The other figure is tiny, blond, and vaguely resembles a yardstick. Must be her.

The picture doesn't bother me. The headline, on the other hand:

They're in Love!

The teaser underneath goes even further: "Costars Andy Pettigrew and Franca Delaney can't keep their hands off each other. Will they go public at the *Churchill's Man* premiere?"

Ugh. Okay, I was not born yesterday. I grit my teeth. "Jeremy."

Jeremy and his minions are hard at work promoting the are-they-or-aren't-they relationship. As I wait for the person in front of me who clearly does *not* have twelve items or less, I flip to the story. It's a couple more pictures. It looks like they're on the set, so the chance that this is from an actual scene in the movie is strong. I know. I know this is not a real story. I would know that even if I weren't dating him. This is the fodder these magazines require as a matter of course, and they fabricate stuff constantly.

What I didn't realize is that the magazines have help. When I was on the set, there was no way anyone could get this close to the filming unless someone gave them a way in.

"Jeremy." The person in line behind me probably thinks I'm a raving lunatic by now. Or is wondering what poor Jeremy ever did to cross me.

Nothing except his job, I remind myself. This is the story of Andrew's life. If I want him to be successful, some of the gamesmanship probably has to be part of the picture.

But I don't have to like it.

The phone rings, and I pick it up before I even look. "Hello?"

"Is this Kelly Reynolds?" I don't recognize the voice.

"This is."

"What can you tell me about your relationship to Andy Pettigrew?"

I end the call. WHAT. THE. HELL? How did this happen? What is going on?

The phone rings again. I jump and then proceed to peel myself off the ceiling of the grocery store in time to answer it. The lady in front of me is arguing about the price of a cantaloupe, but for once I'm grateful. She's bought me some time.

"Hey, it's Andrew."

I try not to yell. "Andrew, someone just called me and asked about you. How?"

"Okay, hang on—"

He must be floored. I ambushed him with the info. This isn't a good way to start a phone call with anyone. I take a breath and try again.

"Someone just called here and asked me about my relationship to you. How would they know? How could they get my number?" My mind is racing. Could Tessa have said something?

"What did you say to them?" He actually sounds unconcerned.

"Nothing. I hung up, and then you called."

"Good."

"What?" He's okay with this? "What about the boys? I'm not ready for them to get any attention. And you'll get in trouble—the whole Franca thing—oh, and I saw the cover with you and Franca. I know it's fake, don't worry about it, but I still don't love seeing you and seeing the headline—"

"Time out! Kelly! Breathe!" Andrew has raised his voice a bit.

"Huh?"

"My phone was stolen. Whoever it was is just fishing."

"What?" Not all my cylinders are firing on this new information yet. I hope the guy behind me isn't listening.

"They have my phone, Kelly. With my numbers in it. They're calling all the numbers. They're fishing."

"Really?"

"Yeah. And they should have about two minutes' more time to snoop, because the phone company is in the process of turning off my cell as we speak."

I'm quiet for a second. "So they don't have anything more than my name?"

"You did good. Hanging up was good—they have no dirt on you. You're just another name from my cell phone."

I guess that's good.

He laughs a little. "You saw the cover, though."

"Yeah."

"I was wondering when I'd hear from you about that."

"It's okay. I know it's Jeremy."

"With a little help from Sandy, my publicist. But she just does as she's told. She's actually a good person."

"As opposed to Jeremy?"

"Naw, he's not a terrible guy. He's just very single-minded. Kind of terrier-like. When he wants something to work, he'll do everything he thinks might make it work. He thinks the on-set romance thing is a good angle."

I'm totally distracted. It's finally my turn in line, and I don't want to be, you know, that person who's on her phone while checking out—even if I'm currently looking at the person on the other end of the phone on the cover of a magazine, which is a weird sensation.

"Hey, I have to go."

"You okay?"

"Yeah. As long as it's a false alarm on the us-being-outed thing. I want the boys left alone. But it's my turn in line at the store."

"Get off the phone! Don't be that person. I hate that person, the one on the phone when they're supposed to be paying."

"Me too. Love you. Bye."

"Love you." And the call is ended, just in time for the checker to ring me up.

The Good Part of a Bad Night

Seriously, everything is good, up to a certain point when it isn't anymore. And kind of in a sudden way.

I fly to LA for the *Churchill's Man* premiere in the early morning. Tucker's waiting for me at the curb, and he drives us through the streets of LA. It's a relief, really, to have someone else handle the traffic. I'm not a baby about it, but I don't want to nervous-sweat right now. It's not attractive.

I sit with him in the front seat of the gigantic black SUV. I resist the urge to fiddle with the stereo and look up at the side of a huge office building. Andrew's face is forty feet tall. He's working a smoldering stare. I smile, because if he were with us, he'd probably make some comment about his lip gloss and the blue steel photo shoot.

The text under his handsome face reads: "Churchill's Man. Coming 1/28."

Tucker points to the billboard. "There's your guy."

"He's not my guy. He's somebody's man."

He smiles. "Careful. You say it that way and it sounds like he and Churchill had a very special relationship."

"That would be a different movie, wouldn't it?" I try to chuckle, but the butterflies in my stomach are threatening to crawl up my throat. I check the backseat for my garment bag and suitcase. Tucker took care of it, but I'm feeling a little OCD. "Tucker, what's this going to be like?"

"Truthfully, premieres make me break out in hives."

"I'm so glad I don't have to do the red carpet thing. I would fall apart."

"Andrew and I bond over our hatred of premieres. They're a necessary evil, but mostly they're just evil." Tucker pulls the SUV into the valet circle of the hotel. He hops out of the car and has my bags at the curb all in one swift, graceful motion.

With a big smile, he hands me a room key. "He's doing press for another couple of hours. He'll sneak up when he gets a chance, I'm sure."

"Thanks, Tucker." He's so nice. I wish he was assigned to handling me. I would be so much calmer by association. Cooler too.

The hotel's very chic—lots of mirrors and glass, high ceilings in the lobby, big fireplaces, and a glossy black piano.

As I'm dragging my rolling bag, which refuses to stay the right way and keeps flopping over, into the elevator, my cell phone rings. I'm distracted by the hoopla, but if Hunter and Beau are calling to check in and let me know they haven't tied Tessa up yet, I want to take the call.

"Hello!" It kind of comes out in a gasp of air.

"Are you okay?" It's Andrew.

"Yeah, I'm just trying to get my luggage to cooperate with me." No one else took the elevator up, and I'm grateful for that, because the bag is now on its side diagonally across the floor of the elevator.

"What room are you in?"

I look at the envelope with the key in it. "Three forty-five. And I'm excited. This is going to be fun."

There is a longer than usual pause. "Me too."

He's quiet. Uh-oh. "Is everything all right?"

"Yeah. I'm just stressed. They're fitting my suit for tonight. Kind of a big crowd. But I'll catch up to you soon. I'm staying here tonight too."

That excites me. I think about what could possibly happen later.

The last time we Skyped, we had a good time doing our super-top-secret spy plan to make this whole thing work out. We'll spend as much time together as we can tonight without actually being together. No public appearances for us as an "us." I never thought for even a second about me walking the red carpet. I know Andrew and I like the way things are right now. We don't like the conditions laid out by Jeremy and his crew, to be sure, but we like that Boise is still our secret place. We like that Hunter and Beau haven't seen a big disruption to their lives.

I find my room. As I get in the door, the phone rings again. I drag the uncooperative rolly bag in on its side and throw it as far into the room as I can, then answer the call.

"Hi, Mom." Beau's on the line.

I'm glad we can talk before things get too crazy. "Hey, hon. How are you?"

"What's your room like?"

The room is very posh. It has two king beds and a little sitting area with a love seat and two chairs. There's a wet bar to one side and a sliding glass door that opens out on to a tiny balcony. I can see the fringe of cliché palm trees that reach almost to the foot of my room's windows.

"It's nice."

"Does it have a Jacuzzi in the living room?" Beau cuts to the chase. This is about the glamour, not about missing me.

"No, Beau. It doesn't have a living room, and it doesn't have a Jacuzzi either."

"Oh. Well, Tessa says everything's fine, and we're about to watch the next movie, so can I go?" He yells something to Hunter with the phone covered.

Tessa's rented them many movies that their mom most certainly would think were too violent or too adult for them, and she's gone to the grocery store and bought them non-Mom-approved junk food to munch while watching the terrible movies. They're not missing me at all.

"Beau?"

"Yeah, Mom?"

"Give everybody a kiss for me. I love you."

"Love you, bye." He hangs up before I can say another word.

I smile and turn back to my mission. My first job is to get my dress out of my bag. If it creases, I'm done for. I called Barb, who is smart about all these kinds of things, to ask her how to pack a dress. I could've asked Tessa, but she was so worked up about the premiere that I got nervous just talking to her about it. Practical information was clearly beyond our capacity in this case. And even Barb wanted to know what was going on, but I told her my mom had a thing in LA that was fancy so I had to dress up. I have still not fully figured out how this relationship will fit into my real world, but I'll be damned if this event is how everybody finds out.

The dress is wrapped in a complex layering of tissue paper and plastic dry cleaner bags. I haul it out of its cocoon and hang it up. It looks like it's survived the trip. I find all the outfit components: the shoes and the various firming, smoothing, and shaping under gear. I think all that stuff cost me more than the dress itself, but I want to feel totally safe. No body part will be making an unplanned appearance. And I don't want to be bulgy in any way.

I've already had my meltdown over this, trust me. There's no way I can compete with the women who will be at this event tonight. And I'm trying very hard to take Andrew at his word. He says he chooses me, so I must believe he chooses me for a reason.

However, I don't know what in God's name that reason is right now. I look at all this battle gear I'll be putting on in a few hours, and I'm not at all convinced I belong here. We can sleight-of-hand it all we want, but I'm a nonfamous, nondescript woman dating a handsome, charismatic, famous person. It's ridiculous.

I try to shake this off. Now is the time to be excited, not self-critical. I need to soak up the atmosphere and enjoy it for what it is, not for what I'm not.

My phone buzzes. It's a text. I know it's not the boys. I just talked to them, and all is well there.

I read the text.

Still doing the business thing. Catch up to you soon.

I text back.

Relax. Come when you can. xoxo.

I glance at the time on my phone. I have four hours. I probably need two to get ready, and that's only if I take the longest shower in world history, which I think they frown on in California 'cause they're running out of water. I'm going on a run.

I get changed and go downstairs, then out the side doors by the pool. There are several guys camped out by their cars. A few sit on little scooters or motorbikes.

Game on. This must be the paparazzi. I examine them. Most are younger than I would think. In their twenties. I don't notice any women—that's an interesting piece of trivia. They all seem to be smoking, which must help pass the time. Several talk or text on cell phones. Some sit with each other, chatting. I count fifteen or twenty guys. Wow.

Oh, hell yes, I'm going to spy on them. This is like being behind enemy lines, or deep undercover, or something. None of these men has a clue that I have any relationship to the man I presume they're stalking. The premiere's at a theater not too many blocks from here, and if Andrew's doing some press, then everyone knows where he is.

I run a little in place, then jog closer to them. This isn't my warm-up routine in any way, shape, or form, but I'm trying to look natural. When I'm within earshot, I pick a palm tree to stop at and stretch out my quads and Achilles. Let the spying begin.

Two young men wearing leather jackets sit on the bumper of a silver sedan. They're smoking. My back's partially turned to them, but I can hear. One of them has a bit of an accent that I would place as Turkish maybe?

"This is shit." The Turkish guy's speaking.

"Well, it's a premiere. All the shots are going to suck ass anyway." The other one sounds resigned, at peace with whatever is sucky about this job.

"Yeah, but he could at least do something before the theater. Walk out and get a damn cup of coffee or something. The guy lives like a freaking recluse."

Non-Turkish guy sounds sympathetic. "Can you blame him?

We're a circus, for Christ's sake. I wouldn't bother with the cup of coffee either, if I was him."

Turkish guy is still grumpy. "His friend is in town, that Todd Ford guy. The musician. They haven't even gone out one night together."

This is something I didn't know. I haven't met Todd yet. Andrew has mentioned him a few times. This makes me nervous. I have the feeling that not all of Andrew's friends are as mature and enlightened as he is, and I remember the asses some guys were when I was twenty-nine. Am I going to be meeting him tonight?

Non-Turkish guy perks up. "Oh, well, there you go. Todd's an absolute animal. They'll be out after the premiere. I guarantee it. We'll make some shots then."

Turkish guy snorts. "Pettigrew's hot or cold. Either they'll tear it up, or he'll have freaking ice water all night and go to bed at eight. It's all or nothing with that dude."

I realize I probably need to run now. There's only so long a person can stretch. I turn my back on the men and trot off.

As I run, I feel nagging worry start to eat at my insides. This is a new bit of information, Todd being in town. I don't know how he might change things. What if he doesn't like me? Does his vote count for a lot with Andrew? And what did the guy mean with that "hot or cold" comment? My gut rumbles with uncertainty.

I scream inside to shut up. I cannot ruin this night. It's going to be great. I kick the run up a notch and feel my lungs burn. Bring a little pain and keep myself working too hard to worry—that's my plan, and for a few miles, I think it works.

I get back to the hotel with two hours to go. I immediately get into the shower. I think I hear my phone buzz, but right now I'm shaving and midleg, so I ignore it.

I'm about to get to the business of my dress when there's a knock at the door. I pull a robe on and open the door a crack. Andrew's there.

"Let me in, quick! I have twenty minutes before I have to be back for the last interview."

I open the door wide, and he sweeps in. He's not even dressed for the premiere yet. He runs a hand through his hair. He looks tense.

"Where've you been?" He slips an arm around me, kisses my neck.

"I went running."

"I wanted a minute alone with you."

He kisses me again, and I start to shiver. "Wait! I haven't done my hair or makeup yet. Don't distract me."

"Hold off on that. I need a smoke, and then I've got a surprise for you."

I wonder if the surprise is his friend Todd. This sets my teeth on edge. I don't know why, but it just feels bad.

He has a cigarette between his lips already. He seems off, out of sorts. Tucker was right—it's clear premieres stress Andrew out.

"I have to say, I wish you'd quit that."

"I am in total agreement with you." He steps to the balcony. "I think you may get your wish." He doesn't open the door, just looks through it.

"What?"

"Your room is a bit inconvenient. Look." He peeks out again.

I join him. The paparazzi are still camped out in the parking lot, right under my balcony. "They've been there all day. I didn't even think about it."

"I'm not in the mood to give them a photo op right now. God." He groans.

I'm starting to get crazy nervous. There's another knock at the door.

Andrew brightens. "It's surprise time!"

The person at the door is a young, sweet-faced woman who is hugely pregnant.

He slips an arm around my waist. "This is Mallory. She's my hair and makeup lady. She's the surprise."

It doesn't click. "Huh?"

He looks worried for a minute. "I thought you might like her to get you all glamified."

Mallory smiles and holds up her tackle box. She looks friendly.

"That'd be a lot of fun. Thanks, Mallory." I give Andrew a hug around his waist and step forward to shake her hand.

She directs me to one of the chairs.

Andrew claps his hands together, glad his plan is in action. "Let the makeupping begin! You two have fun. I'm going to go finish up and get dressed. See you in a bit." He bounds out the door, and I'm left with Mallory.

She does her thing. When she finally hands me a mirror, I have to say I'm impressed. The makeup has a lot of fluttery eyelashes and shiny gold eye shadow to it, but it works. The only thing I'm a little uncomfortable with is the hair. It's still mine, except there's a lot of curl. Ever since my failed perm in the attempt to have *Princess Bride* hair in fifth grade, I'm kind of allergic to curls.

I go get my dress on, and I hear knocking once again just as I smooth the last bits of myself in place.

This time Mallory gets the door. Andrew stands there in a

beautiful black suit. He's clean-shaven, he smells good, his hair is neatly coiffed. He's beautiful.

He comes into the room and stops. "Wow, that's a great dress. You look amazing."

"Thanks." I can't help it—I feel better. Maybe that's what I've been so worked up about all day. My dress is simple, but I do love it. It's a deep eggplant satin. It has a V-neck and little cap sleeves. It just hits the top of my knees. I'm fair, so I think the color looks good with my skin and eyes. I know I'm blushing. "And thank Mallory. She did most of this."

Mallory smiles and gathers up her tackle box. "Nothing doing, Kelly. You were an easy subject. Have fun tonight." She pats Andrew on the shoulder and leaves the room.

Andrew hasn't moved. "Now what?"

Andrew smiles slyly. "Well, I can think of one thing."

He hops on the bed and fluffs a pillow next to him invitingly.

"Um, you should've thought about that way before the dress and the hair and the other froufrouing. I cannot be touched now for fear that everything will fall apart."

"C'mere, pet." He sounds suspiciously like Jeremy.

I put a knee on the bed, pretending to crawl toward him. "Meow." And then I feel the remote under my knee, and the TV clicks on.

It's loud, and it's an entertainment show. The announcer sounds too chipper. "Tonight in Hollywood, *Churchill's Man* premieres. Will it be another hit for Andy Pettigrew?"

Andrew reaches for the remote. "Quick, before it's a total buzz kill."

He can't turn it off fast enough. The announcer continues:

"But more important, will Andy and Franca finally go public with their heated on-set romance?"

He sighs. "Not. Quick. Enough."

He clicks the TV off and rolls over, gets up from the bed.

I can't help but tease a little. "Heated, eh?"

"Jeremy. That man." His phone buzzes. "His ears are burning apparently. He's wondering where I am." He pulls me up off the bed, runs a hand through his hair again, and makes a point of taking a very deep breath. "We're going to pretend I didn't get that text. There's not too much more time. Let's take a ride."

He has his cell to his ear as we leave the room. "Tuck, we're going to the elevator. Can you meet us in the garage?"

I don't know what's up. How can we leave the hotel together? Why are we leaving now? There's just an hour before he has to walk the red carpet.

We take the service elevator by ourselves. I feel uneasy. This feels like a risk. The doors open, and Tucker's right there. The back door to the black Suburban is open. Andrew leads me to it and helps me climb in. He's in quickly right behind me. Then we're moving. The way Tucker looks at the wheel tells me he's on high alert now. This is him working his job in full bodyguard manner.

The black SUV rolls out of the garage, and immediately there are two cars behind us. They give chase—there is no other way to describe it. I have a moment of feeling dizzy. I don't want to ruin things for Andrew.

He can tell. He pats my hands, which I realize I'm wringing in my lap. "Hey. It's going to be fine. This is what Tucker and Dean do for a living. They're very good at it."

"And Dean?" I haven't seen him tonight. Andrew motions to the car next to us.

It's an identical black car, right next to us, and it seems there's another young man and woman in the back. The man, through the deeply tinted windows, looks strikingly like the one sitting next to me right now. That must be Dean in the driver's seat.

"A decoy?" This is, again, beyond what I know from my life. Andrew nods.

We continue down several streets, then side streets, and eventually our tails seem to give up.

"Why aren't they following?" I thought they'd be more persistent.

"Because the other car just went into the underground garage at the theater. They think we're the decoy car." Andrew holds my hand and relaxes back into the seat, throwing his other arm around me.

Tucker seems to relax too. But we keep driving.

I'm confused. Doesn't he have to get back? "Where're we going?"

Andrew kisses me. "Almost there."

We pull onto a residential street, turn into a gated drive, and park. The city's given way to palm trees and canyon and gardens.

"This is Wattles Gardens. The mansion's up the hill a little. I want to show you something." Andrew gets out of the car.

It's as if we have the place to ourselves. The air's warm. The sun sifts through the trees. Everything smells lush, earthy.

"I found this place when I first moved here. I like to run the trails a lot. It's quiet most of the time."

I have a strange moment, because both of us are insanely over-dressed for a hike. But he leaves Tucker with the car and leads me down a concrete sidewalk. The garden looks like it wants to reclaim this trail. It's overgrown and wild looking.

Suddenly the leaves part. We're in front of a Japanese teahouse. There's a pond and a bridge. He takes my hand.

"This is so pretty. Who would have known it was even here?" I stand at the top of the bridge and marvel.

Tucker's behind us again. "You forgot your tea." He smiles. This must have been a plan between the two of them. He holds a carrier with two large iced green teas.

Andrew takes them, and Tucker retreats. Andrew hands me one and toasts, clinking our plastic cups together. "To us."

I love that we have a thing. I take a sip and kiss him. "To us."

After a quiet moment in the gray-green twilight of the gardens, we return to the bustle of the city to drop Andrew off. Tucker has me sit with him up front.

Tucker turns to me. "Ms. Reynolds, you're going to want to put on your sunglasses and look nonchalant. We're about to throw your friend here to the wolves."

Our black SUV pulls into the fire lane in front of the theater, and suddenly there's a frenzy of flashbulbs and noise outside the car. I look in the backseat.

Andrew straightens his tie. "Well, I'm off. I'll see you after the movie."

Tucker and I both nod. The back door of the car opens, and Dean's on the other side of it to walk with Sandy and Andrew.

There's a roar, and then it's muffled again as Dean closes the car door. I watch him take Andrew into what looks essentially like the lion's mouth: a long stretch of red carpet lined with people and equipment and then bleachers that rise up from both sides of the entry to the theater. If running the gauntlet didn't come to mind before, one look at this scene definitely conjures it now.

I see Franca join Andrew on the red carpet, a little way in front of the theater entrance. She looks like a brilliant-colored bird of paradise, slim as a stem.

Tucker notices too. "Look, it's your favorite hyena."

I chuckle. "I'm surprised Jeremy didn't make her ride with us."

"Oh, he tried." Tucker grins. "Andrew put his foot down, but they've got to sit together in the theater. That was the compromise."

"She's not even in this movie. This is stupid." I try not to let it bother me.

"You know, it keeps those people out of your business if they think he's with her. Maybe that's a good thing." He nods in the direction of the huge bank of reporters and photographers.

Tucker always has a good perspective. "True. Now what?"

Tucker pulls away from the curb. "Now we normal people go back to business."

After a short drive, he pulls the car into the underground parking lot of the theater and walks me to the lobby himself. He offers to sit with me during the movie, but I can tell he's really supposed to be working. I send him off to stand guard somewhere. I mill around for a while and go find my seat. The last time I see Andrew is from a considerable distance, as he waves to the crowd from a balcony box, Franca at his side, looking cozy. I give her my best death stare as the lights go down, and I sit in a darkened movie theater and watch Andrew on-screen, like the rest of his admirers, from afar.

He's magnificent. He plays an American, code-named Intrepid, who made himself into Churchill's wingman during the war. He taught himself to fly planes, made his own fortune, helped save the Allies, and looked dashing and handsome while doing it. Actually I don't know if the real man looked dashing while accomplishing these tasks, but Andrew sure does.

It's surreal, falling in love with the person you've already fallen in love with all over again on the movie screen. But it feels especially strange because I'm sitting in the theater all by myself. It feels sort of fraudulent too. Really, what if I turned to the person next to me and said, "That's my boyfriend, you know."

And I almost do, except the lady who sits next to me is very old, and about halfway through the movie, it becomes apparent that she has a little dog hidden in her purse. She watches the movie, but she also feeds the dog popcorn periodically. I'm not sure who would be the crazy one if I claimed Andrew as my man. It's all kind of odd.

Kind of odd, and kind of lonely.

The Bad Part of the Bad Night

The movie's credits roll, and the lights come up quickly. Some people begin to leave, but others stand or turn around in their seats and visit with one another, mingling and chatting.

I, of course, know absolutely no one, so I get up, rearrange my dress after sitting for two hours, and try to figure out how I'm going to look like I belong here for the time it takes me to find Tucker and/or Dean. I have no problem at all deciding when it comes to fight or flight. In my past life, I was the antelope, not the lion.

But I'm trying really, really, *really* hard not to do my best antelope impersonation right now. I remember to walk smoothly and slowly in my heels, and I clutch my clutch for all it's worth as I hightail it to the lobby of the theater.

I spot Dean at lookout on the front door and am making my way to him when I'm intercepted. Jeremy.

"Hey, Kelly!" He sidles up to me.

I feel distinctly antelopeish next to him. "Jeremy! Good to see you again."

He's dressed in a sleek gray suit, with a black tie a little loose at the neck and the uniform cowboy boots. He wears an expensive-looking watch. His brown hair recedes a bit, but tonight it's kind of spiked up, and he's got a carefully groomed five o'clock shadow. Everything about him says "I threw this together" in a way that tells me he didn't. Nothing about Jeremy is by accident. The man is the definition of calculating.

"So! What'd you think?" He sips a longneck Coors. I try to stand up tall.

"The whole premiere thing made it kind of hard to settle down and focus on the movie, to be honest." You know what? I'll be friendly and treat him as though he's a fellow human being. Maybe he'll surprise me.

"It's kind of a spectacle. I think we tend to forget that. We've become immune."

He seems like he's friendly too. Maybe I misjudged him.

"Well, it's your job," I say with a laugh. "It's like working in an ice-cream parlor—after a while, it's just ice cream."

He's next to me now, and he puts an arm at the back of my waist, gently guides me away from where we've been standing. "Let's get you a glass of wine."

As we weave our way in and out of the crowd, he greets quite a few people with "Bro!" or a knuckle pound or a nod and an eyebrow raise at the person's date. He's in his element. This feels very reminiscent of a frat party. "So who'd you sit with for the movie?" he asks.

He knows the answer to this one. *He* sat with my date, Andrew, since I'm still persona non grata. He and Franca.

"No one. My mom was going to come, but she had to cancel at the last minute." This isn't true, of course. Though now I think it would've been a good idea.

We're by the bar now. He hands me a glass of wine, and he's got another Coors. "Well, it's too bad it has to work that way."

I wonder if he means it. His voice is warm, sympathetic. I look up at him and try to see what he's really saying. His brown eyes seem warm too.

"Yeah, it kinda sucks. I guess I'm still getting used to how things work out here." I feel guarded, but it might be good if I could build some sort of rapport with this man. You know, it could be helpful to Andrew somehow.

He looks at me and gives me the full up-and-down appraisal. It's subtle, but I'm sure he wants me to notice.

"You know, that's not always how it works," he continues.

"Oh, I know." I'm not sure how much to expose myself to this comment. I think I'm still supposed to be denying that I'm anything more than a family friend.

I lean on the bar a bit—my feet are killing me in these shoes— and Jeremy touches my elbow. "If you were seeing someone else, it might not have to be that way."

I have no idea what he's getting at. "What?"

"You're a knockout in that dress tonight. I bet he didn't even have the balls to come over and tell you that in front of anyone. Has he even acknowledged your presence here?"

All right, I'm going there. "You know he can't. You're why he can't!"

"Can't he? Or is he too chickenshit? If he were more mature, he'd find a way to do it. And if he weren't an actor, there wouldn't be a problem at all."

I still can't follow. "Why are you telling me this?"

"If you get tired of the cougar thing, I think you're an amazingly sexy woman. And we could date without all this sneaking around bullshit. I'd parade you out on my arm for all of Hollywood to see. And I'd be the envy of every man at this party."

Oh, I see. Wow. I guess I'd be flattered in a roundabout way, if he weren't supposed to be looking out for Andrew's best interests.

"Andrew is your client. You probably shouldn't hit on his girlfriend."

"You'd be my woman, not my girlfriend. You're a lady, not a girl. Give yourself some credit."

I set my wine down and take a step back from him. "Do you have morals?"

He grins shamelessly. "I left them in my other pants."

"I'm walking away now."

"Have a great evening, Kelly."

Thankfully Tucker emerges from the crowd. "I saw Jeremy talking to you. You all right?"

"I think I need a shower. That man is a piece of work."

Tucker smiles. "Did he hit on you?"

"Um, yeah."

"Sadly, that's not surprising."

I feel a pang of loneliness. I check my phone. The movie's been out almost an hour. "Is there any way I can see him now? I can't find him anywhere. Once the house lights went down I lost track of him."

Tucker nods. "He never watches his movies. It makes him crazy. He's back at the hotel at the after party. I'm taking you over right now, if that's okay. Unless you want to hang with Jeremy some more." He grins.

It's the first time Tucker's joked with me, but I like it. It seems our relationship is moving to a new level. Bonding with the body-guard—it's a new facet of this relationship that I didn't foresee, but it's not a bad thing.

We scoot through a side door and out through a service entrance. The big black Suburban Andrew arrived in on the red carpet is parked in the alley. Tucker's a total gentleman and helps me climb up into the passenger side in my ridiculous heels.

"I swear I'm taking these off as soon as possible."

"I had a client once who never wore heels shorter than five inches. Sometimes I had to carry her at the end of the night because her feet were literally numb." He's relaxed and chattier when Andrew isn't around. I guess he's not feeling the need to be greatly vigilant.

"Tucker?"

"Yeah?"

"Is it normal? The whole contract I-can't-date-anyone-publicly thing?" He seems like the right person to ask this question. I feel like he won't lie to me.

He nods. "You'd be surprised. And there are a lot of people 'dating' in LA who can't stand the sight of each other. There are always the rumors too—about people who're married strictly for business."

I can recall gossip headlines alluding to that. "Do you think this is a good idea? I'm not like these people."

He pats my hand. "I think that's exactly why this is a good idea. Because you aren't like these people. But, to be fair, I've known plenty of *these* people who aren't like these people."

"Andrew?" I hope for a good reply.

"Most of the time, yeah, Andrew." He seems like he's about to say something more.

"What?"

He reconsiders. "Nothing."

"Tucker, please."

He sighs. "Yes, Andrew, most of the time. He's young, Kelly, and new to a lot of this. There's a difference between a working actor and an insanely famous actor. Sometimes he loses sight of things. Just be mindful of that. He never means to, I don't think."

"Thank you, Tucker."

"For what?"

"I appreciate your honesty. I'm flying blind here, you know."

"Yeah, I do."

We pull up to the hotel, and he parks. "Sorry, but if we walk in together it's less of an entrance than me letting you out of the car. People sometimes recognize me as his bodyguard. I don't want them to put two and two together."

I slip off the heels. "Screw it. I can walk. Don't you worry about it."

We go in the front lobby, and Tucker takes me into an elevator. "The party's on the roof. It's closed, of course, but you're with me."

I can't help but snort. "Did you know *you'd* be dating me, Tucker? Are you okay with that?"

I think he's blushing a little. "Well, I'm gay, but other than that, yeah, I'm comfortable with our relationship."

He's definitely blushing. I love this guy more and more each moment. "Seriously, though, are you dating anyone for real?"

"Not at the moment. But thanks for asking." He pats me on the back as the elevator arrives at the roof.

As soon as the doors open, the music assails us. It's pounding, literally.

I'm overwhelmed before I've been on the roof for five minutes. It's packed, and it's a young crowd. There are lights flashing everywhere. The DJ plays loud dubstep music. The line at the bar is incredibly long.

Tucker has to yell so I can hear him. "Come on, I'll take you to find Andrew."

We pass through the first set of velvet ropes with a nod from the bouncer. It feels weird to know I wouldn't rate for a second if it weren't for Tucker standing next to me.

We weave through many, many people dressed either very skimpily, if women, or very funkily, if men.

Tucker's quite effective at clearing a path. I fight against the impulse to shrink into the back of him and disappear.

I was never very good at parties, even when I was in school. If a large herd of us went out to dance, I was fine. But in unfamiliar territory on my own, in short order I found myself longing for my pajamas and my bed.

I try to let go and enjoy the scene. It's not very often that I get to be anywhere like this. Okay, it's *never* that I get to be anywhere like this. I'm a widow in Boise, Idaho, with two kids. Let's get real.

Tucker takes my hand and pulls me up alongside him. I see why. We're at another checkpoint. This is getting to be like the Berlin Wall or something. No one here was alive when that existed. Never mind.

He yells into the gatekeeper's ear. They fist-bump, and the guy, dressed in a gorgeous green suit, reaches over the crowd to point for Tucker. He then pulls yet another velvet rope aside.

Tucker threads a wire from his ever-present radio at his hip to his ear. It has the curly earpiece on it, and the mouthpiece attached at his cuff, just like the Secret Service guys wear. He's going into working mode. We must be getting close to Andrew.

There are several pavilions—little tents with chairs and sofas—

surrounded by lots of California greenery. He steers me to one of them. There's another velvet rope. This one is staffed by Dean. When he spots Tucker and me, he smiles for a moment, but only at Tucker. They shake hands.

Tucker leans in and shouts into my ear, "Andrew's been asking where you are. He's on the back couch. You're safe here to hang out. I doubt anyone would be the wiser."

I don't know about that—there's a big crowd on the other side of Dean's rope. I can't even see into the pavilion for all of the bodies in the way. As with the rest of the party, all the girls are less clothed than me.

I give Tucker and Dean a little wave good-bye and weave my way into the cluster of people. Already I feel awkward.

Suddenly, I emerge on the other side of the crowd. There he is.

Andrew sits on one of the couches next to a person I assume is his friend Todd. He's smoking. He has a beer in his hand and is using it to gesture as he talks. Both guys are flanked by girls, and the other couches in the pavilion are filled with women too. Great.

I'm almost all the way over before he notices I'm there.

I have to yell to be heard. "Hi."

He looks up. "You made it!"

He stands to greet me and takes two huge side steps, off balance. I immediately recognize this for what it is: he's drunk. Double great.

He recovers and slips an arm around my waist for a hug. He has to yell into my ear, just like anyone else here trying to have a conversation. I might be deaf by the end of the night.

"How was it?" He steps back to look me in the eye. I lean into his ear.

"It was great. You were amazing."

"Good, good." He's not paying attention. He smells like the boys at college. I have a crazy-strong flashback to Peter's crew parties sophomore year. I just hope the bathrooms aren't as scary.

He motions to the couch. "Come meet Todd."

I straighten up. Okay, Kelly. This is a friend. Time to be warm, time to give everyone the benefit of the doubt. Regardless of what the photographer guys said earlier today.

Andrew waves to Todd, who has to semi-pry himself out of the arms of the girls.

He stands, and I get a good look at him. He's shorter than Andrew, more normal looking. He's still handsome. He has warm, dark skin and tightly curly hair that droops into his eyes. He wears a striped T-shirt and a holey argyle cardigan sweater. The whole look is kind of prepster meets hobo. He's even got duct tape over the toe of one of his Converse sneakers.

He comes and gives me a big hug. "Greetings." He smooches the side of my cheek. He's charming. And charmingly drunk, just like Andrew.

"You guys have been having fun." I leave it at that.

"I'm so glad you could come out tonight. Andrew's told me all about you." Todd plops back down onto the couch and pats the cushion next to him. A girl in a white bikini top with an orange tan shoots me a bitch-kitty stare. I have to laugh.

I wedge in between Andrew and Todd. But Todd is completely focused. He looks at my dress, notices my shoes. "You look terrific. Has anyone told you that tonight?"

I can't help it. "Jeremy, actually."

Todd laughs, blowing the smoke from his cigarette into the night air above our heads. "Did Tucker save you, I hope? You have to tell Andrew."

Right now Andrew is intent on a conversation with two girls who missed curfew two hours ago by the looks of it. Total jailbait, I swear.

"How long are you in town?" I ask him.

"This week. I go back a week from today."

I know nothing about this guy. "Where are you from?"

"New York. I'm in a band there. Andrew and I used to be in a band together, until he went all movie star on us and left for LA."

A high school friend. This is an important person, a person who has history with Andrew. He knows Andrew from when he was *Andrew*, not Andy Pettigrew, superstar. And he seems to know all about me.

"You lived in Pennsylvania too?"

"I lived with Andrew and his folks when my dad got stationed in Germany my senior year in high school. Someday I'll tell you all of our high school exploits—or most of them."

"Don't tell her about how you left me in that tree in the park when the cops came." Andrew has turned around to listen. He puts an arm around my shoulders.

"You were the one who passed out right when the party got busted," Todd counters. "It was every man for himself."

I'm none too keen on hearing the high school drinking exploits. It makes me uncomfortable.

Todd changes the subject, thankfully. "Jeremy put the moves on Kelly tonight." He waits for a reaction.

Andrew looks at me for confirmation.

"He told me to look him up when I was sick of the whole cougar thing." I leave out the other parts.

"The old Jeremy King loyalty test." Andrew shakes his head.

"What?" I'm confused.

Andrew rolls his eyes. "Jeremy doesn't believe anyone could be with me for me. He thinks you're dating me for my money, fame, power. So he tests you to see how loyal you are."

"And if I'd said I was into him?" I'm astonished.

"Oh, he'd jump all over that—or you, more accurately—but it'd be in the name of protecting his client." Andrew takes a sip of beer.

Todd laughs. "Oh, man! You need to watch your back, brother. He's cold." Todd punches Andrew on the arm.

Andrew stubs out his cigarette in the ashtray. "Let's dance." He pulls me off the couch before I even know what's going on.

Play along, Kelly, relax. Don't assume the worst. "Wait!" I let Andrew lead me out to the dance floor.

I'm not sure what to expect when we pass by Dean and the velvet rope. I do notice that he murmurs something into his sleeve. He probably just alerted Tucker that Andrew's on the move.

The dance floor is a small area nearer the pool and the rest of the party. I'm not sure what the plan is here. Andrew has his hands on my hips and sways with me to the music. But my alarm bells are going off. There are a lot of people at this party. They can't all be sworn to secrecy, can they? And I'm sure they can't all be trusted to be discreet. I wonder whether everyone surrendered smartphones at the door. How many people are taking pictures and posting them as we speak? Or in this case, as we dance?

"Andrew." I love the way his hands feel on me, but still . . .

"What?" He looks down at me. His eyelids are hooded. I know that look. He's pretty drunk.

"Are you sure this is a good idea?"

He puts an arm around my neck, pulls me in to whisper in my

ear. "I think this is a fabulous idea." One of his hands strays, heading down to the hem of my dress.

I step back just as he strokes my cheek and reaches out to kiss me. I kiss him even as I grab both of his hands in an attempt to rearrange them.

"Andrew. What about all of the stuff with Franca?"

"Screw it. You're my date. I didn't get to hold you all night."

I'm acutely aware of the crowd. Yes, it's busy, and yes, there's a lot going on, but there are a lot of people. Someone's going to notice who that is in the clinch next to them on the dance floor. It's time for me to be the clear thinker here.

"We need to take this underground, my friend." I lead him off the dance floor.

We get to the fringe, and he shakes me off, tries to circle his arms around my waist and pull me back out again. "Come on, Kelly. Lighten up."

I've already decided this is not a good idea. I think we're being watched more than casually by several of the girls around the pool. "Andrew, we've got an audience. We aren't ready to do this, remember?"

He nuzzles my neck. "It's called fun. You're so serious." This stings. I am not amused.

We've made it back to the pavilion, the couches. He lets go of me. "I'm going to go dance." He walks back toward the dance floor and disappears into the crowd.

I don't know what to do. I'm hurt, but I'm irritated. He's acting like— Well, Kelly, he's acting like a boy. Probably because he is one. Jesus.

Todd's suddenly next to me. "You did the right thing. He's not paying any attention. But a lot of people are." He tosses his head in the direction of the girls by the pool. They have their cell phones out, and it sure doesn't look like they all have phone calls to make. Maybe Todd isn't as drunk as I thought he was.

"You want to dance?" He extends a hand to me. Okay, he might be a dangerous friend of Andrew's, but he's a smooth one. I sigh and take his hand.

He doesn't make an effort to be near Andrew on the dance floor, and I appreciate that. Andrew dances with the bikini-top orange girl, but thankfully, the music is fast, and he weaves around frenetically. Todd keeps me distracted. We have fun, dance a couple of songs together. He tries to get me to do more than a few ridiculous moves. Each one he prefaces with a goofy "And this is the corkscrew" or "This is the going postal." He's funny, and I appreciate his attempts. And he's kind. Without him, I'd be left standing in the middle of a party, stranded.

After a while, we go back to the pavilion. Tucker's replaced Dean at the rope. It's getting later, and the crowd has thinned out a little.

Franca. Franca sits on one of the couches, entertaining a little throng of men and women. She has on a bright yellow jumpsuit now. I guess one outfit isn't enough for an event like this. Her phone is at the ready, and she checks it every other second. Occasionally someone at her side must say something funny, because Franca lets out an odd, high cackle every so often.

"Todd." I'm not sure what to say to him, but I want it to be along the lines of *Quick! Run!*

His shoulders slump. "Oh, God, not her. I hate her teeth. They creep me out."

He takes my hand, and we glide by the pavilion. As we pass Franca, Todd raises a hand in salute and calls out, "Franca! Darling! It's too fabulous seeing you!"

He doesn't even slow down. She gives a little half wave, looks puzzled, and then turns back to her cadre.

I want to hug him. "I think we have something in common."

He nods, but he looks around for someone else. "Where's our mutual friend, the one we do like?"

I look for Andrew. He's disappeared. He's not on the dance floor. He's not on the couches. My stomach flip-flops. Am I going to turn around and see him with someone else?

Todd must have read my face just now, which I suspect is not a hard thing to do, and he finds Andrew in a jiffy. "Oh, there he is." He points to a table closer to the pool where Andrew smokes and talks casually with an older man in a suit. "He's back to business— that's one of the executive producers."

I breathe out in relief. But I don't like it, that worry. I want to trust him. The fact that I thought he might be off with someone isn't a good sign.

"He likes you a lot. I wasn't kidding that he's told me all about you."

This Todd might just be blessed with the gift of second sight. I needed to hear that right now.

"Sit with me," he says. "We'll have a drink, relax."

I pat him on the hand. "I'm not much of a drinker. I think I'm going to bed."

I can't remember if I brought my little clutch up on the roof with me. I think about asking Tucker.

"Be sure to say good night to him, Kelly. Give him a break."

"I'm doing the best I can. It's hard. I'm not good at this."

Todd strolls back to the couches and the young-looking girls who are lying in wait. "Maybe he's not either," he calls over his shoulder.

I see my clutch on the little table at the edge of the pavilion and retrieve it. Andrew's still at the table with the producer. I don't want to interrupt, especially if it's business. And part of me kind of wants to make a point by leaving without saying anything to him. I don't like having my feelings hurt.

I wave good-bye to Tucker. "I'm going to bed," I mouth to him. He waves back.

I walk toward the elevator but stop along the way to slip my heels off. They will be relegated to the back of the closet in punishment for the beating they've given my feet this night.

I bump into someone as I stand back up. "Sorry."

I turn around, expecting Andrew. It's not. It's the orange girl, the one Andrew took for a twirl out on the dance floor. She sways visibly. Her mascara has slid south, giving her sweaty raccoon eyes. She is very drunk.

"What, bitch?" she asks me.

"What?" I stand with my shoes in my hand.

"What's your problem?" She's louder. Well, this should be fun.

"Good night." I turn my back to her. There's no reasoning with a drunk person. Time to leave.

"Hey!" She grabs at me and catches my shoulder, mostly by the cap sleeve of my dress. It tears off, and she takes a decent chunk of my skin with it, thanks to the dragon-lady nails she's sporting.

"Ow!" I'd really like to kick her ass. I don't think I've ever been in a girl fight before, but man, I am tempted.

But I'm also sober. And at least ten years older than she is. Let's see, if I avoided dancing longer with my boyfriend to stay under the radar, would a bitch-slapping frenzy be a good idea? I chalk one up to my wisdom and experience and stay still.

And anyway, suddenly Tucker's right next to me. This guy is good, I tell you what.

"It's time for you to go home, miss." He takes a step in front of me, shielding me from the drunken harpy. There's a quick bustle. The bouncer from velvet rope number one suddenly has the orange girl by the arm and escorts her to the elevator.

"Tucker, you are my favorite person in the world." I lean into him. Maybe that instinct to hide behind him at the beginning of the night was a good one.

He stoops down and recovers the left sleeve of my dress. "Sorry, Kelly." He looks at the skin on my arm. "She got you good. What a little monster." He mumbles something into the microphone at his sleeve.

I touch my arm and realize I'm bleeding. "You've got to be kidding me." I sit down on the half wall around the pool. What a night.

"Here." A waitress has brought Tucker a white bar towel. He dabs at my arm with it.

"Geez, maybe we need to get you a tetanus shot. Or a rabies shot." He laughs a little, and so do I. Things are ridiculous.

Suddenly I'm aware of a little circle of onlookers. They're dissipating now, since the girl fight didn't materialize, but a tall figure pushes through them and covers the distance to Tucker in a few long strides.

"What's going on?" It's Andrew. Todd saunters up behind him.

"Nothing. Some girl tried to get Kelly to fight her. She's been escorted out of the party."

Todd elbows him. "It was the drunk girl you danced with, dude."

I look up in time to see Andrew see the blood on the bar towel.

"It doesn't even hurt anymore," I tell him quickly. "It just bled for a minute there."

His look is agonized. He doesn't say anything. He puts his hands on top of his head, and he turns around and walks away. Todd follows him, but Andrew brushes him off. I can't tell if he says anything before he disappears through a fire door.

I stand up. "Well, that was just awesome. I'm going to bed. Really. I have a plane to catch in the morning." I throw the towel in the trash and stuff the sleeve of my dress into my clutch.

Todd and Tucker walk me to the elevator. "'Night, Kelly." Tucker gives me a hug.

Todd rides down in the elevator with me. "Clearly she did not get the save-the-drama-for-your-mama memo." He smiles and puts an arm around my shoulders.

"Ow." He hits the shoulder the girl tore up.

"Sorry." He pulls a cigarette from a pack in the pocket of his sweater, tucks it behind one ear. "You know he feels responsible."

"Yep." I wonder if I hold him responsible. I think I'm still deciding.

"He'll want to talk to you."

"I want to go to sleep. He'll have to wait." I save the jab about only talking to sober people. It's just mean.

"Okay." Todd hasn't seemed ruffled by anything that's happened tonight.

"You're one mellow cat, Todd Ford."

"You're one tough cougar, Kelly Reynolds."

He walks me to my room. I go inside and go to bed. I set my cell on silent and take the hotel phone off the hook. I'm done for the night and fall asleep, hard.

I sit at a dining table, long and broad, wood warm and worn

from use. I'm surrounded by a group of young men and women. I don't seem to recognize any faces. They're all having a good time — eating, drinking, talking, and laughing. Candles are lit, and a big feast is laid out on the table. Across from me is Peter. His hair is longer—wildly curly like when we were in college. His eyes sparkle, and he's devilishly handsome. He wears his rowing sweatshirt, the one that was always my favorite. The one I stole and wore because it smelled like him.

Peter smiles, toasts me with his wineglass, drinks deeply.

I smile at him, raise my glass. Someone next to me laughs, too loudly—almost screaming with laughter—and a bottle of wine spills, streaming out across the table. I stand up as the red wine flows toward me. Someone tries to stop the flow with a napkin, but glasses are knocked over, more wine is spilled.

The laughing has turned to yelling now, and I can feel my heart revving up. I look over at Peter, looking for help, for reassurance.

He smiles at me in the middle of all the chaos, then takes another deep drink of his wine. He drinks so deeply the wine overflows the glass, pours down the sides of his mouth, his neck. It looks like blood running down his chest and leaves a wide stain in the sweatshirt, like blood blooming from a wound.

I wake up screaming, drenched in sweat. The hotel room is blank and silent in return.

The next morning I get in the shower, get dressed, and get packed before I get over to my cell phone to change the settings.

When I do, it's clear I missed several calls last night from Andrew. Well, good. That was supposed to be an awesome night, and instead I relived the worst parts of my young adulthood.

I brush my teeth and worry. That stuff is all very far behind me, in my past. But I did it, I lived it. That was kind of par for the course.

How fair is it that I expect him to not be that way? Especially with the superhuman pressure he's under. He's supposed to skip all that stupidity because I'm tired of it? Maybe I'm not being realistic.

But the truth is, I don't want to relive any of it. He's welcome to live it, but I'm pretty sure I don't want to be along for the ride. Besides, he's twenty-nine. The days of college partying should be far behind him too. He should be done with that nonsense by now. Maybe the Hollywood scene is different; I don't know.

But one thing I've learned (of the few things I know, because the list is short, trust me) is that it's neither my responsibility to try to change Andrew nor my right to expect him to behave any differently. He is who he is.

I can't help but feel downhearted. Things had gone so well between us. Almost magically. Okay, miraculously. This sucks.

I try to snap out of it. No relationship is without bumps in the road. He behaved badly last night. Maybe I was too uptight about the whole thing. Maybe I need to take a page from the Todd Ford playbook and chill about it.

There's a knock at the door. I feel an immediate jolt of adrenaline. Here we go.

It's him. His hair is wet. He wears a white T-shirt and jeans, with a thick black belt. He's got on soccer shoes that are falling apart. Todd's fashion sense is getting to him. He looks a lot younger this morning than he did in matinee-idol mode last night.

"Are you okay?" His eyes are wide with concern. They also tell me he didn't sleep much last night. They're rimmed red and have dark circles under them.

I swing the door wide, and he walks in, moving past me without meeting my eyes. I'm not ready to say anything. The ball is in his court on this one.

"Kelly, I'm sorry about last night. I was an idiot. You were right to have your guard up."

"I wasn't doing anything except what we agreed on, keeping a low profile." I feel a little defensive, apparently.

"You're right."

"You were drunk."

"I was stressed, I hadn't had anything to eat, and then Todd showed up, and we just started pounding beers."

"I've never even seen you drink."

"If I'm shooting or prepping for a movie, I don't at all. I actually haven't in a long time . . ."

"All things in moderation."

He stares at his feet, runs a hand through his wet hair. "Yeah. Not really my strong point, remember?"

"We're still finding our way around being together. I get that. One night of partying is not a big deal. But the drama? I've done that in my life. And I am really, really over it."

I stand. I hate this part. All I want is for last night to go away and for us to go back to getting along famously. But he doesn't turn around right away, so I flop down on the bed. A nap is in order right about now. I could sleep all of this away, maybe.

He turns around and comes to me, sits next to me on the bed. He reaches out, gently lifts the sleeve of my T-shirt.

Oh, that. Yeah, there's kind of a bruise and a few bloody claw marks. I wince and pull the sleeve back down. "It's nothing. Just a stupid girl. She was drunk."

"It *was* a big deal. Last night was all my fault. I'm so sorry." He leans over and kisses the scratches on my shoulder.

I'm losing focus. He looks at me. I put my hand on his cheek, kiss him. My whole body reacts to the feeling of him close to me. "We'll do better next time," I murmur.

I let go of the worry. Things have gone really well up to now. Last night was just a bump in the road. I'm trying not to overthink, I remind myself.

He kisses my neck. He kisses me on the lips again and slides his arm behind me, lowering me onto the bed.

Okay, I stand corrected. This is a better cure for our troubles than a nap. I close my eyes and try not to purr.

Media Push Comes to Shove

Andrew is tenderly attentive to me the rest of the morning—carrying my bags to the car, making sure I have everything for the airport. He's careful to kiss me good-bye and apologize again. But as I travel home, I find myself unnerved by last night's experience. We have enough unusual complications. I'd like for that kind of thing not to happen again.

Unfortunately, we don't have an opportunity for a do-over anytime soon. Andrew's about to embark on the notorious and much-dreaded media push: travel to Tokyo, London, Paris, Madrid, New York, and finally back to LA to do press for the movie. The premiere was one thing. Now he's got two packed weeks of interviews and appearances.

This worries me.

I can't imagine traveling so much in so little time. That in itself would suck the life out of me. On top of this, Andrew is expected to be charming and look fabulous all the while.

But he did say he does best when he has a schedule and clear expectations.

So I go back to driving the kids to soccer and swimming and making lunches. At some point, I need to start concocting a plan for me. The domestic goddess thing works for now, but the boys continue to grow, and they're threatening to eventually have their own lives, separate from mine. Which will mean I won't have anyone to ferry around anymore, and soon enough, no one will ask me to buy Skippy peanut butter instead of the store brand because it doesn't have lumps in it.

And at that point, unless I'm planning on hoarding fifty cats and doing the crazy-lady thing, I will need something to do. I need something new, a new direction and a purpose.

When I think about it at length, I get a headache, so very often I change the subject and obsess over my boyfriend instead. Andrew does his best to call, but his itinerary is head spinning. Nevertheless, I think I'm doing a decent job of holding it together with him on every continent and then some.

But I worry about how he's holding it together. I catch some of the press coverage. There's a Web site devoted to him that seems somewhat less rabid than most of what's out there, and it posts pictures and clips of him in Tokyo, doing interviews and signing autographs. He looks tired.

In Spain, there's a moment in the airport when the crowd overwhelms the security detail, and that gets some play on *Entertainment Tonight*. They seem to cover things in regard to Andrew with a spin that feels like they're surprised he gets so much attention. They liken him to the Beatles—but with less of a reason for the fanaticism. The report doesn't make me worried for his safety—I can make out Tucker by his side, leading him out a side door by the arrivals gate—but Andrew's eyes look tired. Vacant. He looks like that distracted guy I saw in Ventura County when he was mad at Jeremy.

When the crowd starts to surge, you can almost see him come back to his senses. He looks surprised as Tucker and airport security hustle him away.

Then he's in New York, and I'm glad to have him back in the country. We talk on the phone and make plans about seeing each other, and it feels good.

But I've forgotten one thing—until I see it on the Internet the next day. New York is home to Todd, the animal, and of course the two of them hit the town.

Now that I know Todd, I don't see him as a mustache-twirling villain who leads Andrew into dire situations against his will. But the two of them have a history together, and it involved getting up to no good. Sometimes high school friends bring out high school behavior.

The picture shows them hailing a cab. Innocent enough, but there's a bodyguard—I can't tell if it's Tucker or Dean—who is very clearly holding Andrew upright, as he is plastered. The hooded eyelids are back. All the feelings from the night of the premiere come back to me.

I don't like it. I have a bad feeling about all of this.

And it's so odd, this voyeurism—following Andrew around the world from afar. Am I spying on him? It feels like it. I don't often seek out information, but at the same time, I'm not avoiding it. I can kind of understand the claustrophobic feeling he describes sometimes. A fishbowl. He's in it. Is it right that I'm there along with all the other cats, watching him swim? I don't know.

So I try to keep the cattiness to a minimum and wait for him to come home to me. Or for the next thing to happen.

My Unfunny Valentine

The next thing is Valentine's Day. After being married for forever, Peter and I kind of let each other off the hook about this. It never felt like a very real holiday, and in the dark of winter, finding a babysitter and fretting about the day was more a hassle than anything else.

But I don't know what to expect with Andrew. Part of me is a little excited. The grown-up part of me reminds the rest of me that Andrew is in the thick of automated dialogue replacement (ADR) from the sheriff movie and stuck in a studio for hours on end. The shoot for *The Last Drive* has wrapped, he's done with the tour for *Churchill's Man* and back in LA, but there's still work to be done. After the drudgery of the media junket, this is not exactly the change he's been looking for, and it's not the satisfying work of acting either.

We talk a few days before the holiday. I wash dishes and catch the phone with wet hands. "Hello?"

"Hey." He coughs.

"You're sick." I dry my hands, listen to him struggle to clear his throat.

"Yeah. And working to keep my voice, so I've got to keep this short."

"This is the ADR stuff?" I don't know this technical movie stuff on my own. He already told me what it was all about. The point is to rerecord lines that weren't clear on set.

"Yeah. I'm dead tired."

"Is Logan with you?" I liked that director. Seems like he'd take care of Andrew through all this extra stuff.

"Sometimes. Mostly it's an engineer on the other side of the glass telling me not to breathe so loudly."

"That does sound fun. Are you getting rest?"

"Better than on the media push. At least I'm in town."

"I wish you could come here."

"I wish I knew what my next job was. Then I could take some time and come up there."

"Something will come up. You're amazing."

He coughs again. I can't tell if it's a sarcastic response to my compliment, or if it's because he's sick. "I better go."

"Okay. Talk to you soon. Take care of yourself." I want to reach through the phone and hold him.

So on Valentine's Day I'm a little disappointed when flowers don't come, and neither does a phone call. The boys are already asleep, and I'm getting ready for bed when the phone rings. Okay, it makes me happy. He's thought of it.

I answer the phone. "Hello?"

There isn't a response. I can hear breathing.

"Hello? Andrew?" This is the age of caller ID. I know it's his cell. And it's the new number, not the one that was stolen a while ago.

Still no response, just more ragged breathing. Then a cough. A rough, hacking cough.

"Andrew?" Now I start to worry a bit. "Andrew, are you there?"

"I'm here." He's drunk. Completely drunk. Two words, and I know. My heart clenches into a knot, and I feel adrenaline shoot into my shoulders and straight down my arms.

"Where are you? Are you all right?" The helpless feeling of being two states away is mixed with anger. He's drinking. This is not good.

"Just out." There's a weird little breathy laugh.

I don't even know what that means. "Are you by yourself? Are you home?" My brain races through all sorts of dilemmas: another woman, drunk driving, drunk at home alone, out on the town, in a bar, somewhere embarrassing for his career, you name it. Nothing feels right about this.

"I miss you." Again, this is barely intelligible. "I want you. I want you, Kelly Jo Renaa-reynoldsss." He botches my name, and this makes him laugh again.

Well, I've gone straight to pissed. This is a visceral response from me. There's no straight thinking about it. "Is someone there with you?"

"No. I took a cab home. Jesus, you don't have to worry. I'm not dumb."

Oh, no, I'm not going to be lectured about this from the drunk ass on the other end of the line. I am the wiser, sober one here. "You, of all people, need to be smart about this. For all sorts of reasons."

"Fine."

"You're alone?" This is me at my most insecure.

"There's no one but you. Not that they don't try."

I don't even want to talk anymore. I'm quiet, and there's more drunken breathing on the other end of the line.

"Be safe," I tell him after a moment. "I'm going to bed."

I can't do this. I'm mad, and there's no point in arguing with a drunk. The second I think that, it hurts. I don't want to think of Andrew as a drunk. A *person* who is drunk is bad enough at the moment, but it feels like this is a habit. Has been a habit. I hate it. I want to undo all of this, go back to thinking he was perfect.

There's no response for a minute, and then I hear crying, like sobbing crying. All my anger melts away. "Andrew?"

"I'm sorry. I'm sorry. I'm terrible to you."

"Oh, Andrew. Just go to sleep. You need to stop doing this. You're under a lot of stress, and this is not helping."

"Okay." He coughs again, and he sounds awfully sick. "I love you, Kelly."

It breaks my heart. What is going on there? I can't figure out why he's falling apart so badly. "I love you too. You're at home?"

"Yeah."

"Go to bed. It will feel better in the morning. Call me then."

There's no more crying that I can hear. He's just breathing again. "Okay. I love you."

The line goes dead. Suddenly, I panic. What if he does something stupid?

I pace around my living room, trying to slow my breathing enough to focus. I know dark places and what they feel like. I know how it can seem as if the world is ending. And Andrew doesn't have kids to pull him out of it, like I did after Peter died.

This thought puts me in a tailspin, but in the middle of the dive I might not be able to pull up from, I have a moment of inspiration. I'll call Tucker.

He's not necessarily working, but he's got to be around. The media push hasn't been that long ago. Will he be mad? I feel like we've bonded.

Screw it. Surely he's put up with worse behavior from his clients than a woman worried about the health of a man she cares for. Seems reasonable compared to trashing a hotel room, for instance.

I pick up my cell and find Tucker's number. It's a terrible time of night, but it is the weekend, so even if he's not covering Andrew, he's probably covering somebody. Or he's on a date of his own. In that case, I'm ruining his night. I weigh my options and call. I'm desperate.

It rings once. "Tucker Caldwell." He's working. That's a business voice.

"Tucker, it's Kelly. Kelly Reynolds." God, I hope he remembers me.

"Kelly, is everything all right?" He sounds concerned.

"I don't know. Are you with Andrew?"

"No, I've been working with someone else this week. He's just doing ADR. No appearances."

"Can I ask you a huge favor?"

"Of course."

"He called me just now. He sounded horrible. He was drunk and really out of sorts. I'm worried."

There's a long pause. I'm reminded of our conversation about people in Andrew's business. Tucker said something about Andrew being young, and sometimes losing sight of the big picture. Maybe this was what he was referring to. Maybe I'm right that this is not new behavior. Heck, at this point it's not even that new to me.

"I'll check on him." He pauses again. I can't read his tone.

"Does he do this a lot?" Might as well get all the info I can now.

"Before I worked for him, when he first came out here, some stuff happened. I don't know about that; you'd have to ask Andrew. But I haven't seen him like this before. Maybe a night or two where he overdid it a few times since I've known him, but not like this. He's not handling himself, this last stretch, well. The press and then the post-production. And maybe being apart from you."

"Great."

"Not to guilt-trip you—that's not what I meant. Todd's in New York; you're gone. I think he's lonely. And when he's done with ADR, he has nothing to look forward to. He likes to be planning for the next movie. He doesn't have that lined up yet, so it'll just be an open schedule. He doesn't do well with downtime."

Andrew told me that himself, right at the beginning of things.

"Thank you, Tucker. Thank you for being so honest with me."

I can hear voices. Tucker is somewhere different from when the call started. "I'll check on him, Kelly. I have to go."

"Thanks, Tucker. Thanks so much."

There's a dry laugh. "Happy Valentine's Day, huh?"

"God. After all this I totally forgot. Yeah, you too."

This might be one of the crappier ones.

The Visit

Andrew drunk-dials me like this two more times in the next three weeks before I make the decision to go see him. It's not an intervention exactly, but I need to assess this situation from up close, not from Boise, Idaho. He still sounds terribly sick, and once when he calls during the day, he doesn't remember the call from the night before. This is bad.

It's spring break. The boys have soccer camp, and Andrew's tied up with post-production, so we hadn't planned on anything special. Which is good, because I need to do this. I prepare to go to him. I leave the boys in the capable hands of Tessa on a Friday evening and gear up to face down whatever's waiting for me in California.

When I get to LAX, I call him.

"Hello?"

"Hey, Andrew."

"What's up?" His voice still sounds sick, and he coughs, barking.

"I'm here in LA. Where are you?"

"I just got home. You're here? Why?"

I thought it would be obvious. Maybe not to him. "You've sounded so sick. I thought I'd come and take care of you a little. Help you get well."

I'm only partially talking about the terrible cough. And there's a nagging in the back of my head. This might not be something I can fix. I should know that. I'm an adult with a brain. Magic wands can't be waved to put people right.

"Are you staying with your folks?"

Uh-oh. Did I assume too much when I figured we were at the stay-at-each-other's-house stage of our relationship? It felt like that's where we left off.

"No, I thought I'd stay with you."

"Oh, okay. Great. Do you need a ride?" He's coughing again.

"I'm taking a cab. I'll see you in a while."

When I arrive, I have the cab drop me at the house across the street. I wait, puttering with my luggage, and then pull my roller over to the gate and press the buzzer. The gate clicks open without a word from inside.

Parked in the courtyard is a brand-new Tesla, sparkling white, with the vanity plate GD2B KNG.

Jeremy.

He strolls out of Andrew's front door. He's got on a pink Polo, collar popped, cuffed chinos, and very expensive-looking driving moccasins. Good lord.

"Look who it is!" He grins and opens his arms for a hug.

I can't believe it. "No hug." I shake my head.

He laughs. "You crack me up. I'm sorry about the premiere."

"I'm with Andrew. Despite your best efforts."

He leans on the hood of his car. "Aw, now, give me a little credit. I'm just making sure he's not getting used. No offense."

"How is he?"

"He's sicker than shit. Are you here to help?" He swings his car keys around his finger. He always looks so calm, collected. I wish I could rattle him.

"That's the plan. What're you here for?"

Jeremy's lips tighten into a smile. "Same thing you are. I think, my friend, that you and I may be on the same team."

"I thought you were Team Franca."

He snorts. "I'm Team Andy-Sells-Tickets. I could give a rat's ass about Franca, but until that movie premieres, I'll continue to keep the two of them in the headlines, on the top of the Web searches. Because I'd like my client to have a job. And after that, another job. That's how I have a job."

I actually feel bad for a second. "I understand you have a job to do."

"Listen, right now I'm running late for a meeting where the female studio head is going to metaphorically kick me in the balls for two hours straight. You go take care of Andy. Believe me that I will take care of his business."

"Okay."

He pops open the door of his car. "And tell Tucker to stop with the pained expression. He looks like he swallowed a yardstick sideways."

"See you."

"'*Asta*." He gets in his car, revs the engine, and peels out.

Tucker walks out the door. He smiles wide when he sees me.

"Hey, Tucker!" I leave my bag and go to him, giving him a big hug. "What're you doing here?"

He looks tired. "I gave Andrew a ride home from downtown. He's almost done with post, but he's been so sick, I drove him."

I feel the worry crawl its way into my belly. I kept it at bay on the way here, justifying calm because I was taking action to fix things.

"Has he been to the doctor?"

"Just today. It's walking pneumonia. He's got to take it easy for a while."

"I only have the week. Can his mom come out? She could help when I leave."

Tucker shrugs. "She doesn't fly. I don't even think she gets out of the house much. And Todd would come out, but his band just left for a tour in Europe two days ago."

"Well, I guess I'll have to whip him into shape in the time I have. Is he off for a while at least?"

Tucker nods. "In two days, he will be. They have some pickup shots to do. Thank God it's just some tweaks for the CGI guys. He can't talk, much less act. But I don't know if it's a good thing or not for him to be done. You know he likes to be busy."

I do, but beyond Andrew saying just that, I've never been able figure out why. I know, I could quote various adages about idle hands and devils, yadda yadda, but where is that coming from with Andrew? He's always seemed so together . . . Well, until recently. I don't know.

Tucker gives me one more hug and leaves me in the driveway. I'm surprised Andrew hasn't made it out to the courtyard. He must be really sick.

I let myself in. The house is quiet. The living room looks the way I saw it last. The kitchen is empty and doesn't look like it's been used much. It includes an array of cereal boxes much like the one Andrew had in Ventura County. Some mail is on the kitchen island.

I go upstairs. As I get nearer the master bedroom, I can hear him coughing. He still sounds terrible. His cough is a bark like a seal's.

"Hello?" I swing the door open.

There's a humidifier in one corner. On the bedside table is a collection of Kleenex, cough drops, pill bottles, cough syrups. The bed is strewn with scripts, magazines, and newspapers. Andrew's propped up on pillows in the center.

He looks terrible.

"Hi." He tries to focus on me. His eyes are sick, his skin grayish-white.

I am genuinely scared. I sit on the edge of the bed and take his hand. I can't help it, I start to cry.

"That bad?"

I can't say anything.

He smiles. "It's okay. It's just a bad cold."

"It's pneumonia. Tucker told me."

"I'm fine. I already feel better." He coughs again, like his body can't help but tell me the truth. "Listen, I promise, this isn't a reason to worry."

"It's just, I have to say, this is the worst kind of déjà vu."

His face registers. He gets what I mean. Peter.

He runs a hand through his hair. "God. Now I feel like a total ass for not taking better care of myself."

I shake my head. "No, no, I didn't say that to make you feel bad. It just sort of knocked me flat when I walked in the door."

He sits up. "Here's what's going to happen. I'll hibernate, you'll try to make some chicken soup—and who are we kidding, it'll be out of a can—and then it'll all be good. No worries."

I grip his hand. "You're right. We'll fix it. I'll make you soup, make you some tea, and we'll get you better."

He closes his eyes. "I hope so, 'cause honestly, I feel like shit." His face seems to relax. "I'm glad you're here."

"I wish you could just come to Idaho for a while. I could take care of you."

"This is where the work is. Could you stay here for a bit?"

"The boys go back to school next week. Spring break, you know."

"Yeah. I guess you can't play house. You've got a real one to go back to and all."

"Maybe someday it'll all be the same thing." I'm trying to say something here, I think, that involves the two of us living in the same place. Not that I'm saying it clearly, or anything, but . . .

"I don't know." He's noncommittal. Or too sick to focus. Either way, it doesn't feel good. Time to change the topic.

"Sleep."

I take a minute and clean up the whole room. I commandeer the stuff by the bedside. I make sure the humidifier is clean. I pull all the towels from the bathroom to wash in scorching hot water and bleach. I dig around and find him a new toothbrush and throw out the one from the cup on the sink.

I will do battle with his illness. This is something I know how to do. And the encouraging thing here? Pneumonia is something people recover from. Especially young, healthy men. This thought takes a little of the panic out of my head.

After I get a very basic pot of chicken noodle soup on the stove, I mill about for a while. The house is basically clean. I don't think Andrew's been spending much time here. Besides working, I try not to think too much about where else he's been of late. I find a can of orange juice in the freezer and whip that up, but there's not much more to do.

He's still sleeping. This is a tempting opportunity. I know I've been wavering about invading his privacy. But a little looking around his house is irresistible. I make a bargain with myself that I won't open drawers. Maybe that makes it okay.

In the living room, I spend a little time at the piano. There are sheaves of sheet music with assorted scribbles. I hope he's been writing. I suspect it's therapeutic for him. He needs something, I can tell. I can only pump him full of chicken soup for a few days, and then he has to work out on his own whatever is bugging him.

On the top of the piano are photographs. Most of them I can tell are his family: his folks, his sisters, pictures of him with all of them. There's one picture that intrigues me, though. It's a young girl, high school age or so. Cute, curly blond hair. No one who looks like him. It looks like a senior picture.

My interest is piqued. We haven't had the discussion of the exes. My discussion is short, I guess, and involves basically just the one whopper of a former love, Peter. So I guess we've had that talk. But I haven't asked him about his past loves. Because why? I need to know about the drop-dead gorgeous models and actresses he's been with? I don't know if I need more fuel for the freak-out fire.

I flip the picture over. The frame's nondescript, but there's writing in gold pen on the back: "Emily Waylon."

It's not Andrew's handwriting. I try not to freak out. This is someone important.

Now, try not to judge me. I go to my laptop. Yes, I'm looking her up. Is it snoopy? Yes. Should I just ask him? Yes. Am I afraid to, especially since he's been in such bad shape lately? Yes.

I fire up my computer. I type in her name and his home state, Pennsylvania. There's an obituary. I click on it.

It makes me physically sick. She had recently graduated from high school, was a sophomore in college. Midyear. It's a beautiful death notice, and it most notably does not list a cause of death. I've read enough obituaries (hell, I've written one) to know that often a family leaves off that detail if the loved one took her own life.

My hands tremble, but I go to IMDb and type in Andrew's name. I've never actually looked at his bio on here. Now I'm looking for Emily's name.

There she is. It actually has quite a poignant paragraph, even quotes him from an early interview. She was a good friend in high school. I click on the interview citation and go straight to the magazine archives for the article.

It's long. It's about his role in the remake of *Camille*, about where Andrew's inspiration might have come from for such an emotional movie. There are very few direct quotes from him besides the one IMDb mined. Much of it seems to have come from "sources." I wonder who would give up such a sensitive part of Andrew's life to a national magazine. Someone who didn't care for him too much.

They dated, he and Emily, according to the article. They broke up when he moved to LA and she went off to college. They remained in contact, remained good friends. When she was a sophomore, she sank into a deep depression. She was planning to come out to LA to see him on her spring break that year. In February, he canceled on her, having just landed a role on a soap opera. He received word on his birthday, the first of April, that she'd been found in her dorm room, dead. She'd taken too many of her prescription sleeping pills. The death was ruled an accidental overdose. Andrew did not attend the funeral, and the article goes on to quote a "Hollywood insider" who relates that his agent had to haul him out of a hotel room to report for his first day of shooting on his first real acting job. He'd apparently been drinking heavily.

I stare at the screen. His birthday is in three weeks. It all falls into place. Yes, the movie tour; yes, the constant work; yes, the illness; and maybe missing me and/or Todd. But Tucker left out one big thing: an anniversary that he probably doesn't even know about. All of this makes sense to me now.

What am I going to do with this newfound information? Not a thing. It was a breach of privacy. I shouldn't know about it. I'll take this information and use it to deepen my patience and understanding, but unless Andrew decides to confide in me, as far as he's concerned, I know nothing of it. Everyone is allowed a few secrets. And the trouble is, no one seems to allow Andrew any secrets.

I spend the rest of the afternoon feeling like the heel that I am. When Andrew finally wakes up, I tend to him. I try to give him as much tender care as he must have needed ten years ago, and I hope it's enough to help him out of the quicksand he seems to be slipping into right now.

Blue Midnight

Andrew struggles through another day of post-production work, and I clean his house from top to bottom. Clearly something is wrong—I never clean. And his house isn't even dirty. Jeremy contributes to the cause by sending over dinner. Once Andrew is home, we eat a little, talk a little, drink tea, and Andrew collapses into bed, exhausted.

I fall asleep in one of the other bedrooms, but only after I spend a good amount of time staring at the ceiling, clutched in panic. I worry about having left the boys to come down here. I worry they're mad Tessa is running them to spring break camps instead of me. I worry about the Emily information. I worry about Andrew. I fidget with the fringe on the bedspread, and I'm pretty sure I've gnawed all of my fingernails down to the nub.

I do actually sleep, because I wake up in blue moonlight. I sit up. It's not a nightmare that's woken me. It's sound. I don't know what it is at first. Then I listen, fully awake.

It's the piano.

I slip quietly down the stairs. Andrew sits at the piano. He plays softly, making little notes on a sheet of staff paper on the top of the piano every so often. There is a lit cigarette in an ashtray next to the sheet music.

"Hey," I announce myself.

He startles. "Jesus. I didn't know you were up."

"Why aren't you asleep?" I touch his hand. The feel of his skin stirs something in me, but I keep my focus on his eyes, looking to read them for a clue.

"No reason." He looks away from me, busies himself stubbing out the cigarette.

"Andrew."

"I'm so tired, but I lie down, and there are too many things." He leans into me, draws me to him, and I feel his breath on my neck.

"You can't get better if you don't rest. All those things? I was boring a hole through your ceiling earlier, worrying about them. Let me worry for you. You rest."

"A designated worrier." He smiles, then frowns as a coughing fit comes on.

I rub his back and wait for it to subside. "Come to bed."

"I want to, and what I really want to do is lie down and kiss every inch of you. I don't think I have the energy, of course, but still." He laughs a little. Then another thought must come to him, because his expression clouds over again.

"Stop. Stop and rest." I take his hand and lead him away from the piano. He follows me up the stairs, to his bedroom. He climbs into bed, and I sit on the edge.

"When I'm better, we have a lot of lost time to make up for." He traces my cheek down to my lip with his thumb, thinks for a moment, and lies back, arms over his head on the pillow. I think he's about a second from sleep.

"What were you writing?"

His eyes suddenly fill with tears. "I promised someone a song once. I never got a chance to write it. I was thinking I might write it now."

Emily. That's the someone. My heart might break for him. "I think you should. It's never too late to keep a promise."

"I don't know about that . . ." His voice trails off. He's finally let go, and he's asleep.

I go back to my bed and cry myself to sleep.

Castles in the Sand

I know the party in Malibu is a bad idea from the get-go. But it's been four days, Andrew seems to be feeling a little better, and I want to be supportive. Plus, I wonder if getting out might be a good distraction. He's an adult, and if he says the house party is a good idea, I'll trust he's right. I want to trust him.

"It's mostly going to be networking." Andrew's talking while he drives. I'm riding shotgun in the black convertible. The spring weather is warm today, and his cough is sounding better. We have the top down. Maybe he'll get a little color in the afternoon light.

"This is the producer from *Churchill's Man*?"

"Yeah. He never wants to let it go. It's been like six weeks since the premiere, but he'll probably invite some writers to the house to-night too, in hopes that one of them'll wheedle an interview out of me. More press for the movie." This makes Andrew seem tired again.

"But the other guy?"

"Yeah. Greg Nero'll also be there, and he's shopping a movie around that I'm interested in. It's about Northern Ireland in the eighties. I guess it was bad then."

I skip the part where I tell him I was alive and old enough to remember how bad it was. But that movie is enough reason for us to go to this party. This party means his next job, potentially, and by all appearances, he needs to go back to work.

I think again about Emily. In a normal relationship, I wouldn't know about her. I'd just be confused about why he's been falling apart, and really worried. Now, through the magic of the Internet, I'm still really worried, but I know where some of this might be coming from. I wonder if he's intentionally skipped mentioning his birthday to me too.

"You know, you've got a birthday coming up." I think I can mention this safely.

"Don't remind me. April Fool's, isn't that rich?" His tone seems bitter.

"What do you want to do for it?"

"You mean, me and you?"

Uh-oh. Are we not thinking in me-and-you terms? "What do you usually do for your birthday?"

He doesn't take his eyes off the road. "Out here, not much. Sometimes Todd's around and we go out, or once we went to Mexico for the weekend. Usually my folks call, my sisters send me cards their kids have made, Jeremy sends me a gift basket full of stuff I hate, and that's about it. To be honest, Kelly, there are a lot of reasons why my birthday always sucks. Some of them I should tell you about."

My heart jumps. "You know I'll always listen."

"I want to tell you. Maybe not on the way to a party in Malibu, but . . ."

"Well, we should do something for your birthday before I go back home. You're almost thirty—maybe you'll catch up to me soon. I've stopped aging, you know." I'm trying desperately to put a smile on his face. "Maybe we can make it a good occasion again."

He doesn't take the bait. "Yeah, we could do something."

I'm changing the subject. If that wasn't the most lackluster response, I don't know what is. "As soon as you start feeling tired tonight, we should leave. You're finally feeling a little better. No reason to overdo it."

He nods absently, eyes still on the road. "Yeah."

When we get there, a valet takes the car, and we go around to the back of a beautiful beach house. It's perched on a bluff overlooking the ocean. There's a long, winding staircase that leads down to the shore. The whole house is open to the warm sea air, and candles float in the azure swimming pool.

I'm relieved because this is nothing like the wild crowd I encountered at the premiere after-party some weeks ago. Apparently producers know more people who are around my age, because some of them are in attendance at this function. And the tone is mellow. I relax a little bit. Maybe this will be fine. I think I've been bracing for something ugly. Maybe there's no need to worry this time.

Andrew hands me a glass of wine, and I notice he has a beer in his hand. I speak before I even realize what I sound like. "Be careful. The cough syrup you took this morning packs a punch."

He rolls his eyes. "Okay, Mom." But he gives me a little side squeeze and a smile.

Jeremy materializes next to me. I jump. I forgot to ask Andrew what our story is. I don't know the protocol for tonight. Is a private party a safe place to conduct ourselves as boyfriend/girlfriend, or are we still stealth-dating?

"Kelly Reynolds. So fabulous to see you." Jeremy gives me the kiss-on-each-cheek hello. What a snake. A charming snake, but still.

He steps back, both of my hands in his. "You look radiant. How's your visit been?" He apparently wants something.

"It's been fine. Thanks for asking." I give him the up and down, since he just did it to me. He's wearing a linen shirt and slacks, Italian loafers. Again, Jeremy's general style says "I'm playing it cool," but behind that is a very careful decision to look relaxed and casual.

"Andy, good to see you. You still look like shit, my friend." Jeremy shakes his head.

"Thanks." Andrew gives him a nod.

Jeremy turns to me. "Let me show you the house."

I look at Andrew. He shrugs. Oh well. I'll have little to do at this party, and this'll buy Andrew some time to visit with that producer he wanted to chat up about the role.

Jeremy takes my hand and leads me in through the patio doors.

"How are you?" he asks.

"I'm fine. What's up?" We walk through the huge living room to a stairway, which I can see leads to a large mezzanine area that overlooks the pool.

"Let's go on up here where we can hear ourselves think."

Once we're up the stairs, he goes to the railing out on the deck above the pool. I stand next to him, rest my arms on the edge. We can see Andrew from here. He's on the other side of the pool, close to the spa area and the overlook to the ocean. He's out of earshot. Of course he is. Jeremy is calculating. He meant for us to be out of earshot.

I look at Andrew. He looks tired. He's too thin. His color is still not good. He stands, talking, but his shoulders slope forward. It's barely perceptible, but still a sign of his general state of fatigue. I want to drag him out of here and back to bed.

"He looks a little better." Jeremy says this gently. I would even venture to say with a caring tone.

"He shouldn't be here. And not with a beer in his hand."

A couple comes up next to us. Jeremy's clearly not comfortable with them as close as they are. He takes me by the elbow. "Let's go somewhere more private."

I feel like I'm in a spy movie. We retreat inside, and he pulls me over to a couch tucked into a corner of the second level.

"Kelly, this is a bad time of year for him. Always."

Jeremy knows. He knows about Emily. "I know."

"He told you?" He sounds surprised.

I feel ashamed. "No, I found out about it."

He thankfully doesn't press the issue. "Well, this year it's worse than usual. He's been working really hard. Now he's sick. And he doesn't have a role to get ready for yet."

I wait to see if he's going to reference the drinking.

"Kelly, I was there the first time. I'm the one who dragged his ass out of the hotel room and to his first job. He came this close to never even getting a chance in this business because of it." His index finger and thumb are perilously close to one another for emphasis. He considers for a moment, and then goes for it. "You seem like you're good for him."

"I don't know." I don't know where this is going, but with Jeremy, I can be sure it's going somewhere.

"Well, I do. He can't drink the way he has been. It almost ruined him once. I can't tell him. Maybe he'll listen to you. I won't have it affecting his career, and if he's this sick, it's going to."

"Being sick is human."

"Being sick because you haven't been sleeping because you've been out tearing it up isn't human, it's juvenile. And not good for business."

"He's a person, not just your business."

"Fuck, I know that. Of course I know that. I care about him. I want him to be well. Just talk to him, please. Remember, we're on the same team."

Jeremy's up off the couch and headed to find a new conversation before I can respond. Sharks have to keep swimming, I tell myself. They always have to be moving. After a few moments I see him down by the pool, and lo and behold, Franca Delaney materializes next to him. For a second I almost feel sorry for Jeremy, getting cornered by the human hyena. Almost.

Now I fully intend to go find Andrew. I don't think my plan involves the Jeremy-endorsed lecture, but I do want to check and see how he is.

Instead, I'm intercepted again. This time it's by Gerry, Andrew's costar in the sheriff movie. He's a sweet man. He strikes up a conversation, and then takes it upon himself to introduce me around to a host of people he knows at the party. I do actually appreciate it, on the one hand. I should be giving Andrew the space he needs to do some business. On the other hand, if he's not up to business, then I'm just giving him time to get into trouble.

But for crying out loud, he's a grown-up. And if he doesn't have that self-control, I need to think about what that says about him and his drinking.

Maybe it's more accurate to say drinking problem.

This interior monologue gnaws at my skull for most of the time I spend with Gerry. Finally, I notice the deepening blue of the sky above the ocean, and I find a way to excuse myself. I return to the pool terrace in search of Andrew.

I can't find him. I have no idea where he is. I text him, but get no response. I go back inside and make several laps of the upstairs and down. Where is he? I start to shake a little.

I hate this. It's fundamentally clear that I have no trust in him. That's no way to build a relationship, and that's more my problem than his. We need to have a serious talk. I've been trying to leave him alone since he's sick, but this can't wait.

As soon as I find him. I drift back out to the pool.

Jeremy sees me and steps away from his conversation. "What's up?"

"I can't find him." I sound panicked. I am panicked.

"He's probably in the house. He was in there chatting up some producers earlier."

"No, I was just in there."

"Check the stairs. Maybe he's down on the beach. I'll make another swing through the house." Jeremy looks at me, and I can see it in his eyes. He's worried too.

I walk to the far edge of the bluff to look out over the ocean.

There's a bonfire on the beach, some distance below the house at the bottom of the winding staircase I noticed earlier. I've checked everywhere else, so I start down the stairs.

As I descend, I can hear the surf more clearly, but I can also hear voices. It sounds like two people. It sounds like Andrew and someone else. A female someone else.

My teeth chatter. Yes, it's a cool evening, but this is in response to the fight-or-flight surge coursing through my body. I long to be in full antelope mode and flee, but I force myself to keep putting one foot in front of the other all the way down the stairs.

"And Franca?" The woman's speaking. Her voice is clear and clean above the surf.

"She's a friend." Andrew's voice is muddled by his cough.

"Friend with benefits?" The girl laughs, but something's not ringing true.

"No, no, no." He laughs hard. Too hard. He's drunk. I look at my watch. Yes, it's been probably two hours. But this is a man with a problem. Someone told me once that to an alcoholic, the first drink is like falling off a cliff. There's no going back. I remember Andrew's comment to me about no switch. He can't turn it off. I want to weep. This sucks, and this is the reason he and I won't make it together.

That realization hits me hard, but I press forward. I still need to get him home tonight. He's sick, and drinking problem or no, his first problem is getting over pneumonia.

As if on cue, he coughs.

"I should take you home," the woman suggests. "I have a cure for that cough."

"I've got a ride." He's coughing again. This fit is a longer one.

I can see them, silhouetted by the orange ball of fire behind them. The woman is sitting close. She's patting him on the back now, trying to still the coughs.

"He does, that's true." I announce as I'm approaching. I call it announcing. It's probably more like yelling, but let's not split hairs.

The woman straightens up, surprised. "Who're you?" She's beautiful: huge black hair and dark eyes, luscious full lips.

"I'm the one who's taking my sick friend home." I put myself between them.

She stands up. "Interview's over, I guess."

"Are you a reporter?"

"Maybe." She looks around, uncomfortable. Good.

"I think maybe you should leave now."

"Whatever."

I stand my ground and consider growling at her. Behind me, Andrew tries to laugh but loses it to another round of coughing. He's not on his feet yet, and I'm glad. I'll deal with him in a minute.

She stalks away, back up the staircase. I don't know how Andrew's going to make it. I don't know if he can catch his breath to climb. This is a sick déjà vu to standing with another man I loved, listening to him try to catch his breath. I have to sit for a second to bear the brunt of the feeling.

Andrew stands. "Nice." He thrusts his hands clumsily into his pockets, and he tries to walk off down the beach. He stumbles a bit and stops.

"Nice, what?" I am mad. I am steaming mad.

"She's just a reporter."

"Yeah, I noticed. And you're a drunk talking to a reporter." I pull up even with him.

He turns to face me. "Nice." He takes off down the beach again.

He's got a bigger stride, but I'm sober, so we're an even match in the storming-off competition. "No. No, you're not going to be all self-righteous with me."

He stops, and I grab him by the elbow.

"Look at me."

He does. Why I'm talking to him, I don't know. He more than likely won't remember this in the morning.

"What?"

"You're on a dangerous path. You're sick, and you're drinking. Plus you're talking to some vulture. And she's flirting with you . . . or something."

I shouldn't have added that last part, because that's the part he latches on to.

"Do you think I'd even take that bait? You give me no credit." He shakes off my hold on his elbow and starts down the beach again.

This has to stop. He's going nowhere, and I need to get him home. We can argue tomorrow. Or whatever. Right now it's getting colder and colder, and he's got pneumonia.

"Andrew. Andrew, stop." I try to get him by the elbow again. I use a softer tone. "Andrew, we need to get you home."

He shakes his arm up and out of my grasp with a hard jerk. I catch the business end of that hard jerk and lose my balance, falling backward. My hands go out behind me, and I feel something sharp under my right arm as I land in the sand.

I sit there for a minute. The pain comes quickly. I see the glint of broken glass. Great. Andrew stands above me as I turn my arm over, revealing a sizable gash.

Yes, Andy Pettigrew just pushed me down and cut me. Not on purpose, but I can see the headlines now. His life is over. I feel a trickle of blood on the inside of my elbow and immediately get up and look around for a place to run.

"Kelly—"

I shake my head. "No, Andrew. Look." The reporter woman has turned around and is coming back down toward us.

This is not how this is going to end. I will not allow it.

I break into a run, fumbling for my cell in my pocket. I look back to see him crumpled, kneeling on the sand with his head in his hands.

I lengthen my stride to put as much distance between us as possible. The crash of the waves becomes the only sound in my ears, and when I turn to look back, the bonfire is a distant dot behind me on the beach. I finally stop for a moment, try to collect my thoughts. I call Tucker.

"Hello?"

"It's Kelly. Tucker, call Jeremy. He needs to find Andrew, down on the beach. Now."

"What happened? Where are you?"

I look up at the lights in the distance, kick off my shoes to run faster in the cool, loose sand. "I'll call you back when I know where I am."

As usual, running finds me in my time of trouble, and I'm rescued by the rhythm of it. There's blood down my arm, and I can tell there may be stitches involved. It hurts, but that's not why I'm crying. Obviously. But the sand is soft and smooth, and I try to focus on that.

There's a road. I run to it, looking for a sign. The brightest lights on the street are a fancy little restaurant. I run up the beach access road to the parking lot and make the call.

"Tucker?"

"Yeah. Jeremy got Andrew. What's going on?"

"I'm at Geoffrey's in Malibu." I walk around the parking lot, trying to look normal as I dust the sand from my bare feet and cover the cut on my arm.

"I'll be there in a minute and take you to Andrew's."

"Tucker, I'm staying at a hotel. Any that you can recommend would be great. And I can get a cab."

There's silence. "I'm coming to get you. What about your things?"

"We can figure that out tomorrow. I'm going to see when I can get a flight out."

Tucker's in the parking lot in his plain little sedan in record time. He swings the door open without getting out, without leaving his seat. I climb in.

He looks at me, at my arm, and his face falls. "What the hell?"

I've never seen Tucker drop his guard. "I fell."

"Bullshit. We're calling the police." His cell phone is in his hand.

"Tucker. Stop. He didn't hit me—he didn't push me. He elbowed me. And he didn't mean to. I fell on some glass. But I know how it looks, which is why you're picking me up in the parking lot of a restaurant."

He's grasping the phone so tightly there's a strong possibility it will be crushed. "You just took off?"

"Running's kind of a reflex. Look, you called it. He's a mess."

He's quiet. We're driving now, but he still hasn't put his phone down.

"It's everything you thought was wrong, plus one more thing Jeremy knows about."

Finally Tucker speaks. "Jeremy told me today. A girl he knew, on his birthday."

"Ten years ago in a few weeks."

Tucker looks at me and my arm again.

I shake my head. "I know it's not an excuse. I can't be a part of his drinking. He needs help."

"Jeremy got him. He said he was completely wrecked and calling your name. Jeremy had to sit with him on the sand to get him to quiet down."

I like the image of Jeremy getting his perfectly casual outfit all sandy. I'd laugh if I didn't hurt—and if I didn't want to sob out loud right now.

"Thanks for coming to get me."

We're returning to the city, and Tucker doesn't look away from the road. "I'll always come get you, no matter where you are, Kelly. Right now you need stitches and a tetanus shot."

I can't answer. He takes me to the ER, gets me fixed up, checks me into a hotel, pays for it with who knows whose credit card, and doesn't leave until he knows my flight number out in the morning. He will be the one who collects my things from Andrew's, picks me up from the hotel, and puts me on the plane home the next day.

I will be the one who covers my stitches with a long-sleeved shirt when I dress in the morning and ignores the phone calls and texts from a very flawed young man. If there was a line to be drawn in the sand, getting hurt might have been it. As much as l love him, and as much as I know he's suffering, I can't be an unintended casualty of that suffering. I have responsibilities beyond myself. I send him one last text before I board the plane back to my old life. It's simple:

Don't call me again.

Unraveling

There are many reasons I do not wear mascara on a regular basis. Number one, I never did jump on the makeup bandwagon. I had no older sister to teach me, and my mom was a strictly au naturel hippie chick. Also, since then I have streamlined my morning routine to take as little time as possible. At some point I wisely admitted that waking up early is one of the worst things in the world, and I now do everything I can to avoid it. So skipping the mascara is my two minutes or thirty seconds or whatever time shaved from when I have to get up in the morning.

Plus, I'm that terrible person who doesn't always wash her face at night. If you don't use a trowel to load on the makeup in the morning, it's not the biggest deal at night to collapse on the bed without your face washed. And I'm also the person who, when applying mascara, either pokes herself in the eye or leaves a smudge smack in the middle of her eyelid that won't come off.

I'm getting to a point here. The biggest reason I don't wear mascara except for oh-so-special occasions is that I cry.

As Tessa says, I ugly cry. Not a little moisture out of one side of an eye, it's fat tears falling down my face, snotty nose. All of it meeting on my cheeks until I use a tissue or convenient sleeve. If things are especially bad, this will also be accompanied by lots of odd snorty sounds.

I cry at commercials. I cry when someone sings "The Star-Spangled Banner" and doesn't mangle it. I cry at assemblies when I see how much fun the kids are having. I cry from total sleep deprivation and exhaustion when I've been up trying to fix and save the people I love.

It's safe to say I've not been wearing any mascara lately.

I'm back to full-on worry mode about the future. I know—just because things have taken a turn, as my reserved English friend who doesn't exist would say, I shouldn't abandon the freedom and joy of living in the moment. But it's hard right now.

When I get home, I rally the troops. I need Tessa.

She brings the boys home, and she sits with me at the kitchen table long after the boys have gone to sleep.

I don't know how to tell her. I pull up my sleeve. That's the best I can do.

Her face goes white. "Kelly Jo, what happened?"

"He's in trouble." The tears start. It's probably not realistic to expect them to stop anytime soon.

"Did he hurt you?" Tessa is gentler than I've seen her since Peter died.

"No. No, but it was too much. That kind of drama, it sucks other people in. Getting hurt was my sign. I can't be in the middle of a storm like that. I have to protect myself and my kids."

"Are you sure?"

"No. Not at all. But I need to stay away until I can think straight. I can't help him right now."

She picks up my phone. "He hasn't texted you since you've been home?"

"I told him not to. I just can't, Tessa."

She nods and fiddles with my phone. "I could block the number if you want."

"It's okay."

She gives me a big hug instead.

She stays with me most of the night, but at some point she has to go home. And I lie down to stare at the ceiling. There's no way I can sleep, despite how exhausted I am.

I'm worried sick about Andrew, of course. I'm terrified by his behavior and completely unwilling to go anywhere near it for fear that his vortex will somehow pull me down with him, but I'm still worried.

I also worry about the boys. How much have they noticed? Are they worried about Andrew? Are they worried about me? Have they been scarred somehow by my brief foray into dating? Is something like Andrew's behavior in their future as young men? Could they turn into this brooding kind of person because of losing their dad? How do I steel them for the angst young American men apparently can't handle? I don't know. Too many questions.

Here's the nightly OCD anxiety routine I develop: Get the boys home from school and handle assorted homework and lessons, practices, etc. Feed them. Make sure they've bathed or at least halfheartedly promised to shower in the morning. Try to clean the kitchen, though I have to admit I've never been very enthusiastic about dish washing, so that often gets put aside for the following day. Hang out with the boys and watch TV or read together. Get them to sleep.

Then I lie in my empty bed. Ditto snores. I lie there. I look at the clock repeatedly.

Then I get up, go out to the kitchen, and fire up my laptop. Usually I fight against doing this until after midnight. Usually.

Once the laptop's on, I do normal mom Internet surfing. I check Facebook, my email. I check the weather and the headlines on the local news Web site.

Then I stop the pretenses and Google him.

The Andy Pettigrew results pop up. The worst days have images posted first. He has a beard now. Not scruff, not stubble, but a Unabomber-worthy beard. It's unkempt. His pallor is bad. If his eyes are visible, they're dull and very often unfocused.

So far, just one time the news was bad enough that a mug shot popped up first. I choked. I walked away from the computer for about twenty minutes—crying my eyes out, basically. That would've been a time to witness the ugly cry in action. When I pulled myself together, I came back to read about his DUI arrest. The cops found him asleep/passed out at the wheel of his car, which was idling at the gate in front of his rented house.

There's lots of news about the friends he's been seen with. None of them are people I remember him telling me about. Todd's not one of them. I wonder how he's met them. I wonder if they're predatory. I wonder if they drag him out to clubs and let him do the buying.

But really. The man is thirty now. He's an adult. The worst predator is his addiction. It'll eat him alive. He doesn't need any frenemies for that—he can destroy his life all by himself.

Which is how I've left him. Alone. I don't know if I'll be able to forgive myself.

Every night I do this. I watch from afar as he spirals downward. Then usually I cry myself to sleep.

Several of these episodes have involved me trying to decide if I should call. He's not called since I forbade him to (gee, wonder why?), but part of me keeps hoping he will. I'm also terrified that he will.

I sent him a note on his birthday, writing that I hoped he was taking care of himself. I considered calling that night to check in on him, apologize for leaving him in his hour of need. Then I woke up the next day and remembered my travels down this road before. I'm just not strong enough. I have to be strong for me and two other people already. I feel like I'm carrying a steamer trunk full of baggage and the weight of the world for the boys, and I can't carry anything more. I wish I could.

Instead I Google him and see the path he's tearing through the celebrity landscape. I wonder how long it'll be before he's the butt of late-night jokes and the cliché of the Hollywood washout.

I can't stand it.

But I can't help. I can't do this for him. I can't.

So I wander around, blind to the world, running on empty, trying to pretend I'm normal. The boys probably figured out long ago that I'm not firing on all cylinders, but they've ridden out some tough patches of depression with me before. They know from experience to set my running shoes by the back door and call Gran if they need someone to give me a good snap-out-of-it lecture.

When they ask after Andrew, I tell them he's very busy, and we might not see him for a while. I've told them as little as I can beyond that. And I try to smile when I'm around them, as hollow as it may feel.

Depression is a terribly mundane way to exist. It's like death by paper cut. Or non-death by paper cut. There's nothing as dramatic as an end. It's just a dusk, a dimness to what used to be bright and in focus.

It sucks. Most days, after my nightly sad habit, I wake up feeling like one of the boys is standing with a ski boot to my chest, compressing me into the coils of the mattress.

If I could sleep forever, I would.

Sleeping sometimes involves dreaming, though. And sleep's necessary to have the coping skills I seem to be lacking, but I can't stand seeing Andrew in my life again, even if it's just a dream. It hurts. And when I dream of Andrew and Peter in the same night, the pain's almost unbearable.

I don't know if I'm still talking in my sleep, but if I am, I hope I'm asking someone for help. We need reinforcements. Fast.

Still No

I don't know which day it is, but the boys are doing their home-work when I see Andrew's picture pop up on *Entertainment To-night*. I turn the TV off. I don't want the boys to see him like this. I don't know if they've been paying attention, but they don't need to know he's struggling, suffering. They don't need that.

Later that night I clean up after dinner and try hard to act nor-mal. But I'm really waiting for the boys to wander away from the kitchen table so I can get on the computer and find out what's hap-pened to Andrew. Finally, mercifully, they drift upstairs to get ready for bed.

There's a knock at the door. I can't even answer it before Tessa charges in.

"Kelly! Kelly, turn on the computer!"

"Have you lost your mind?"

She is a woman on a mission. She opens the laptop herself, types. "You're going to want to see this."

"Is it something bad? Oh, Tessa, my God—"

She spins the laptop around. "Look for yourself."

Suddenly I feel the tears in my throat. "Rehab. Finally." It's rehab. He's safe in rehab. For now, he's somewhere I don't have to worry about him. I get up to get a glass of water, blow my nose, and regroup.

Tessa pushes me back into the chair. "There's more."

"Did he get arrested?"

"No, Kelly Jo, oh no, it's not that. Look. Look at the pictures."

He's got his usual hoodie on. He's shaved. That might be a good sign. It's night, and he's walking with Sandy, his publicist. I read the caption—says it was taken as he entered rehab in Malibu for an indefinite stay for indefinite reasons.

"Look. Look at the last picture. The one with his other hand out in front of him."

"What am I looking at?" I scroll through more pictures. Each is pretty much the same: Andrew with his head down, walking next to Sandy, who often has her hand up to keep the person taking the pictures at bay.

The last picture, though, makes me freeze.

He's holding a book. *In Our Time.* It's my Hemingway book.

I snap the laptop shut.

Tessa grabs me by the shoulders. "You've got to go to him."

"I can't." My heart pounds.

"Kelly, come on. He's got your book. He's getting help."

"I don't have the strength for this."

"Yes, you do. I'm not saying go back to him. I'm saying go see him. I'll watch the boys for you. Take the time you need. Do what you need to do."

I try to fill my lungs, but my chest feels crushed. "Let me think. Just give me some time to think about what to do."

Tessa rubs my back, comforting me. How many times is she

going to have to help piece me back together? "I love you. You do what you need. When you're ready, I'll take the boys."

"I don't know what to do."

"Maybe he'll reach out to you. If you talk to him, maybe then you can decide what to do." She gives me a good squeeze, reassuring and warm.

Then she walks out and leaves me to my nervous breakdown.

I spend the next seven days in absolute, abject terror of the phone. My poor children—they watch me jump about ten feet each time it rings. They do their normal routine, since, you know, they're still normal, and let it ring a couple of times before walking over and checking the caller ID to see who it is. Then they call out the identity, and whoever it's for takes it.

This has happened a million times in our house. Now, however, I have the mental fragility of a cat in a dog kennel, and every little thing sends me into arched-back mode.

For seven days, Beau and Hunter get calls from friends, and assorted unaware people call me—bill collectors, the firefighters' association, the lady from the PTO—and each of them has to talk to a crazy, breathless, agitated madwoman.

I'm beginning to wonder if the boys will commit me when the phone rings for the thousandth time.

Beau walks over. "Unavailable. I'll just let it go to voice mail, Mom. It's probably a salesman."

I launch myself over the kitchen table to answer it. "Hello?"

There's a long pause on the other end of the phone.

"I know you told me not to call, but I need to talk to you."

My chest goes numb.

"Hang on. I'm going into the bedroom."

I take the phone and look at Hunter. Beau will probably figure it out, but Hunter already has. He knows enough to realize Andrew and I have been having troubles. He might know more. He's a bright boy. He nods as I disappear into the bedroom.

I sit on the bed and put the phone back to my ear. "I'm here."

There's breathing on the other side. I wait.

"Kelly, I'm getting help."

"I know. I saw." I try to hold the phone still, but my hands are shaking badly.

"You and everybody, I guess."

"Are you okay?"

"I think I will be." He coughs. I hope he's not too sick.

I wait. I don't know what to say. I'm afraid to talk, actually.

"Are you still there?" He sounds concerned.

"Yes. I won't hang up."

"I need to see you. I mean, I'd really like to see you."

"I don't know." Despite everything, I immediately think about how I could get down there, if the boys would be all right with Tessa, but I don't know how to make my brain slow down to process any of it. This is not a good idea.

"Please. I can fly you down. Please." His voice cracks a little, and my eyes fill with tears.

"Oh, Andrew, I just don't know."

"Please."

I try not to cry. "Okay, yes. I'll come."

I almost tell him to stay where he is, but then I remember he's safe. It might be the only reason I can keep it together while we make the arrangements.

It's a little unusual to tell your sons you're making an impromptu trip to LA at six thirty the next morning, but the boys seem to roll with it. I tell them Andrew needs my help. They seem to get it, and they go get ready for Tessa's. Then I call Mom.

"Hello?" She's in her cocoon of normal life. I'm calling from the land of insanity, but I try to remember what her world is like so I don't scare her.

"Mom, it's Kelly."

"Hi, hon. Are you okay? You sound upset. Are the boys all right?" So much for not scaring her. I've put her in a panic.

"Mom, I'm coming down there in the morning."

"What on earth for?" Her voice goes up a register. Not a good sign.

I don't even want to say. "Andrew." There. I brace for the reply. She doesn't know the details of the last trip. I didn't let her and Dad know I was there when I went to help Andrew last time. I didn't want them to know about his struggles, but I suppose now they know, along with the rest of the world.

"Oh, honey." It's quiet for a second. "We'll be at home. Will there be a car for you, or should we come pick you up?"

I'm shocked. I was ready for the lecture. She sounds sympathetic. "There's a car coming. You're not mad at me?"

"Kelly Jo, I think you probably need to come. We'll see you in the morning. Now try to get some sleep."

And just like that, the call's ended. For some reason, this gives me a little peace.

The next morning, after a brief sleep, I board a plane for California.

When I get off the plane and walk out to the arrivals area, Tucker's there. I could cry.

"Hi, Kelly." He smiles at me. He's a good friend.

He takes my bag and leads me to the car. There's not much

conversation between us. We go to my parents' to drop my stuff. Mom gives me a wonderful hug. I tell her I'll be home as soon as I can, and that's about all I can muster.

"Honey, you go. We'll be fine. We'll see you tonight." She pats me on the back and sends me out to the car.

I can see Tucker drop the composed face he'd apparently been wearing. Now he looks very tired, and possibly worried too.

"When are you going back?" He's gotten right to it.

I'm worried about my answer. "Tomorrow morning. I need to get back to the boys as soon as I can." I hear the excuse in the words. It feels like a cop-out even as I'm justifying it.

Tucker's very kind and lets me off the hook. "You were great to come. Andrew appreciates it, I know. He needs friends like you right now."

I know the unstated thing there is *as opposed to friends like the ones he's been with lately.* Or maybe the unstated thing is *as opposed to absent friends like the one you've been lately.* The guilt grabs a little corner of my gut and starts to gnaw.

"So it's too early to visit yet, but I figured we could get some breakfast while we wait. The visit will feel a little weird because it's a lot of spy versus spy. They'll sneak him off campus, and we'll go to where they are. He's concerned that no one finds out you're here."

I'm almost 100 percent sure this is what my heart breaking feels like. It's interesting because, you know, I've been here before, but the circumstances were not quite the same. I guess I'm surprised to find myself in this spot again. I wonder if I'll just go under and drown in all of it.

But I have to kick to the surface. My life is more than me. It has been for a long time now. Giving up is not an option.

"Tucker." I think he knows what I'm trying to say. If he doesn't, he can probably read it in the sick look I know I have on my face.

"It's enough that you're here, Kelly. I think he knows that too. Just be the friend you can be for him right now. You have yourself and your boys to think about. I know that. He knows that."

I nod and follow him into a coffee shop. Tucker's about to order for us, but he turns around in line to look at me.

"But you know he's going to try, right? You can't fault him for trying."

"Tucker, I love him. It's not that. It's everything else. Lots of reasons."

"I know." The barista is waiting for our order now. Tucker looks at me for one more second, then turns around. The conversation is over, and he and I won't speak of it again.

After breakfast I find myself in the car again with Tucker, headed to an undisclosed location. We enter another underground parking garage. I try not to read too much symbolism into the descent.

Tucker and I ride the elevator up to a very generic office suite. Lord knows what kinds of strings were pulled and logistics required to make this happen. The place is very California beige and still has new-carpet smell. Tucker leads the way down a hall of empty offices and stops at a door.

"Thanks for coming, Kelly." He opens the door for me to walk through.

Andrew stands up from a couch. He's clean-shaven. He's wearing a white dress shirt and black dress pants with a skinny blue tie. I wonder for a second if he has a court appearance tied up with the rehab, but maybe he's just making an effort—maybe an effort for me, I don't know.

His hands are stuffed in his pockets. This is his awkward sign. "Hi."

I have to fight not to cry. "I'm glad you're safe."

We stand there for a long time, still not speaking. Then he steps back and offers me the chair next to him. I sit. I should have an enormous handbag or something to prop on my lap, pull tissues from, but I don't. For once I wish I was a purse person. I don't know what to do with my hands.

He takes a huge, deep breath and exhales. "I don't know how to start. I guess I'll just jump in." He sits on the edge of the couch and leans forward. He's trying to close the distance, but I feel like I need to scoot back to maintain some sort of control over myself. I resist the urge and stay still.

"Okay." I manage to squeak out.

"I want to make amends and apologize before I say anything else."

"I'm not okay with the way you've been behaving. I'm fine, but you're pissing me off, treating yourself the way you have been."

He's still. He looks me straight in the eye. "I hurt you. I am sorry."

I look at him for a moment. He's steady. So I go on. "I know about the girl, Emily. About the first time. Don't destroy yourself. When you said you have no switch—I get that now."

"There's no moderation with me. If I start, I get swallowed up by it, consumed. I thought for a long time if I just kept a lid on things, I could stay in control. But lately everything is just too much and I lose myself again and again. I guess I thought I'd handled the Emily thing a long time ago. And I thought I could just stay busy when everything started getting crazy. But I didn't think I had a problem. Now I know I do."

"I should've figured it out. You tried to tell me, and the smoking, and the rumors."

"Thanks for giving me the chance to tell you how sorry I am."

I nod. I'm fighting a nauseated knot in my stomach, but it feels so good to be here. To be talking to him, close to him. I want to crawl onto the couch next to him and curl up in his arms. I'm startled by that. This is why being near him is dangerous. I can't lose my head about him, about this. I can't afford to.

He reaches forward. He takes my arm gently, pulls up the sleeve to reveal the scar where the stitches were. "The sight of you running away on the beach was a low point."

"That woman, she would've eaten you alive if she'd seen me. And I couldn't reason with you. I had to get out of there. The paparazzi would've had a field day."

He lets go of my arm. "I hope you might forgive me someday."

I nod again. The words just aren't coming.

He looks at me, waits for my permission to continue. I don't say anything, so he goes on. "I've been thinking a lot. Things got really bad, obviously, but when I was done, totally done, one night I left whatever pointless house party I was at and just started walking. I kept walking and walking, and the sun came up, and the ocean and the sky turned this shade of pink."

He stops for a second, gathering his thoughts maybe.

"Anyway, for whatever reason, I finally got why you like that story."

I'm lost for a second, and then I realize. "The Hemingway?"

He nods. "Yeah, 'Big Two-Hearted River.' It was pretty basic, at first. Then I read the whole book of short stories, and I liked them, so then I read it again. And I appreciated it more for the way Hemingway writes. It's simple and spare. I like that."

Tears stream down my face, but my strategy is to ignore them. They land in little plops on my clothes.

He goes on. "I liked it, but I still don't think I got it. And then, walking on the beach as the sun rose, it struck me."

"What?"

"So the soldier fishes, and he doesn't do it for a reason except that it's quiet, it's a good routine. He's so wrecked by the war that it's the only thing that holds him together. He can't think about what's happened to him, what he's seen, what the trauma is."

He threads his fingers together, stares at them intently while he thinks. I try to continue to breathe.

"And then when he thinks about fishing the swamp—you know, when I first read it, it just struck me as, okay, don't fish there, fine. But then I realized: that's his memories, his mess. He can't delve into it that day. He chooses to hold to his routine, not go there, and that's how he copes. That's how he's keeping it together, keeping himself in one piece after all the shit he's been through."

He's quiet as he looks up into my eyes. "Kelly, the thing I realized? That guy is you. You're holding it all together, you run—but those dreams you have, the nightmares? You can't think about Peter, what happened, because you're afraid. You stick with the routine because you need to keep it together. You can't fish the swamp."

I suck in a breath between my teeth. I never thought he'd figure it out from my perspective. I thought he'd see the symbolism, but not how I applied it to myself.

He's up on his feet. His hands go back to his pockets, and he walks to the other side of the room before he turns around to face me.

I'm suddenly mad. "Why are we talking about me? I'm not the one who's been trying to kill myself."

His eyes go wide. "No, there's a point to this, I swear. Damn it, I don't want to hurt you more. The point is, I figured out that story, what it meant to you, and all I wanted to do was get to a place where I could help you instead of hurt you. I knew I wanted to help you, and I needed to be whole for you if I wanted to be part of your life. So I called Tucker the next day, and we started all of this."

He smiles now. It's all clear to him. He thinks he's figured everything out.

"I can't. I can't do this, Andrew." I get up and walk out the door.

I resist the urge to run down the hall, but I do duck through the next door, into a conference room, and cover my eyes. This may be a throwback to my toddler days when if I covered my eyes, I believed I was invisible.

The door swings open. "Kelly, please."

Well, that didn't work. He sees me.

He takes me by the shoulders. "Kelly."

I'm sobbing now. Who knows if he can even understand what tumbles out of my mouth. "You're right, but you don't even know, Andrew. You don't even know."

He searches my face for a clue. "What? What don't I know?"

"Andrew, I am so beyond fixing. I can't fix you, and you can't fix me."

He still holds my shoulders. "Kelly, we don't have to be fixed. We can help each other. I finally wanted to get better. *Me*, no one else. I was the one who wanted to change. I want this."

I close my eyes again. Maybe I can will it all to go away. I feel faint.

"Sit down. Tell me." He steers me to a chair around the conference table.

It comes out as half crying, half yelling. "Peter was an alcoholic. I left him for a year when the boys were little. He sobered up, and things were good, but then he got sick . . ." I can't even finish. I bury my face in my hands, double over in my seat.

I hear his chair push away. "Jesus." He's silent for a minute. "Oh, Kelly."

"After everything, he promised me we were through the worst of it. And then I was alone again."

"I wouldn't leave you."

"You can't promise me that, not really. I'm a broken person. I barely survived the last time. I can't go any more to pieces than I already am. I'm not strong enough for this." I inhale as deeply as I can, sit up, and wipe my face with the sleeve of my shirt. I've got to get out of here.

He stands, looks out the conference room window, but he turns to look at me before I walk out the door. I don't know what the expression on his face means, and I don't give him a chance to say anything else. This time, I do run—all the way to the car. Tucker is waiting for me. I suspect he heard some of what transpired, because he offers a Kleenex and wordlessly drives me to my mom's house.

When I get out, I come around to the driver's window. It opens. "Tucker, take care of him for me. You're a good friend." I want to kiss him on the cheek, like people do in movies, but instead, I just turn and walk into the house.

My Truth

If I was being flippant, which is certainly not appropriate for the moment, I'd quote Ricky of *I Love Lucy* and admit that I have some splainin' to do. I've never been good at handling ugly truths in anything but a roundabout way.

I very rarely wade back through all of this, but now it seems I'd better. It's out in the open, and I feel like I've had my chest cracked open, so I don't know how it could get any worse. I sit down to write Andrew a letter. He deserves the whole story. I want him to get well, and I certainly don't want my mess to be the reason he can't.

The letter is hard. All this was hard to live, but it's almost harder to replay it in my mind another painful time. This is why I leave it alone. It is my swamp, and no, I don't fish it. I can't.

The memories all come back to me as I try to think what to write. Peter and I met at school. I was instantly smitten. He was curly headed, charismatic, funny. He had a way of running his hands through his hair when he was excited about an idea. I just loved it.

We dated a little, but he lived in the crew house, a big, rambling mess of an old, white farmhouse with a bunch of his rowing teammates. They had wild parties—really wild parties.

I was never much on drinking. I watched him out of control at more than a couple of parties, and I was distinctly uncomfortable. So the next time he called to see if I wanted to meet him somewhere, I had other plans. And that was it in college.

Then the dinner party. Here we were, all grown up. I was newly teaching; he was working on a Ph.D. in public policy. He seemed different. We dated for a year before we got engaged. Life was good. We got married, Hunter came along, and Peter got a job teaching at a community college. Beau was born.

Then we moved west. Peter had a new job teaching at Boise State. That's when the drinking started again.

I guess it had never stopped altogether. When we lived in Virginia, more than a few nights each year, old college buddies of Peter's would call up and meet him for a drink. He'd call and let me know at the end of the day, say he'd be home a little late. He'd come home at two. But when the boys were babies, he kept it limited to a few nights a year. He just couldn't step away when the opportunity was presented.

Out west, though, it didn't matter. First it was when the department had tailgate parties. Then it was when people invited him out after classes. Then it was always. More nights than not ended with me putting the kids to bed and him not home yet.

When I found out he was drinking during the day too, I left. I found an apartment close to the school where I taught, and I moved out. The boys were three and six. We were separated for a year. The depth of my depression was one of the scariest things I've ever lived through. The only reason I survived was the boys. If they hadn't needed me, I wouldn't have fought to get better.

Peter came to me on our anniversary that year and told me about rehab, and his sobriety. We bought a new house, the one where the boys and I live now, and moved in after a year apart. He never had another drink.

Three years later, he got sick. And five months after that, he died. I was more ready for the way I felt then than the way I'd felt when Peter was drinking, but it didn't hurt any less. I had a lot of support after he died. But when he was drinking, I felt a lot of shame and didn't tell very many people what was going on. It hurt too much.

I pour all of this into my letter to Andrew. I don't know if he'll understand, but I try to explain. It comes down to this: yes, I have been here before, but I am not personally strong enough to do it again. What if rehab doesn't work this time? Or what if it does? It did last time, and I lost Peter anyway. I can't bear that again. Also, I have the boys. They've been there, done that as well, and though we can tell ourselves they were too little to remember, I think children are like wet clay—everything makes an impression on them somewhere. I will not put them through any of that again. I will not risk it. I will not risk them. I know he thinks he won't leave, but what if he's not the one who gets to decide?

Anyway, I tell him again that I love him, and that I know he can find strength in his family, his friends, and himself to get through this fight.

What I leave out—but what I'm ultimately saying—is that he can't find strength in me. I don't have any to spare. If this is another moment for a skiing metaphor, this is a chute I won't go down again. I'm not a good enough skier.

I write about half a dozen drafts, trying for the right tone and throwing away the ones that are too wet from tears. Everything with

Peter is back up at the surface again, and then there's the look I keep remembering in Andrew's eyes. His face as he told me about the sunrise, and how he knew he could help me, and how he was going to get past this. There was so much optimism. And I stomped on it because I'm a coward.

I get in my car and drive to the nearest mailbox. I send the letter. That's my weakest moment. This is my surrender. I'd rather stay safe, take the long way around—or the lonely way, in this case—than risk loving someone again. Instead of joining Andrew in the fight, I have run as far away as I can.

A Running Partner

I wake up—or actually, I decide to stop trying to sleep and get up. The dawn is still gray. I feel gray. The inside of my mouth tastes gray.

I'm fairly confident I will not be able to run this morning without a little caffeine. I'm hardly ever able to in the weeks since I fled LA. At least the weather is calming down a bit. There's no snow. It's late May, but that doesn't matter in Boise. Until the end of June, anything can happen.

This morning the gray air is calm. I look out the window. Maybe I'm brooding, or thinking. Or just staring.

"Mom." I jump, startled. It's Hunter.

He doesn't need to be up. It's Saturday. "Go back to bed, hon. I'm going running. It's a day off."

He pulls the kettle off the burner. "Your tea was boiling."

I give him a big hug. He's always been a sweet kid. He takes care of people by managing little things.

"What are you doing up?" He's in the T-shirt and pajama bottoms he's slept in all year. Next Christmas I will give him a new set, and he will wear holes in those too. Or outgrow them ridiculously fast, like he and Beau always do.

"I thought I'd run with you today."

Seriously, I am stunned. My jaw's probably on the floor. But delightedly stunned. It never occurred to me that Hunter might want to come. "Really?"

He blushes a little. The freckles on his nose stand out on the pink. "Geez, Mom, it's not a big deal."

I try not to screw this up by being overly mother dorky, which I know he despises. "Go get changed. I've still got to get my shoes on and have a little tea."

He comes back down a few minutes later, so cute I can't stand it. My little boy has a sweatband, Bjorn Bjorg style, around the mop of sandy blond hair he's started to grow out. He's wearing his soccer sweats and running shoes.

"Let's go." I bounce out the door.

Ditto's ecstatic. The boy is going too? The dog hops back and forth, then off the top step of the back stoop.

We lope around to the quiet street. I'll run a short loop today, down the street to the cul-de-sac and along the little flat trail into the hollow below. I want Hunter to like this. Who knows, maybe he'll come out with me another time . . .

We jog to the cul-de-sac. Hunter seems fine. He's played soccer since he was little, but I don't think I've ever seen him voluntarily do any exercise outside practice. He's an easy athlete—a great skier like his father—so he tends not to work too hard at what comes easily.

When we come to the dirt trail, he pulls up. "Can we walk a little?"

"Sure." He doesn't seem particularly out of breath, but I'm

doing things his way. Ditto's happy not to run. He can't cheat on this route and sit somewhere till we pick him back up.

We walk a little way up the trail. "Mom, can I talk to you about something?"

I rummage through my brain for what he might need to talk about. Girls? Grades? I try not to tense up. "Always. Shoot."

He seems to hesitate, but then he goes for it. "Mom, I know something's going on with you and Andrew."

Well, now, this is a total surprise. We're having a talk about me. "Yeah, honey, there is. What do you want to know?" I'll be straight with him. I suspected he might be more astute than I thought.

"Is he your boyfriend?"

"He was. I think." That doesn't sound very grown up.

"Beau and I like him a lot. Is he in trouble?"

"He was, honey. I think he's going to be okay now." I appreciate that we're walking. I try to keep my breathing in time with the rhythm of our feet so I sound calm.

"Then how come you're not dating him anymore?"

"Well, it's complicated, honey."

"Is it because of me and Beau?"

"Andrew likes you guys—of course it's not that."

"No, I mean, are you trying to protect us or something?"

Geez, who raised this kid? He's too perceptive. It's killing me. "Kind of. I mean, all three of us have been through a lot. It's a thing between Andrew and me, honey. But us—you, me, and Beau— we're going to be okay. Don't worry. Everything is going to be the same as it's always been. I'm not going to change things on you right now. Andrew's going to take care of himself just fine. He has a lot of friends and family to help him right now."

Hunter stops us from walking. "Mom, you can help him. Beau and I are fine."

I hesitate. "We've all been through a lot."

"You always handle it, Mom. You take good care of us. You're strong. And we can take care of ourselves sometimes, you know. We aren't little anymore."

"I know you aren't." I feel the cold morning on my face and breathe it in. I can hardly make sense of this discussion.

"Dad's been gone almost three years. Beau and I are okay. If you like Andrew, maybe you should try a little more."

I want to laugh at the absurdity of my almost-twelve-year-old sounding more sensible than I have behaved in probably the last nine months.

"We'll see." I don't tell him I'm fairly positive I torched that bridge when I literally ran away. And that even with him and his brother out of the equation, I may not possess the strength to help anyone but myself.

Hunter adjusts his headband and starts to run again, at a brisk pace he seems way too comfortable with. "Well, think about it," he says, looking back at me. "We'll really be okay. We've been okay for a while now, Mom. All of us have."

He runs off ahead of me with the dog. I stand there, stunned, until he turns around again and throws his hands up, wondering what my deal is.

I run back to the house, trailing him, thinking.

I spend most of the day stewing over our conversation. Dang that kid. He's too smart.

Last night I was too exhausted to even worry about the mail. I realize this in the afternoon when I see the mailman stop and stuff our mail in the box. I trot out to the curb and pull out the stack to throw away junk and weigh the pile of bills. There's a padded envelope among the pizza coupon mailers. It's not a normal piece of mail.

I stand in front of the mailbox and examine it. It's addressed to me. I don't recognize the handwriting.

Inside is a small note card with another envelope. The card says:

*Andrew will be back at work in LA this week. He wanted
you to have this. Hope all is well. He's doing as well as can
be expected.*

— Tucker

I tear the other envelope open. Inside is my copy of *In Our Time* and an index card. The card has a few lines written on it in a hand I do know:

*I'm reading "A Farewell to Arms" now. It makes me think
of you.
Life can crush you, ruin you, kill you.
Or it can break you and make you stronger in the process.
You are strong, Kelly Reynolds. And you are strongest in
your broken places.*

Andrew

I hold on to the items for dear life and walk inside. I stare at both notes, the one from Tucker and the one from Andrew, for a long time. Thankfully Hunter and Beau are in their rooms and are spared witnessing this odd behavior.

Then I touch the spine of *In Our Time*. It makes me sad to think that Andrew was holding this, now it's in my hands, and that's the last connection between us.

I open it to "Big Two-Hearted River." I scan through it. I think about what Andrew said. How I hold on to my routine—cling to it for dear life might be more accurate. I run my finger over the words Hemingway uses as his character finds comfort in fishing, and then I force myself to think for a moment.

The man in the story focuses on his fishing, avoids thinking, stays safe—where nothing can make him feel. Is this what I want?

I can hear Peter now. I can feel him, standing next to me at the top of a run, asking me if I'm skiing it or going around.

Most of the time I'm a complete and total idiot, but for once in my life, I recognize Andrew's note and Hunter's pep talk for what they are: signs that it's time to figure out my mess of a life.

And I think I know where I need to go to do that.

Indio Again

I stand somewhere with wet grass. I can feel it between my toes. The mist is thick. It's morning. I step forward and find the water's edge at my feet. I look out into the mist and see the sun breaking through. I've been here before. Pilings of crumbled docks stand out of the water, and I can hear the lapping of the river now.

It's the river near school—near college. As I realize that and my brain begins to form a prediction of where this dream is headed, a scull parts the mist like a knife. It's probably fifty yards downriver from me, but I see the thin line of it pushing through the water even before I can hear it. The single rower has his back to me.

I stand on the shore and wait. The boat slices gracefully through the gray water. It is suspended, the line between air and water blurred in the morning mist.

I'm wearing the crew sweatshirt he gave me one night, when we were walking back from a lecture and I was cold. I can feel the cold of the steel zipper against my skin.

His broad back pulls with the oars, driving the boat closer. The rhythm of the boat, the man, the water, is beautiful.

He shoots past me now and turns to look as he goes. It's Peter. He is as he was: young, healthy, his curly black hair moist from the river's mist and the effort. His arms and shoulders are strong under his jersey.

He smiles at me. He breaks rhythm long enough for a quick wave. Then he turns back to the oars and resumes his work, pulling the boat seamlessly along the river's surface. As fast as he appeared, he disappears again, the scull swallowed by the mist as he glides up the river.

I open my eyes. I lie quiet in bed, thinking. I sit up and swing my legs over the edge. My wedding ring sits on the bedside table. I pick it up, kiss it, and put it down again. It's been almost three years since I lost Peter.

As soon as school was out June first, the boys and I flew to LA to see Mom and Dad. That's where they are now. But I needed the space of the desert. I wasn't ready to run into Andrew by chance, so Mom let me sneak away to Indio. She told me to "sort things out," if I could. I've been puttering the days away and running my loop in Indio all week. But I'm not running my loop today.

I'm in the car. That dream has stayed with me. I cannot shake it, even as the afternoon sun starts to cast long shadows. I definitely need to run, but I'm going to Joshua Tree. I need every ounce of spiritual scaffolding I can get, so I'm going to run in the most sacred space I know. If I can't come to a resolution here, then I'm truly lost. And I cannot be lost.

I crank up the Coldplay. If I want to completely fall apart, I'll play "MLK" by U2, but I can't run if I have a nervous breakdown. Anyway, bawling while running got me into this jam in the first place.

After a short while, the desert floor crunches under the pounding of my soles. I feel my lungs expand. The rhythm sets in. I run hard.

I honestly don't know how far I've gone. But suddenly, I'm done. I stop. I pull out the earbuds. I listen to the empty heart of the desert.

What am I here to do anyway?

Love.

I can love.

I can't fix, but I can't run away from it either. Love might not heal. Love might not last. But it might.

I think I'm calling his name when I turn around. I cannot run back quickly enough.

The sun is setting as I drive the way I came, descending into the valley. The heat of the desert shimmers off the valley floor, and I see storm clouds rolling into town. By the time I turn down the street to Mom and Dad's condo, I have the wipers on high. Thunder rumbles and the light of the day dissolves into a wet, angry dusk.

I get out. The urgency makes me tremble, and now I'm struck with a terrible feeling of panic. How can I find him? I know in the marrow of my bones that he needs me, and I need him, but I don't know how I'll get to him in LA quickly enough. The impossibility of it pushes me to the edge.

So when I walk up the path to the door, I cry out at the sight of him. I wonder for a moment if I've gone delusional, but he's real. He sits on the front stoop. Tessa must have intervened, told him I was here. Thank God for her. He stands as I approach. He's soaked to the bone, in a hoodie and baseball cap, as always. His beard is a short scruff, and his hands are stuffed into the front pockets of his jeans.

I run to him. My hands are around his neck. Strength fills me.

I try to pour the intensity into him, hugging him tightly. His head is bowed.

"Andrew."

"I love you." His hands are still in his pockets.

"I'm so sorry." I kiss him. The rain soaks us. He cries, his shoulders rising and falling in shudders. His arms come up, hands pulling me in at the shoulder blades, pulling me as close as he can.

The rain falls, and I feel strong. I can hold up to this, and I can help him. I can't fix him, but I can love him. He can't fix me, but he can love me.

He leans into me, and we walk inside. I'll run a hot shower for him. We'll talk about the next steps—how to help him get better, stay better. We'll talk about me, my past, the things I've held just under the surface for too long. Maybe we'll talk about finding a new place, a private place that's safe for all of us.

We'll go meet the boys and fly home to Boise. We'll be together. All of us.

Do-Over

Red carpet done right—that's what Andrew wants to call this. I
do feel a lot less freaked out the second time around. I think
it helps that we're at Andrew's rented house, and that the boys are
downstairs having pizza with Andrew, Jeremy, Todd, and my folks
right now.

Which, by the way, is a complete rip-off. I've been primped
and prodded and preened for an hour and a half, I won't be able to
eat because I'm terrified of messing up the dress, and they're all
hanging out like we're going to a football game or something.

Finally Mallory is done. I'm happy, because I convinced her a
shiny ponytail would be a good red-carpet look. Actually, I probably
didn't convince her, but she acquiesced. So that part of me is comfortable. And the makeup is tolerable. There was a brief discussion
of false eyelashes, but we got real and gave up on that idea.

I walk down the stairs to the kitchen.

"There she is!" Dad likes to announce things that are obvious.

"Here I am." I look at Andrew to see what he thinks.

"My date!" He leaves the pizza and comes over. "I'd hug you, but I think I'd get pizza on you." He's wearing a gray suit with a spring green tie that matches my dress, but it's obscured by a huge napkin stuffed into the neck of his shirt.

Todd puts his pizza down. "Don't let Andrew near you. He was shoveling it in, so he's definitely saucy." He smiles and wipes his hands on his torn-up jeans.

Jeremy isn't eating. He's on his phone. But he puts it aside long enough to comment: "Kelly, you're a vision. Leave him immediately."

Andrew rolls his eyes.

Mom comes over and gives me a hug. "Oh, Bug, you look amazing. Now you-all go have fun. And don't be nervous."

"I'm not nervous, Mom. I'm not the one who has to talk about myself for the length of a football field."

Andrew carries his plate to the kitchen. "You have to stand next to me and endure it, though. That might be more painful. And I'm not going to win."

Jeremy claps him on the back. "Blasphemy! I called this one, son."

Yes, we've decided to go public. It's awards season. Andrew threatened to leave the agency if Jeremy didn't drop the dating clause in the contract. A client with a nomination can throw his weight around a little, I guess. So we're putting the Franca-and-Andy-are-they-or-aren't-they debate to rest. It's not going to be a big deal anyway. Except maybe to Franca, but she's about to star in a new movie with the latest incarnation of the Justice League, so she'll be plenty occupied with a bevy of leading men. The press really prefers famous people to date other famous people. It sells twice as many magazines. But we decided as a family, and then we did a few things to get ready. We changed the phone number. We told the school.

What will be weird is when we get home. Two weeks ago we drove around with Andrew in our part of town and picked out a new house. So when we get home, we'll drive past a gate to get in the neighborhood. We'll pull into a new driveway and see Ditto going crazy in a new backyard. We'll walk into a house that has been decorated by no one, but waits for both of us to put our mark on it. And the boys too, of course. They're very comfortable laying claim to bedrooms and hanging posters with tape that will ruin the walls.

But new is good. Different is good. Taking a risk is good. Andrew held my hand very tightly when we signed the papers. We're pretty strong when you put the two of us together.

That's what I think again when I step out of the black Suburban with Andrew holding my hand to steady me. Wearing heels is still not a skill I've mastered. Tucker gives me a big smile. He doesn't have much of a job tonight—awards shows have their own security detail—but he walks in front of us anyway.

It's good too, because I need a minute to figure out how to see. The flashbulbs are just like the ones I remember from when I was little and they took school pictures with big lights in the gym. I have little gray-blue spots all over my field of vision. And it's loud, really loud. People are screaming, bellowing, "Andy! Andy!" From the public bleachers across the street, I can hear kind of a generalized, high-pitched squealing.

"How do you even see to walk?" I ask Andrew. I have to yell. I'm clinging to him, I'm pretty sure.

"You'll be mostly blind for the first minute or so. Just look out at some point in the distance, or pretend to. Or just look at the back of Tucker's head. Or me, you can always look at me." He looks right at me and flashes his million-dollar smile. The flashbulbs go crazy again.

"Everybody else is. You're going to get spoiled."

He squeezes my hand. "Are you ready for this?"

"No."

"Too bad. Here we go!"

And we plunge down the next chute of our lives. Together.

About the Author

B eck Anderson believes in the power of perfectly imperfect women and in the healing power of love. Her new novel, *Fix You*, grew out of those beliefs and the time to write afforded by the worst Thanksgiving blizzard she's ever witnessed in West Yellowstone.

For Beck, the path to published novelist has taken lots of twists and turns, including a degree in anthropology, a stint as a ticket seller at a ski resort, a much-loved career as a high school English teacher, and a long tenure as a member of the best writing group ever, hands down.

Beck balances (clumsily at best) writing novels and screenplays, working full-time as an educator, mothering two preteen males, loving one post-forty husband, and making time to walk the foothills of Boise, Idaho, with Stefano DiMera Delfino Anderson, the suavest Chihuahua north of the border.